BLOND HAIR, BLUE EYES

CHRIS KELSEY

Black Rose Writing | Texas

The author grants the final approval for this literary material.

First printing

This is a work of fiction. Names, characters, businesses, places, events, and incidents are either the products of the author's imagination or used in a fictitious manner. Any resemblance to actual persons, living or dead, or actual events is purely coincidental.

ISBN: 978-1-68513-409-9
PUBLISHED BY BLACK ROSE WRITING
www.blackrosewriting.com

Printed in the United States of America
Suggested Retail Price (SRP) $21.95

Blond Hair, Blue Eyes is printed in Chaparral Pro

*As a planet-friendly publisher, Black Rose Writing does its best to eliminate unnecessary waste to reduce paper usage and energy costs, while never compromising the reading experience. As a result, the final word count vs. page count may not meet common expectations.

This book is dedicated to my sister, Juliette Kelsey Chagnon, who was always my best friend when I needed one the most.

ACKNOWLEDGMENTS

As always, thanks to my faithful beta readers, Judy Kelsey, Gisele Bryce, and Lisa Kelsey.

BLOND HAIR, BLUE EYES

PROLOGUE

If I was more revenge-minded and not allergic to the idea of spending the rest of my life in jail, I might've killed Burt Murray myself.

I'm disinclined to use violence if I can avoid it, however, and while some things might be worth going to prison for, killing a slimy bastard like Burton Murray isn't one of them.

In my duties as police chief in Burr, Oklahoma—a little town in Tilghman County in the western part of the state, snug up against the Texas panhandle—I've had occasion to visit the repository of notorious reprobates and malefactors known formally as the Oklahoma State Penitentiary at McAlester. Said visits taught me something important: I'd rather use a Colt .45 to clear my sinuses than spend a night behind those walls.

I once had a chance to shoot Burt with the law on my side. I didn't do it. Nine years later, someone else did. They didn't have the law on their side, but I don't think it mattered to them either way.

Burt Murray was sheriff of this county from the mid-1940s to the mid-1960s. County sheriff is an elected office. Burt ran every four years and won every time. To a large percentage of our tragically misled voters, Burt could do no wrong. In fact, he'd probably still be sheriff if it hadn't been discovered that 25 years earlier, when he was a deputy, he killed a family in cold blood. For most of those 25 years, it looked like he'd gotten away with it. Unfortunately for him, there's no statute of limitations on murder.

To be fair—and to the best of my knowledge—Burt never personally killed anyone after that. That's nothing to sneeze at. I can't even say it about myself. That's not to say he didn't try. He went after me when I confronted him with evidence of his misdeeds. It was a close-run thing, but I was able to hold him off.

The difference between me and Burt is that the folks I shot were crooks. The persons he shot were law-abiding citizens who simply had the bad luck to be a threat to his ambition. If they'd been white, I expect Burt would have gotten the electric chair. They were Black, however, so he got off with his miserable carcass more or less intact. Many of his constituents thought the case against him a lie from beginning to end. Burt stayed popular among them. Sadly, in Tilghman County, they may have been in the majority.

Truth be told, it's entirely possible Burt Murray was Oklahoma's most beloved cold-blooded murderer since Charles "Pretty Boy" Floyd. Like Pretty Boy, Burt had an uncanny ability to pull the wool over the public's eyes. In his prime, Burt could charm the panties off a Sunday school teacher. Sometimes it seems like every voter in the county has a story about our ex-sheriff sweet-talking a judge into ruling in favor of a wealthy campaign contributor or looking the other way after one of his political cronies had beaten the daylights out of his wife. Hell, he might even convince the wife she'd had it coming.

Burt had a certain *je ne sais quoi*. That's French for "inexplicable ability to bullshit." In my early years on the job, I was as susceptible to his appeal as anyone.

I'll give you an example: 20-some-odd years ago, not long after I'd been hired, I ticketed a local VIP for driving under the influence. His name was Ed Cecil, and he was a big-shot in Republican Party circles. He was also a friend of Burt, who, by then—with Ed Cecil's help—had been elected and twice reelected as County Sheriff. It's hard to believe now, but back then, drunk driving wasn't considered as big a deal as it is now. If it had happened today, I wouldn't give a damn who he was.

I'd haul him in and drag him in front of a judge. But things were different back in the '50s. The worst punishment you'd expect for such an offense is to be written a ticket, which is what I did.

Most fellas would've paid the fine and be done with it. But Ed Cecil was used to getting his own way. Even a slap on the wrist was intolerable. He called Burt to complain, and Burt called me.

"Emmett, you know ol' Ed ties one on, now and again," he said, as if Cecil driving drunk was merely a slightly distasteful thing he did once in a while—like cussing in church or breaking wind in a crowded movie theater. "He only does it late at night when no one else is on the roads," said Burt. "He never hurts no one."

I put up some resistance, saying something like, "There's always a first time," which was about as mouthy as I'd ever gotten with Burt. Keep in mind, I'd only been on the job for less than a year. Burt was a local legend.

He said, "Ed's already promised me it won't happen again. Ed's a man of his word."

I hemmed and hawed, not wanting to give in. Burt sensed my weakness and bore in.

"Listen, Emmett," he said like he was imparting top-secret information, "Ed's got his eye on being County Commissioner. A drunk driving ticket might not sound like much to you, but it could jeopardize his election. Ed'll do good things for Tilghman County. Mess things up for him, you're messin' things up for your friends and neighbors. You don't want that on your conscience, do you?"

I knew he was twisting me around his finger, which I didn't like, so I tried to hold strong. "It's not like I'm crucifying the man," I said. "I just gave him a ticket."

Even I could hear the doubt creeping into my voice. If I could hear it, you'd better believe Burt could, too.

Sure enough, he jumped on it like Reggie Jackson on a hanging curveball. "Don't you see, Emmett? You *might as well* be crucifying him. If you don't tear up that ticket, Ed can kiss his political career goodbye. Heck, he might as well kiss the rest of his life goodbye."

You can see where this is headed. I was a kid. Burt was Burt. I didn't know about the bad things he'd done; I only knew he'd been in this business a lot longer than I had. As hard as it is for me to believe now, I actually looked up to him.

I gave in and tore up the ticket.

Fast forward to the next Halloween, when Ed Cecil broke the promise he never intended to keep.

He ran over and killed a trick-or-treater. I answered the call that night. There was booze on Ed's breath and an empty Jack Daniels bottle on the front seat of his Chevy Bel Air. It was all I could do not to pull my gun and put one through his skull, except if I'd done it, by all rights I'd have to do the same to myself.

Instead of Ed Cecil's ruined career, I had the death of a little five-year-old girl on my conscience.

After that, I always took what Burt said with a grain of salt. Sometimes he could be convincing; sometimes I could be convinced. He'd flatter me and I'd allow myself to be flattered. Over time, my anger towards him faded. It never went away completely, but it's fair to say I eventually more or less forgave him. There were even times I kind of liked and admired him.

It wasn't until I discovered he'd killed at least three—and maybe four—people back in 1940 that I turned on him for good.

***

Like I said, at the time, Burt was a Tilghman County sheriff's deputy. He and another deputy by the name of Frank Sallee shot three members of a family in cold blood. For 25 years they managed to evade the long arm of the law, which wasn't too hard, since they were the long arm of the law. It also didn't hurt their cause that the folks they killed—the Youngers—were Black.

Initially, Burt and his cronies were just trying to run off the Youngers like they'd done to every other Black family in town. The Youngers were the last holdouts. Burt, Sallee, and a couple of other fellas fire-bombed their house in the middle of the night—not intending to kill them, necessarily, although their physical well-being obviously wasn't of paramount concern. They'd done similar things to the other Black families they'd scared away: burnt crosses on their lawns, thrown bricks through their windows. Before the Youngers, they never set anyone's house on fire, but I reckon since they were the last Blacks in town, Burt and his buddies wanted to get it over and done with. The others they'd intimidated just up and left. There was no reason to think the Youngers wouldn't do the same.

Even after the fire had been extinguished and the Youngers disappeared, no one suspected they were dead. It was assumed they'd gotten the heck out of Dodge like those other families. But they hadn't. They'd been murdered. Burt Murray and Frank Sallee shot them, then disposed of their bodies, their car, and everything else connected with the crime.

The two men kept their secret over the years. Their careers thrived in the meantime. Burt was elected sheriff. Sallee climbed the ranks of the Texas Rangers. Years passed. They must have figured they'd never get caught.

They hadn't counted on Rufus Kenworthy.

One day in 1966, I got a call from the warden at the state prison telling me an elderly inmate dying of cancer had something important he wanted to tell me. His name was Rufus Kenworthy. He was serving a life sentence for murder. I recognized the name, although I hadn't heard it since I was a boy. Rufus Kenworthy killed a Pullman porter by the name of Ike Butler here in Burr back in 1932. The fella who was the Tilghman County DA at the time thought it would be bad politics to prosecute a white man for killing a Black man, so he blamed Bonnie and Clyde—who were in the news a lot back then—and let Rufus off the hook, on the condition he leave town and never come back. Rufus took him up on the offer, only to be convicted of killing another Black man in a different town, some years later.

I figured Kenworthy wanted to cleanse his soul about that, but I was wrong. Instead, he wanted to talk about the Youngers. He told me the real story, or at least he gave me the bottom line: They'd been shot, and their bodies dumped in Burr Lake. Rufus insisted he didn't shoot them, and there was no evidence he did. He just had guilty knowledge, is all. Unfortunately, he didn't feel guilty enough to tell me who actually did it. The reason he gave for telling me at the time was that, as a way of getting right with the Lord, he wanted to make sure the Youngers finally got a good Christian burial. I did some detective work, though. It didn't take long for Burt and Sallee to rise to the top of my list of suspects. I arrested them, albeit not before Burt tried his best to fill me full of bullet holes.

The case went to trial. It was hard to find an unbiased jury. For a quarter century Burt had kissed pretty much every baby born in Tilghman County. A lot of those babies had grown up. Quite a few were registered voters. Most of them loved Burt. If I was a gambling man, I wouldn't have bet a nickel on him getting convicted, yet somehow the DA managed to seat enough folks on the jury who either didn't know or didn't care who Burt was, or who secretly nursed a grudge against him. They convicted him of second-degree murder. The judge gave him 15 years to be served at the aforementioned Oklahoma State Prison. Nobody believed he'd serve the entire sentence, of course, but he was behind bars for eight years, which was longer than I would've predicted. It took him that long to find a lawyer savvy enough to convince the presiding judge to vacate his conviction.

The DA who originally prosecuted Burt was a Democrat. These days, a Democratic elected official is rarer than a dodo bird. The current DA, Harry "Hopalong" Hawpe, is a prominent Republican, like Burt. To no one's surprise, once the judge vacated Burt's conviction, Hopalong declared Burt had suffered enough and declined to retry the case.

That's politics in Tilghman County.

Officially, it's like Burt never killed the Youngers. Or tried to kill yours truly.

Trust me. He did both.

***

That could've been the end of the story. Should've been, in my opinion. But it wasn't.

You might think that after spending so much time in jail and being nearly 70-years-old at the time of his release, Burt would retire. Maybe take up needlepoint or raise petunias.

Or put a gun to his head and pull the trigger, which would've been my advice.

But Burt Murray didn't care for flowers, and he wasn't the type to shoot himself in the head unless he did it by accident while trying to shoot someone else. Burt was a politician. Asking him not to run for office was like asking a dog not to lick his privates.

Of course, he came back to Tilghman County to do it. He started making noises about it the day he got out of jail, holding a press conference covered by all the Oklahoma City TV and radio stations and even a few from Tulsa. He'd been treated poorly, he said, but he was in a forgiving mood. He said he was "saddened and shocked" to find Tilghman County had gone straight to hell while he'd been in jail and claimed to be eager to get back to serving the citizens of western Oklahoma. Everyone thought he'd run against the fella who replaced him as sheriff, my friend Keith Belcher. But Burt raised his sights. Being sheriff was too puny. He wanted to be the United States Congressman from Oklahoma's Eighth District.

You might say it takes a lot of nerve for someone like Burt to run for a seat in Congress after being convicted of murder. You'd be right, but you'd be giving away the fact you're a Yankee, or at least hail from someplace far away. Folks around here are pretty quick to forgive one of their own, especially if he's accused of something that not everyone is convinced is a crime—like killing Black people. Back in the early '20s, Tilghman County had a greater concentration of Klansmen than any county in the state. I'm both sorry and embarrassed to say it hasn't changed much.

The bottom line is: When it came to Burt Murray, it didn't take much for the good people of Tilghman County to let bygones be bygones.

I should also point out that a lot of them thought trying to kill me wasn't much of a sin, either. I'm a liberal and a Democrat, which in this state is like confessing to having sex with Leonid Brezhnev and liking it.

All that time in jail gave Burt plenty of time to think up a few phony issues to run on. One of them was the Equal Rights Amendment. Burt called it, "a scheme to make it hard for ugly girls to find husbands." Another was welfare; one side of Burt's mouth would say, "Getting something for nothing ain't American," while the other would promise tax cuts to the owners of the same corporate outfits putting our family farmers out of business.

Unfortunately for Burt, carping on the ERA and welfare didn't exactly light a fire under the electorate. In fact, his comment about the ERA probably cost him votes; no daddy thinks his daughter's ugly. His spiel about welfare didn't help much, either. I've never in my life met a single person willing to turn down a helping hand from the government. There are still a lot of folks around who remember how FDR's New Deal programs saved them from losing everything. Growing up as I did during the Great Depression, Franklin Roosevelt was a hero in my house.

It was like that in a lot of houses.

Without a major issue for people to get excited about, coupled with the fact he'd been out of the spotlight for so long—out of sight, out of mind—Burt's campaign looked to be in trouble. In desperation, he turned to the one issue that never fails: a little old-fashioned racial prejudice.

Despite being located smack dab in the middle of the continent, in many ways, Oklahomans are every bit as southern in our attitudes as Alabamans or Mississippians. Given Burt's record, you'd think he'd hit on racism as a tactic right off the bat. It took him a while, though. Of course, once he did, he rode it like a champion quarter horse.

Maybe it took him so long because there are so few Black people in his district. Where there's a will, there's a way, however. Instead of focusing on Blacks, Burt made villains out of the Southeast Asian refugees who've settled here in recent years—the Vietnamese, Laotians, and Cambodians the United States allowed into the country after we'd trashed theirs in our most recent war to make the world safe for General Motors.

Most of those folks worked at the Little Piggy meat-packing plant outside the Burr city limits. The plant opened with great fanfare a few years ago, but fell onto hard times when the original owner couldn't find enough locals willing to scald the hair off live pigs and slit cow's throats and chop large animals into bite-sized nuggets for two dollars and thirty cents an hour. The plant was sold to a Texas corporation called Little Piggy Meats, who worked a deal with the government to settle several busloads of Southeast Asian families in the area. Those people needed jobs. Little Piggy had jobs to give. Filthy, stinking, bloody, back-breaking, low-paying jobs.

Initially, the refugees were welcomed with open arms. Their willingness to do those jobs kept the factory open and helped shore up the local economy. Unfortunately, the populace's goodwill lasted only as long as it took for one of Little Piggy's few remaining white workers to get fired. Instantly, longtime residents were bitching and moaning about foreigners taking jobs away from *real* Americans—forgetting or ignoring the fact that the one white guy who got fired was a thief who left work every day with his dinner stuffed in his coat pockets. Those bitching and moaning the loudest would sooner chugalug a bottle of kerosene than work at Little Piggy.

Burt was on it like stink on a skunk. He came up with a rallying cry—Oklahoma for Oklahomans—and resurrected his old fib about being related to former governor Alfalfa Bill Murray, who was the kind of all-things-to-all-people shit-stirrer Burt aspired to be.

I stayed away from Burt's rallies on general principle. In fact, I hadn't seen Burt since he got out of jail, but from what I understood, when it came to scapegoating those poor Asian families, he pulled out all the stops. It's not like the white folks came in contact with the immigrants; most of them lived in a company-run trailer park near the plant and almost never came into town.

That didn't matter to Burt. He'd rant with counterfeit outrage about how Alfalfa Bill wouldn't have put up with illegals taking away jobs from native Oklahomans, and that, by God, neither would he. Before long, people whose only crime was to work jobs native-born Okies refused to do were getting their tires slashed and having epithets spray-painted on the walls of their trailer homes. So far, none of them have been physically attacked, but at the rate things were going, it was only a matter of time.

Meanwhile, passion for our ex-sheriff rekindled. Women threw panties on stage at his rallies, like Burt was Elvis Presley instead of a five-foot-six, 250 lb. ex-convict with a face like a buffalo's scrotum and a bucket of water moccasins where his heart ought to be. His primary opponent—the dull-witted son of an out-of-state oil millionaire who aspired to be a right-wing version of Bobby Kennedy—tried to out-race-bait Burt, but realized it couldn't be done. He dropped out. Democrats were too scared to even put up a candidate. For Burt, the coast was clear.

"Wrongly Convicted Lawman Redeemed," read the headline in one Oklahoma City paper, the day after Burt captured the nomination. He kept campaigning even after he had the election in the bag. Maybe he didn't want to count his chickens before they hatched. I expect the real reason was he craved attention like a junkie craves dope.

Burt even scheduled a rally in Burr, despite knowing it most likely would attract only a few die-hards. Sentiment might've played a part. His wife Kath is from here. Most likely, however, it was his addiction to adulation. I'm sure in his mind, getting fussed over a little is better than not getting fussed over at all.

The rally was scheduled for Friday, June 25th, 1976, only a few days before his scheduled Fourth of July shindig in Temple City on the bicentennial of the nation's birth. By comparison, the Burr rally was a minor event. The Temple City rally promised to be the real blowout, with thousands of proud Americans waving flags, ingesting vast quantities of barbeque and beer and line dancing to a Buck Owens and the Buckaroos tribute band. At the end, they'd set off the fireworks as Burt whipped the crowd into a patriotic lather.

That was the plan, anyway. It didn't happen.

If you're a history buff like me, you might recognize that date to have a significance of its own.

June 25, 1976, was the 100th anniversary of Custer's Last Stand.

CHAPTER ONE

"Don't forget, Emmett," said Karen. "You've got a dentist's appointment this morning."

I tried to open my eyes, but they'd glued themselves shut overnight. I pried them open with my fingers.

"Not exactly the first words you want to hear when you wake up in the morning."

She yawned. "Would you prefer, 'Congratulations, you've won a lifetime's worth of free accordion lessons?'"

Her yawn made me yawn. "I wouldn't go that far."

I stared at the ceiling above our bed. There's a water stain shaped like the Virgin Mary that I've been keeping my eyes on. "I'm going to be pretty busy, Red." Sometimes I call her that, owing to her hair. "I might have to reschedule."

She made a sound like she was spitting out a bug that had flown into her mouth. "You canceled last week and the week before. If you don't get that filling replaced, buster, you're going to have real problems."

"Don't worry, I'll get it done."

Truth is, I'd rather take a length of string, tie one end to the offending tooth and the other to a doorknob, then slam the door,

Three Stooges-style. That way the tooth would be gone, and I could quit worrying about it.

There's nothing wrong with Dr. Rader, my dentist. He's good at his job, plus I'm pretty sure he's the only person in Burr besides me who knows who Thelonious Monk is. Our conversations about music take some of the edge off having my teeth worked on.

But only up to a point.

"You're worried about the pain, I guess," said Karen.

"You're not wrong."

"Maybe you should try hypnosis. I hear it can cure a multitude of ills."

"That'd be great. Let me know if you run into Count Dracula."

The trouble is, I'm allergic to Novocaine or Lidocaine or whatever it is that makes your mouth numb. It makes me throw up and break out in hives and gives me heart palpitations. The last time I had work done, Dr. Rader tried giving me laughing gas. It made me feel like someone had stuffed a chloroform-soaked rag in my face and lowered me into my grave. He had to finish with no anesthesia except oil of cloves. You might as well give baby aspirin to a man having his leg amputated.

"My appointment's at 9:30. If nothing comes up, I'll go."

"Oh, Emmett, not again," she said, knowing as well as I did that something always comes up when there's a dentist appointment on the agenda. She sighed and shook her head.

That's how a lot of our conversations end.

We rolled out of bed and got dressed. There was a moment of confusion when I tried to pull on my uniform pants but couldn't get them up over my thighs. I realized they were hers. I handed them over and found a pair of my own.

We adjourned to the kitchen. "Bacon and toast?" she asked. Left to my own devices, I'll usually have a glass of orange juice and a couple of powdered donuts for breakfast, but if Red wants to cook me up some bacon, I'm not going to argue. "Sounds good, thanks."

"Oh, and don't forget, you also need to take Mr. Paws to the vet."

"That's going to have to wait if I'm going to the dentist."

"Tomorrow, then. I want to let him go outside, but we can't until he gets his shots."

Mr. Paws is the newest addition to our family.

A while back, Karen decided she wanted a pet. We hadn't had one since our dog Dizzy died. I didn't want one, necessarily, but I went along with it to make her happy. Her first choice was something called a "hedgehog." They look more like little porcupines than the hogs I'm familiar with, but Red thought they were cute. I said, Fine, let's get a hedgehog. We looked into it. Turns out you had to send away to New Zealand to get one. Shipping a hedgehog from New Zealand costs about the same as if you flew there and picked one up in person.

We put the hedgehog plan on hold.

Then, one day about a month ago, I was walking down Main Street and came upon a little boy and girl trying to give away a box of dewy-eyed kittens. I took the only male; a year from now, I didn't want to find myself camped out on the sidewalk trying to unload kittens of my own. The hedgehog problem disappeared the second Karen laid eyes on Mr. Paws. She's his mama. I'm his I-don't-know-what. The only time he has any use for me is when he's hungry.

Karen left for work while I ate. She's my second-in-command, so we alternate days going in early. Today was her turn. I ate my breakfast and read the newspaper. Mr. Paws tried to crawl up my pants leg, which I took to mean I was supposed to feed him. I opened up a can of that godawful-smelling food of his and mushed it up in his bowl. I also took a couple of steaks out of the freezer to thaw for dinner. Household chores out of the way, I buckled on my gun belt, put on the fedora I wear instead of a cowboy hat, and left for work.

Karen was talking to someone on the radio when I arrived at the station. She saw me and said, "Emmett, I've got Bernard on the horn." Bernard is the county sheriff's deputy who works our neck of the woods. "There's a fire out at Indian Valley. He thinks you should get out there."

Indian Valley. Damn.

Indian Valley isn't a valley, and it doesn't have anything to do with Indians. It's an abandoned schoolhouse. More than that, it's the first school I ever went to. I attended kindergarten at Indian Valley.

It closed over 20 years ago. There was talk about making it into a museum for antique farm machinery, but when that didn't pan out, people seemed to forget about it. Years of neglect turned it into an empty husk occupied by rattlesnakes and prairie dogs and an occasional cow looking for some shade. With summers getting drier and wildfires becoming so common, it was only a matter of time before the place burned down.

Don't ask me why they named it Indian Valley; the surrounding land is as flat as a pancake. I guess it's just one of those Oklahoma place names that don't make any sense, like Pink or Slapout.

I asked her to cancel my appointment with Dr. Rader. She rolled her eyes but said she would. On my way out the door, I asked her to call the vet, Dr. Skeehan, and ask if it's ok to bring in the cat tomorrow morning. She said she'd do that, too.

Our department motor pool comprises two blue and white AMC Javelin police cruisers and an old Plymouth Fury we don't actually drive anymore but treat like a museum piece. I requisitioned a Javelin and headed out. This being Oklahoma in the summer, I turned on the air-conditioner full blast. It was already hot and muggy and promised to get worse. The weatherman had said there was a possibility of thunderstorms. Frankly, I think he was pandering to the farmers.

I could see the thinning cloud of smoke a mile away. By the time I got there, the worst was over. Indian Valley School had burned to the ground.

I parked on the road next to the mailbox. By the smoldering remains was a pumper truck with its red emergency lights still spinning. Parked next to it was a white station wagon with "Burr Fire Department" on the side. A few men in protective gear smoked cigarettes and talked among themselves. The fella who called it in, Bernard Cousins, was walking gingerly inside the ruins, dodging hot spots and snapping pictures with the camera hanging from his neck. Bernard started his law enforcement career as one of my officers. Today, he's a Tilghman County deputy sheriff. Karen and I don't have kids, but if we did I'd want them to grow up like him. Over the years, I've had a couple of young men work under me who I felt especially close to. Bernard's one of them.

Darrell Moore, the fire chief, called out, "Hey, Emmett!" I waved back and walked through the high grass toward the scene. Grasshoppers flew ahead of me, crisscrossing in the air like stunt pilots. Close to the building, the grass grew sparser, until the ground was nothing but red dirt and anthills higher than the toes of my boots. To the left side was an ancient cottonwood tree. It was practically a twig when I attended Indian Valley. Now it was at least forty feet high, maybe taller, with massive branches sagging to only four or five feet above the ground. Small leafy growths sprang to life near the massive roots, peeking out like baby kangaroos in their mama's pouch. A pencil-thin lizard with lengthwise yellow and black stripes saw me and skittered away.

The tree was untouched by the fire. Would have been a shame if it burned, too.

As for the building itself, nothing much was left except a red brick chimney and the scorched remains of a corrugated steel building that had once been used to park a school bus. The fire had been dowsed, but wisps of smoke still rose from the rubble. Blackened shingles from the collapsed roof covered what had once been the floor.

I noticed one more thing, something I hadn't expected: a sicky sweet odor, like a burnt pork roast, but with a metallic tinge. I'd experienced it just a few times, and only once since I finished my military service.

You never really get the smell of burnt human flesh out of your nose entirely.

***

I stepped over the remains of a wall and walked over to Bernard. He was bent over something on the floor that resembled an overdone Thanksgiving turkey. It wasn't. It was human. Or had been, anyway.

He raised the camera, circled the body, and snapped photos from every angle.

"I wasn't expecting this," I said.

"Yeh," he said, glancing up at me. "I didn't want to say anything about it over the radio."

The body seemed to be male, but that was far from a sure thing. Beside it was a tin can and an empty wine bottle. The can was burnt almost completely black. The bottle was scorched, but I recognized it as a bottle of Boone's Farm Strawberry Hill.

"Any ID?" I asked.

"Not that I can see. I guess he might have a wallet, but I'd have to lift the body to find it and I didn't want to do that. It'd probably be burned up, anyway."

"Any idea who it is?"

He shook his head. "I was hoping you might know."

"No way to tell, is there?"

"I'm guessing it's some hobo," he offered. "No sign of any other belongings other than these." He nudged the can and bottle with the toe of his boot. "That's a Sterno can. Looks to me like he got drunk and passed out while cooking his dinner."

Strawberry Hill is pretty weak stuff, but I reckoned he was probably right.

"What's Darrell think?"

"The same thing."

I scanned the area around the body. "If he'd been cooking, you'd expect to see something else. A pan. A fork and a knife. A can, even."

Bernard shrugged. "Could have been roasting something on a stick."

I shrugged back. "Maybe," I said. "I'd best go talk to Darrell." We walked over to the pumper truck. The chief had his back turned. I tapped him on the shoulder to get his attention. "Hey Emmett," he said. "Sad business, ain't it?"

I nodded, then asked him what he thought had happened. He gave me the same answer as Bernard.

"Pearl Eller called it in about an hour ago," he added, pointing to the nearest house, barely visible, several hundred yards away. "It was basically gone by the time we got here," he said. "All we could do was keep it from spreading."

"Who found the body?"

Bernard and Darrell looked at each other and shrugged. "I guess we all did," said Bernard. Darrell nodded his agreement.

I asked Darrell if any of his men had handled the body. He said his boys knew better than that. Before I could ask, he said he hadn't found anything that might help identify the victim.

"Arson, maybe?" I asked.

He shrugged. "It's possible, I suppose, but not likely. No one was ever going to torch this dump for the insurance money. Like I told Bernard, I reckon what happened was, he drank too much and passed out while cooking his supper."

The radio in Darrell's station wagon kicked on. Darrell excused himself and went to see what was up. He said a few words into the handset, then called out, "We're needed on another call, chief." The fire was as extinguished as it was going to get. I told him he could go.

Bernard used his radio to call the medical examiner's office. He was told it might take a while; they were tied up with something else. We spent a few minutes walking the scene, not knowing what we were looking for, but hoping we'd know it when we saw it. That smell of cooking flesh started to get to me, so I forced myself to breathe through my mouth. I thought of those steaks I'd taken out to thaw. Now I was thinking a salad for supper might be nice.

Before long, the crown of my fedora and the underarms of my shirt were soaked in sweat. We still hadn't found anything. I suggested we sit in my air-conditioned cruiser and wait for the medical examiner. "Sounds like a plan," said Bernard.

We luxuriated in the cool air for a minute. Bernard asked, "Didn't you go to school here when you were little?"

"Yup. Kindergarten. The elementary school in town didn't have one, so my mamma brought me here. She wanted me to get a head start on reading. Drove me here in that old Model A of my father's. Not a lot of women drove back then."

"Your daddy always was a Ford man, wasn't he?"

"He was. He'd turn over in his grave if he knew I'd bought Ramblers for the department." Javelins are American Motors products; around here, any American Motors product gets called a Rambler.

Bernard brought up Burt Murray's rally, scheduled for the next day. I made it clear by my silence I wasn't in the mood to talk about that. We listened to the engine run and the AC blow in awkward silence.

"Hey," he said, "did you hear old Pete Kuhlman passed?"

Pete Kuhlman was an elderly, tight-as-a-gnat's-ass oil and gas millionaire who lived in a tiny house and bought groceries with money he got from returning Coke bottles for the nickel deposit. "I hadn't heard that," I said. "What'd he die of?"

Bernard shrugged. "I'm not sure. He was failing pretty steady the last few years. Myrtle Dennis has been going over there once a week to check on him, although from what I understand, he kicked her out a couple of weeks back. She was concerned about him, so a few days ago she went out to check. Found him dead."

"That's a shame," I said, knowing not many would agree. Pete had the reputation of being someone you'd be wise to stay clear of.

"Pete was all alone in the world, wasn't he?"

"He was," I said. "His wife died when I was in high school. His daughter Jane died a year or two after."

"Maybe losing them is why he got so mean."

"I'm sure it didn't help," I said. "I remember Jane had a young son. Pete was the child's only living relative, but he didn't want to raise the boy, so he was put up for adoption."

"It might've been good for Pete to have someone to spend all that gas and oil money on."

"I doubt Pete would've looked at it that way. I'll bet that old bastard still had the first penny he ever made."

I saw something move out of the corner of my eye. A stray dog skulked toward the smoldering remains, probably attracted by the smell. I honked, but it didn't pay attention, so I got out and shooed him away.

We waited some more. The air conditioner was turning my sweat into little ice cubes. I adjusted the vent so it wouldn't blow in my face. "Any idea what they're going to do with Pete's estate?"

"Probably the same as they did with Earl Calvert's," said Bernard. Earl was another old farmer in the area who died earlier this year. I didn't know him very well, but I remember he was a lot nicer than Pete. "Why do you ask?"

"Because he had a lot of oil money with nobody to leave it to," I said. "Old Earl wasn't as cheap as Pete was."

"You got that right. Ever see that fishing boat of his?"

"Don't believe I ever did."

"He kept it out to Burr Lake. Dang thing's as big as a battleship."

In the distance, a pair of vehicles kicked up dust. "Must be our ME," said Bernard.

"So what's going on with Earl's estate?"

"No idea."

It momentarily struck me as strange that two rich old farmers without family to leave their money to would die within a couple of months of each other. I guess some folks outlive everyone they care about.

I sure hope that doesn't happen to me.

A white Ford Econoline van with "Tilghman County Medical Examiner" stenciled on the side in green block letters pulled up. Close behind was the vehicle this county still uses for medical emergencies: an old bronze-colored Chrysler combination ambulance/hearse from Pate's Funeral Home.

I should say here, as a public service: If you value your health, you'd best try not to have any medical emergencies when you're in Tilghman County.

We got out to greet them. I knew the boys in the ambulance by sight, but I didn't know their names. The woman getting out of the Econoline, however, was new to me.

She had dark brown hair woven into a braid and tied into a bun on the back of her head. She wore large oval sunglasses and green doctor scrubs and was at least an inch or two taller than me. I was initially struck by her elegant manner, until she tripped over a rock and almost fell on her face. She recovered nicely, though, casually nodding to the ambulance attendants as she approached.

"Dr. Annie Childers," she said, offering her hand. Her accent suggested she was from a northern state; which one, I couldn't say, but it had to be a long way from Oklahoma. We shook. "You must be Chief Hardy."

"I am," I said. "Good to meet you. I heard they'd hired someone."

She nodded. "Yes. Me."

I started to introduce Bernard, but he said, "Dr. Childers and I have already met." They exchanged faint smiles.

Bernard and I explained the situation. Dr. Childers took off her sunglasses and leaned over the body. After taking a quick look, she went to her van and came back with a black bag. Bernard and I stood aside as she worked. She examined the body, touching it lightly and with great care. I didn't ask questions. The cause of death seemed plain enough. After a while, she asked Bernard if he'd gotten enough photos. He said he had, so she instructed the ambulance attendants to ready the body for transport. She told us her thoughts, which aligned with ours, although she did add, "You never know what you'll find once we get him on the slab."

The attendants seemed to be having trouble getting the corpse on the stretcher. Its arms and hands were raised to shoulder level, like a dog on its hind legs begging for food. Bernard asked Dr. Childers why the arms were like that.

"It's called a 'pugilistic attitude.' It's caused by the shrinkage of body tissues and muscle due to dehydration caused by the fire. It's very common in cases like this."

The attendants finally got the body secured. They rolled the gurney to the door of the ambulance and tried to load it. One of those raised arms got in the way. One of the attendants grasped the hand to lower it. The hand broke off at the wrist and fell to the ground.

"Idiot," said Dr. Childers softly and resignedly, almost like she expected it. I bent over and inspected the hand. I saw something we'd previously missed: a ring, charred nearly as black as the victim's skin. I used a fingernail to rub away a spot. Underneath it was silver.

Bernard knelt beside me. "That looks like a class ring of some kind," he said.

Dr. Childers saw what we were looking at. "Don't try to pry it off," she said. "I'll do it later."

Bernard took close-ups of the amputated hand and the ring. When he finished, the attendant who broke it picked up the hand and placed it in a large plastic bag. Dr. Childers apologized for calling him an idiot. "That's ok," he replied. "I kind of am."

"Give us a call if you find out where that ring's from," I said. "If we can find out the school it's from, it might help us ID this poor fella."

"It might not be a fella," she said.

"Fair enough," I said.

She reached into a pocket. "Here's my card. If you don't hear from me in a day or two, give me a call."

I said I would. We said our goodbyes and she and the hearse drove away. Bernard wanted to stay and take a few more pictures. I told him to let me know if he found anything. He said he would.

I pondered the tragedy on the drive home, wondering who the victim was, and what he was doing there. I hoped the ring might help us discover the poor soul's identity.

I didn't give another thought to the deaths of Pete Kuhlman and Earl Calvert.

CHAPTER TWO

Most folks know about the Battle of Little Big Horn, where Crazy Horse's band of Sioux warriors wiped General George Custer's Seventh Cavalry off the face of the earth. Fewer are familiar with Old Yellow Hair's second-most-famous military encounter.

It occurred eight years before Little Big Horn. At the time they called it The Battle of the Washita River, although calling it a "battle" is a stretch, to put it mildly. It was a slaughter, an act of genocide— not the first inflicted on American Indians by white men, but definitely one of the most savage. Custer and his boys butchered a village of freezing, near-starving, peaceful Cheyenne, most of them women and children. It happened an hour or so south of here. Today at the site, descendants of the Cheyenne who died that day tie little scraps of colorful fabric in the trees as a physical manifestation of their prayers for the dead. I've visited the place many times. It always gives me chills.

George wasn't only a blood-thirsty maniac; he was also a few beers short of a six-pack in the brain department. Put it this way: Custer more than earned that last-place standing in his class at West Point. The things George was best at were blowing his own horn and kissing the rear end of anyone who could give his career a boost.

As far as I can tell, the only difference between George Custer and someone like John Dillinger is that Custer's murders were sanctioned by the United States government.

That Burt Murray's rally fell on the 100th anniversary of Custer's unwilling day of atonement escaped my notice until much later. Sometimes I wonder if Burt himself had known. He probably wouldn't have cared even if he did. Burt always considered himself immune to consequences of any sort.

He was like Custer in that way. Neither of them thought they could be touched.

***

For me, June 25th started off as a typical day, except that I had an errand to run on my way to work.

I'd lain awake much of the previous night, thinking about the fella who'd died at Indian Valley. I had no idea who he was. I'd probably be the one to break the news to his next of kin, so part of me hoped he wasn't from around here. It's hard delivering bad news anytime, but even worse when it's to someone you know.

I tiptoed around as I got dressed for work, not wanting to wake up Red. I managed to find my own uniform pants this time.

I ate my powdered doughnuts and read the paper. The lead story was about a jailbreak at the state prison. Sometimes I think McAlester has a revolving door only the inmates know about. There was also an article about Jimmy Carter, the ex-governor of Georgia, locking up the Democratic nomination for president. He's a Democrat, which means—unless it comes out that he's killed somebody or committed an act of treason somewhere down the line—he'll get my vote. Mine might be the only one in Tilghman County he can take for granted.

Before going into work, I had to take Mr. Paws to the vet. Karen had forgiven my canceled dentist appointment but insisted I take the cat in for his shots. I opened up a can of food to get his attention, then wrestled him into the cat carrier. He wasn't happy, but there wasn't much he could do about it.

Sweat sprouted on my forehead as soon as I walked out the door. The sun was a pink ball in the eastern sky and the air smelled of smoke. The blaze at Indian Valley wasn't the only one we'd had recently. Wildfires were springing up all over the place.

I loaded the cat carrier into my pickup and turned the ignition. It made a sluggish sound like it didn't want to start, but it finally did. I made a mental note to take into my mechanic the first chance I got. If it's not one thing, it's another.

This would be my first visit to Dr. Jess Skeehan. My take on him, based on nothing but conjecture, was that he's one of those bright fellas who made his way in life by discerning a need and filling it. Most vets in these parts specialize in large animals because there's a demand for it, and because that's where the money is. There aren't as many who treat dogs and cats and guinea pigs and such. Before Jess Skeehan moved to town, Burr hadn't had one for as long as I could remember. His arrival fell under my radar when he moved here a year or two ago. Our dog was long dead, so we had no need for his services. Now we did.

Skeehan's clinic was a converted house—a low-to-the-ground, one-story dirty-yellow brick job a mile or so east of town. Stenciled on the mailbox was: "J. Skeehan, DVM." The lot was surrounded on all sides by rusty barbed wire held up by rotting fence posts. The fence was lined by a row of arthritic blackjack trees. The front and side yards were made of hard-packed red dirt with patches of weeds here and there. In the back yard there was a strange-looking dumpster contraption with a big tube sticking out of the top. In the driveway was a cream-colored Pontiac Bonneville.

Mr. Paws was cowering and trembling and had backed up as far as he could in his little cage. I apologized for having to put him through this and carried him to the front door. I tried the doorbell but didn't hear it ring, so I raised my hand to knock. Before I could, the door was opened by a short, skinny man with a pale complexion and wispy red hair. "I wasn't sure if it worked," I said, nodding at the doorbell.

"It works," said Dr. Skeehan. His smile revealed teeth so white, you'd think he was a dentist and not a vet. "Come on in."

I could see right away he was one of those men who you can't really tell how old they are. He could be in his 20s, he could be in his 40s, or anywhere in between. If he was tall, you could say he was built like a beanpole, but I had to bend my neck to look down at him, and I'm no Wilt Chamberlain.

The floor of the waiting room was covered with worn gray industrial tiles and a ratty fake Persian throw rug covered in animal hair. The ceiling sagged, making it seem like we were walking under an old mattress. Red molded plastic chairs lined the walls. Lysol tussled with the smell of cigarette smoke and cat pee for domination. A Formica counter cut the room in half. On the wall behind the counter was a poster. Above a picture of the Cheshire Cat, it said, "Have you checked your kitty's teeth lately?" That cat looked an awful lot like Jess Skeehan.

On one wall was the stuffed head of a good-size elk. Skeehan noticed me looking at it. "That's a beauty, ain't it?" he said.

I agreed it was. I asked if he was a hunter.

"Yup. Every fall, I take a trip to Colorado and hunt elk." He gestured toward his trophy. "That one there's my pride and joy. Six points. Got it last year. Shot and stuffed it myself."

"A vet that does his own taxidermy, huh?"

"Yeh," he said with a grin. "I tell people, 'Bring your pet to me, you're guaranteed to get it back—one way or the other!'" He was wildly self-amused by his witticism; his laugh sounded like a braying donkey. I smiled politely and glanced nervously at Mr. Paws. "Don't worry," he said. "I've never had to stuff a cat."

That didn't comfort me much.

I followed him into the examination room. He pulled out three syringes and told me what diseases they were for. The only one I recognized was rabies. Mr. Paws hissed when Dr. Skeehan opened the cage. "That's ok, kitty-kitty-kitty-kitty-kitty," he said. "Nice Dr. Jess isn't going to hurt you." He reached in, then jerked out his hand and cursed. Mr. Paws had laid a nasty scratch on him. Skeehan's face clouded over for an instant, but he recovered. He fake-smiled and fake-laughed and said, "Maybe you should do it." I could almost see the smoke coming out of his ears. You'd think he'd be used to recalcitrant animals.

Mr. Paws didn't like it any better when I reached in, but at least he didn't scratch me. I held him as gently as I could while the doctor gave him his shots.

"All done!" said Dr. Skeehan, his eyes and teeth bugging out like a carnival geek. He gave me one of those I'd-love-to-stab-you-in-the-face-with-an-ice-pick-but-the-rules-of-society-frown-on-that-sort-of-thing grins and told me a few things about how to care for Mr. Paws. I wasn't really listening. I couldn't get away fast enough. We settled my bill. Mr. Paws and I went on our way.

***

I drove back home to drop off Mr. Paws. Karen still hadn't left for work.

"How'd it go?" she asked.

I described the visit.

"Huh," she said. "Sounds like a nut."

"Next time I'll take him to a vet in Temple City."

"That's probably a good idea."

When I got back in my truck, it wouldn't start. Karen told me if I'd wait, she'd give me a ride, but I said I'd just as soon walk.

In the old days, a walk to work from our house took maybe five minutes. Our new station is further away, however, at the far end of the downtown business district. It's more of a hike than a leisurely stroll. Not that I miss the old place. It had more in common with a Porta-Potty than a proper police station. The worst thing about it was that the holding cell was located in my office. Criminals tend not to be excessively well-groomed, and our lock-up had an unfortunate tendency to retain the stink of whatever villain had last taken up residence. Sharing a space the size of a walk-in closet with someone who's recently downed a case of beer, thrown-up and peed all over himself isn't as much fun as it sounds.

There was still smoke in the air from the wildfires outside town. After fifteen minutes, I felt like I'd been French-kissing a diesel stack. I walked through the door of the station and was hit by a blast of cold air, which in the summer is about as good a feeling as there is that doesn't involve carnal pleasure. The old place only had an under-powered and overworked window unit, which occasionally caught fire, for reasons we never discovered.

The air-conditioning isn't the only good thing about our new headquarters. It's got wall-to-wall carpeting. I even have an office separate from the holding cell. There's a good-sized squad room where my assistant-chief-slash-wife has her desk. We even have central heat and air, so we can make it hot in the winter and cool in the summer, as Mother Nature intended.

Our dispatcher and receptionist, Cindy Barrett, sat at her post behind a Formica counter facing the twin glass doors. I greeted her and asked if there was anything I needed to know.

"There's another wildfire in Butcherville," she said, "but it's mostly been contained."

That explained the haze.

On the way back to my office, I ran into Joel Carter, our most recent hire, walking out the door leading to our holding cell. He'd arrested someone for DUI at the end of his shift. We talked a bit. I reminded him that the rally was scheduled to start at noon. "Go home and get a couple of hours of sleep, but be back by 10:00. This is one of those all-hands-on-deck deals."

He saluted. "Aye, aye, Captain."

I called Wesley Harmon over at the Sinclair station and asked him to tow my truck. Wes works on all the city vehicles. He'll talk your ear off when you're not in the mood, but he's the best mechanic in the county. He said it'd be a while before he could get to it. I told him there was no rush, that I could drive Karen's car or one of the Javelins if I needed transportation.

I spent time signing a pile of documents Red left on my desk. A sheriff's deputy showed up to escort Joel's DUI to the county jail in Temple City. At one point, a self-employed small-engine mechanic by the name of Jessie Ray Sloan showed up to complain about a ticket he'd been written for the enormous pile of junk accumulating in his backyard.

"It's a planter, Chief Hardy."

"It's a bunch of worn-out tractor tires piled around a rusted-out Volkswagen."

"It's modern art," said the man who wouldn't know a Picasso from a pitchfork.

"It's an eyesore and it attracts rats. Y'all have a nice day."

Red clocked in at 10:00. I'd kept her up all night with my tossing and turning, so I didn't begrudge her an extra few hours of sleep. Joel showed up soon after, having gotten no sleep at all.

Joel's been on the force for a little over a year. We hired him in the wake of a certain catastrophic event I don't want to get into right now, although I expect I'll need to explain it soon enough. For now, let's just say he's a wonderful young fella and we're lucky to have him.

There is one other thing I should mention. Joel is also Black, which—depending on where you were raised—might or might not seem like a big deal. Around here, it definitely is.

Before Joel, Burr had never had a Black cop. That probably wouldn't surprise anyone with even a tiny speck of knowledge of how things are in this part of the world. What might surprise you—if you grew up in a place a little bit less racist than Burr, Oklahoma—is that before Joel moved here, this town hadn't even had a Black resident since the Youngers, the family Burt Murray and Frank Sallee killed.

Red, Joel, and I met in my office and discussed the rally, which was scheduled to begin in a couple of hours. Basically, all we did was confirm the plan we came up with the day before. We'd be stretched pretty thin, but I reckoned that with three of us plus my part-timer, Pat Bragg, we'd handle it alright. Burt's campaign manager told me all they needed us to do was direct traffic. They'd provide their own security. Since Burr doesn't have a town square or even a decent public park, the campaign got a permit to set up a stage in the middle of the business district, directly in front of Miller's Drugstore on the south side of the street. They hauled in a flatbed trailer overnight for that purpose.

At 11:00, we made the short drive downtown. Pat and I rode in one Javelin, Red and Joel the other. The plan was for Pat and Red to use the cruisers as roadblocks at either end of the business district, while Joel and I monitored the crowd in case we needed to augment Burt's security force. Folks had already staked out spots in front of the stage when we got there. Most dressed like they were going to a picnic—the women in modest dresses, the men in jeans and short-sleeved shirts. Teenage girls in halter tops and cut-offs grabbed the attention of teenage boys, as well as a few old farts whose days of ogling young girls should've been long over. The sign at the bank said the temperature was 102. The combination of heat and smoke had me rationing my breaths.

A couple of minutes before noon, Pat backed up his Javelin and let a car through, prompting the multitude to cheer their ever-loving heads off.

Everyone was happy. Things were under control.

I don't know a lot, but at 12:00 pm on June 25th, 1976, I thought I knew one thing for certain: Burton Murray, late of the Oklahoma State Prison in McAlester and soon of Washington, D.C., was as safe as a newborn in a bassinet.

Of course, I've been wrong before.

CHAPTER THREE

Strictly speaking, Burt didn't drive; he was driven. His chauffeur was a bored-looking uniformed state trooper in mirrored sunglasses. The car was a showroom-new gold Cadillac Eldorado convertible. Burt had on a short-sleeved, white western-style shirt that defied the laws of physics by somehow staying buttoned. On his head was a wide-brimmed tan Stetson with an ostrich feather sticking out of a beaded Navajo hat band. Burt doesn't have a drop of native blood in him, but plenty of voters do.

The crowd swelled to 200 people, maybe more. Except for a handful of our Native American brothers and sisters, every face was as white as George Washington's wig. None of our Southeast Asian neighbors chose to attend. Considering the racist drivel Burt was likely to spout, that was undoubtedly for the best.

At least half of those in attendance waved American flags. Many wore *Vote Burton: Stop the Hurtin'* or *Oklahoma for Oklahomans* buttons. As the car inched toward the stage, it was surrounded by a ring of admirers three or four deep, reaching into the car, trying to touch the hem of his garment. The trooper kept the car moving slowly but not too carefully, apparently willing to accept any squashed Murray supporters as the cost of doing business.

I looked up and down the street for the promised security detail but didn't see one. It was looking more and more like the ill-tempered trooper in the mirrored sunglasses was all we were going to get.

The car finally made it to the stage. My nerves were starting to fray. Everyone seemed to be in a good mood, but it only takes one Lee Harvey Oswald or Arthur Bremer to spoil a party like this.

I motioned for Red to keep her eyes peeled. Joel and I elbowed our way through the crowd to the passenger side of the car. I noticed Mr. Mirrored Sunglasses wasn't wearing a badge or nameplate, presumably because he was working private security without permission.

Joel did what he could to hold back the crowd while I helped Burt out of the car. It wasn't easy. He'd never been the picture of health, but he must've gained 50 pounds since the last time I saw him—at his trial nine years ago, being led away in shackles. Prison food must be better than they say.

Burt smiled and shouted over the din: "Emmett Hardy! Good to see you, buddy! Where've you been keepin' yourself?" Like we were lifelong pals. I couldn't help but admire his *cojones*. Burt's always had a way about him. Like Huey Long, or the man Burt claims to be his cousin, Alfalfa Bill.

"Staying clear of you is where I've been."

"That's nice, that's real nice," he said, more interested in shaking hands and swapping howdies with his army of well-wishers. I could have told him Martians kidnapped President Ford and gotten the same reaction.

Joel and I walked on either side and led him to the back of the stage while he bestowed head-pats, handshakes, and kisses on the cheek to anyone who got close. We reached the steps leading up to the stage, and he held out his hand for me to shake. "Emmett, I just want you to know, I ain't got no hard feelings."

"Burt, I want you to know that I do."

He pulled his hand back and looked at me squinty-eyed, then laughed and clapped me on the shoulder. He said, "You're a good man," which I knew from experience was his stock response to anyone who disagreed with him.

He looked around for steps to climb but none had been provided. He made a half-hearted attempt to pull himself up onto the platform but realized he couldn't do it without looking ridiculous. He asked Joel and me for help. Somehow we managed to give him a boost without giving ourselves hernias.

Meanwhile, the Caddy had driven away. I looked down the street in time to see it disappear around the corner. Apparently, the trooper's duties began and ended at being a chauffeur. In terms of security, we were on our own.

Burt planted himself behind the speaker's lectern and took in the scene, occasionally reaching down to shake more hands or add to his Guinness Book of World Records for most babies kissed. I tried to keep one eye on him and the other on the crowd for signs of trouble. His speech was scheduled to start at 12:00, which is when the noon whistle goes off. He knew to wait until it was over before he started his speech.

Burr's siren is perched on the top of the water tower, on a side street about 50 yards behind Miller's. It went off at the stroke of twelve, as usual. It cranked up gradually, then at a certain point got louder than hell. I was standing at the front of the stage, scanning the audience as the siren howled. At the peak of its volume, there was a huge bang. For a split second, I thought it might be a sonic boom, then I saw a puff of smoke rise from the center of the crowd and knew I was wrong.

Folks scattered until only one person remained in the street—a small, shabbily dressed young woman clutching a long-barreled Colt revolver. Joel, Karen, and I drew our weapons and shouted for her to drop it. I looked up at the stage and saw Burt had been hit in the upper right arm. His sleeve was soaked in blood, but he didn't appear to be mortally wounded. He yelled, "C'mon back, y'all! I'm alright!" but no one listened. Folks screamed and cussed and hid behind parked cars or whatever other shelter they could find. The woman wouldn't drop the Colt. Joel yelled at her again. She looked at Joel, smiled sweetly, and lowered the gun, seemingly ready to comply.

I guess she changed her mind.

The woman raised the gun quickly and fired again. Joel fired at her in the same instant. She dropped where she stood. Burt fell backwards. Joel rushed to the girl's side and tried to kick the gun away, but her finger had gotten tangled in the trigger guard, so it remained attached to her hand. I scrambled across the stage to where Burt lay on his back. The second shot hit him in the chest. His eyes were closed, and blood trickled from his mouth. His fancy Stetson had fallen off, revealing sparse hair separated into oily little snakes.

Burt never took off his hat in public. Close to death, his baldness was revealed to all. I almost felt sorry for him.

I knelt beside him and grabbed his wrist. He had a pulse, but it was faint. I put my mouth close to his ear and yelled to make myself heard.

"Do you know her, Burt?"

His eyes opened and he tried to speak, but only blood came out.

"Who is she, Burt? Do you know her?"

The front of his shirt was solid crimson. Blood puddled around his body and soaked into the knees of my pants. I yelled for a doctor, but even if there'd been one, he wouldn't have been much help.

"Hang in there, Burt, help's on the way," I said, but it was simply one of those pretty lies you tell a man who's about to die.

He tried to speak once more. Maybe he was trying to tell me who the girl was. Maybe he wanted comfort. Maybe he wanted to apologize for the bad things he'd done. Whatever it was, he couldn't get the words out. With one final effort, he curled his lips in a grisly smile. One eye twitched like he was trying to wink. Then his face went slack.

Burt Murray's baby-kissing days were over.

CHAPTER FOUR

Chaos ensued. Everyone with vocal chords used them at top volume. Toddlers ran around with pee stains on the front of their pants. A photographer for the Temple City paper hustled over to Burt and tried to take some photos. I grabbed him by the belt and dragged him backward across the street while he continued to snap. A few little boys ran up to take a peek at the body of the dead assassin, then scampered away and hid behind their mamas' skirts. Pistols and rifles appeared in the hands of civilian males. I assume they saw this as a long-awaited chance to shoot something bigger than a squirrel. Unfortunately for them, it was all over but the shouting. Joel told them to put their guns away. They gave hum a mean look, but did as they were told.

Karen radioed Cindy and told her what had happened, then helped Pat rope off the area with crime scene tape.

Camera shutters clicked. Conversations overlapped. You couldn't understand what was being said, but the emotions were raw and easy to read.

I wondered what Burt would've thought about it if he hadn't been the victim.

I left his side and joined Joel beside the shooter.

"Dead?" I asked.

He looked agonized. "I had to do it, Chief."

"You don't have to convince me."

He nodded toward Burt. "What about him?"

"He's done."

"Great. So I killed her for nothing."

I knew how he felt. I have a couple of notches on my gun I wish I didn't.

"I'd have done it myself," I said, trying to give him the comfort I couldn't give Burt. "You were just faster."

He shook his head.

I would've given him time to get hold of himself but there was too much going on and we were already under-manned. I sent him across the street to help Pat keep folks at bay, then kneeled to get a closer look at the dead woman.

She wore a soiled pullover shirt with red and yellow stripes. Her pants were pinkish-red and as filthy as the shirt. On her feet were a pair of worn-out sneakers that at one time had probably been white but were now the color of Oklahoma red clay. Her face and hands were as dirty as her clothes. She reminded me of the bag ladies I'd seen on the streets of New York City—sad, defeated women with no place to go, standing in line on the sidewalk outside a church mission, hoping for a bowl of soup and a warm place to sleep. During the Great Depression, people like that used to hop freight trains and ride the rails. Sometimes they'd get off in Burr, looking for work. They seldom found any.

Karen joined me. "From the city, you think?"

I nodded. "Those clothes look like she dug 'em out of a garbage can."

"Was she carrying a purse?"

"She doesn't look like the purse-carrying type."

I lightly frisked her without finding anything. Her only possessions seemed to be the rags on her back and the gun still connected to her hand. I noticed her belly was kind of big.

I asked Red if she looked pregnant.

"Oh, Lord. I think she might be."

As if things already weren't bad enough.

I took stock to make sure things were getting done that needed getting done. Red began canvassing the crowd. Joel played Whac-A-Mole with youngsters trying to slip under the yellow tape. Pat's our unofficial staff photographer; he made a run back to the station to get his camera.

I turned my attention back to the woman.

She'd fallen on her back with her legs twisted at strange angles, like a marionette with its strings cut. There was a bloody hole under her right armpit but no exit wound. The slug must've still been lodged in her chest. She appeared to be in her early 20s. Her hair was short, blond, and unwashed. It looked like she'd hacked it off herself with a dull knife. Her fingernails were long and jagged. She had a birthmark the color of grape Kool-Aid covering most of her chin. One side of her mouth was scarred, like it had once been seriously burned. Blood from her mouth and nose had started to dry. Pink foam seeped out of the corners of her mouth. Her light blue eyes were wide open, staring at nothing. I couldn't bear to look at her stomach; the possibility that she was with child was almost too hard to take.

People continued to mill around. Pat returned with his camera and snapped photos of both bodies. I made sure he took plenty of close-ups. We needed to cross every i and dot every t. Pretty soon, the higher authorities—Oklahoma State Bureau of Investigation, Tilghman County Sheriff, Highway Patrol—would show up. These days, they tend to let me take the lead on violent crimes in my town. Given Burt's status, however, I knew they'd be all over this. I didn't want to give them anything to gripe at us about.

I had Pat reinforce the roadblocks with sawhorses when he finished taking pictures. Cindy Barrett showed up with a couple of army blankets. "I wasn't sure you'd be able to cover them up," she said. "I thought, you know, with all the little ones—"

"Good thinking," I said. There were still too many kids around, and they'd already seen more than they should. I felt like arresting their parents for not taking them home.

I draped one blanket over the dead woman, carried the other over to Burt, and covered him. Across the street, Karen put her arm around Joel's shoulders and spoke in his ear, obviously trying to buck him up. He'd never fired his gun in anger, much less used it to kill someone. By the time I became a cop, I'd already fought in Korea and seen up-close my share of blood and gore. Joel was denied that dubious privilege. By the time he was old enough to serve, at the tail end of the Vietnam War, the government had done away with the draft. Good for him, although I reckon if he'd gone to Vietnam like so many other young men his age, he'd have developed a callus over his feelings that would've made this easier to deal with.

The clock outside the First National Bank read 12:11. Had it really only been eleven minutes? Already I felt like I'd lugged a buffalo on my back from Tulsa to Boise City.

After I'd gotten a grasp on the situation, I started to wonder: How could such a miserable-looking little gal kill such a powerful man? And why?

Burt screwed over more people in his lifetime than Albert Einstein could count, but he had a knack for talking his screw-ees into believing whatever harm they'd suffered was their own fault. I couldn't imagine what he might've done to this little elf of a girl to make her want to kill him. I'd have understood if he'd been done in by a jilted lover—despite his distinct lack of physical appeal, Burt was a ladies' man of some repute— but this scruffy little thing wasn't exactly his type. He could have forced himself on her, though, in which case, if she was indeed pregnant, Burt might be the father. That could be enough of a motive.

Soon, a pair of Highway Patrol cruisers arrived, followed closely by Tilghman County's resident Oklahoma State Bureau of Investigation agent, Isabel Cruickshank, and the county sheriff, Keith Belcher.

Keith's been sheriff since Burt was convicted and thrown out of office in 1966. I'm hoping he'll keep his job for at least another election cycle or two, and not just because he's a friend: He's also the sole remaining elected Democrat in Tilghman County. People have gotten comfortable with Keith, like they were comfortable with Burt back in the day—the difference being, Keith's an honorable man. He's running for reelection now and having a hard time with it. There's been a rash of car thefts in Temple City lately, and people are starting to blame him.

As for Isabel, she and I get along like a brother and sister. We bark at each other sometimes, but when the going gets tough, it's us against the world.

The two of them took a long look at the girl then joined me up on the podium. Isabel lifted the blanket off Burt. She didn't flinch. Isabel's seen some things. I gave them a condensed version of what happened. She raised an eyebrow at the part about Burt's one-man private security detail disappearing right before the shooting.

"That's suspicious as hell," said Keith. "Any idea where he went off to?"

I shook my head. "Nope. I haven't seen him since he dropped off Burt."

"Did you catch his name?" asked Isabel.

I shook my head. "Nah, Burt didn't introduce him, and he wasn't wearing a badge or a nameplate."

Keith bent over and examined the gun. "Colt Buntline," he said.

"What was this, the Gunfight at the OK Corral?"

The gold Cadillac appeared at the end of the street behind Pat's roadblock. Mr. Mirrored Sunglasses got out and said something to Pat. Pat said something back. Mr. Sunglasses threw the cup to the ground and yelled a cuss word I could hear from fifty yards away.

I pointed him out to Isabel. "There's the bodyguard." She collared one of the other troopers, gave him a gentle push in the direction of Sunglasses, and said, "Tell that guy I want to talk to him."

She rejoined our conversation. "Let me make sure I understand this. Her first shot got him in the arm?"

"That's right."

"Then you looked down and saw she was still holding the gun on him."

"Not exactly. She'd dropped the barrel. It looked like she was trying to decide what to do next."

She gave me long look. I knew what she was thinking, or at least thought I did: Why didn't I or one of my officers shoot the girl before she got off a second shot? I was the most experienced officer present. I had time to bring her down. Why didn't I?

If she'd asked, I probably would've said: There was something about the way she smiled at Joel that made me hold off. It was the smile of a child expecting praise for doing something special. In that second, I felt compassion for her, and that second was all it took. Isabel would've understood, but I'm not sure everyone else would. Even I could see why, given my history with Burt, someone might think I hesitated so the girl could finish the job.

But in the end, Isabel didn't ask. She just nodded, said, "Got it," and strode away to question Mr. Mirrored Sunglasses—looking like Jimmy Cagney itching to slap around a dim-witted henchman, except Jimmy Cagney didn't have waist-length blond hair coiled in a braid down his back.

"How's your tooth, by the way?" Keith asked.

"How'd you know about that?"

"Karen told me about it. You should go to the dentist."

"There's just a hole there where the filling used to be. It doesn't hurt."

"You should go to the dentist before it does. You don't want to have to get a root canal."

"Yeh, I know," I said. "How's the campaign going?"

"It's going," he said gloomily. He nodded down at the body of the young woman. "I'm guessing she's not a local."

"I've never seen her. My people are asking around to see if anyone recognizes her."

"You think Burt did?"

"I tried to ask him there at the end, but he was too far gone. There was a second right after she winged him when I thought he almost smiled at her, but I wouldn't bet my life on it. Mostly, he seemed pissed off at losing his crowd."

"Burt loved being the center of attention," he agreed.

Isabel rejoined us. "The chauffeur's name is Randy Harden. He works out of Enid. He said it looked like you had things under control, so he went to get a hamburger. We'll brace him later, but I don't think he was part of any conspiracy. He's just a moron."

"Burt's campaign staff said all they needed from us was to direct traffic," I said. "They said they'd provide the security."

"Apparently he was it," she said. "They didn't expect trouble because everyone around here loves Murray so much."

A deputy said something to Keith and Keith told us, "So far, no one has recognized the shooter. No one claims to have noticed her at all until she got off the first shot. It's like she appeared from out of nowhere."

"I've got troopers writing down names and phone numbers of witnesses," said Isabel. "I'll have my men follow up."

"Karen's doing that, too," I said.

Keith nodded down at the dead woman. "Maybe one of those cars belongs to her," he said, referring to several vehicles slant-parked across the street from the stage.

Isabel said, "She doesn't look like a car owner to me, but it's worth checking out."

She and Keith broke away to supervise their people. Joel gave his preliminary statement to an OSBI agent. I sent Pat out on patrol. After Joel gave his statement, he, Red, and I had no one to talk to but each other.

Joel could barely speak, except to say, "I'm sorry," over and over.

"You did your job," I said. "You kept other people from getting hurt."

Nothing I or anyone else said made a difference. He would not be consoled.

By mid-afternoon, the street was mostly empty. The bodies had been photographed. An assistant medical examiner—not Dr. Childers, but one of her co-workers—had attended to them, and Pate's hearse carted them away. Onlookers had gotten bored and/or overheated and ran off looking for a place to get cool. Isabel told us we could get back to our normal business. Isabel made an appointment for Joel to make his official statement to one of her agents the next morning.

Half-kiddingly, I asked if he needed a lawyer.

She answered, dead seriously: "I'll let you know."

"You're not saying he was in the wrong here, are you?"

"No, I'm not saying that, but these things have to take their natural course. There's a process."

I could've gotten angry—I guess I did, on the inside—but I managed to keep it under wraps. I told Joel not to be shy about asking for help, and Karen escorted him away. Isabel said, "There's something I need to tell you, Emmett," but one of her people called to her from across the street. "Never mind," she said. "We'll talk later."

After a spell, Karen came back. I asked what she'd done with Joel.

"Bought him a Coke and sent him home." She asked about my tooth. I said it was fine.

I realized I had an appetite. I asked Red if she was hungry. She said, "No thanks," like I'd suggested she wash her hair in the toilet. I put my arm around her, and we walked toward the car. She shivered despite the heat—the first time today she'd shown any sign of being upset. Red's tough. One time she pulled the trigger on a man in the course of saving my life. What she did wasn't much different from what Joel did, except she got the bad guy before the bad guy got me.

"Why don't you call it a day?" I said.

She gave me a hopeful look. "Are you sure?" she asked. "We've got a lot to do."

"I can handle it."

She gave me a relieved smile. "Well, if you're sure."

She's tough, but even Muhammad Ali takes a break between rounds.

CHAPTER FIVE

I should probably tell you something more about Joel Carter and how he came to work for us. But first, I'll have to fill you in on a little history.

A few years ago, we had a young man working for us by the name of Kenny Harjo. Kenny was an Indian, a member of the Muscogee Creek Nation. Kenny's being an Indian shouldn't have mattered, but of course it did.

We brought him on board as a part-time officer in the early '60s. Until we were able to make him full-time, he held down a second job at the local hardware store, and a third as Burr's Animal Control Officer. In those days, the only other full-timer besides me was Bernard Cousins. Bernard was my protégé, but pretty soon Kenny was giving him a run for his money. Before long, it got to where I held both young men in similarly high regard.

A few years ago, I started thinking about retiring, and who would replace me when I did. I wasn't close to being old enough to collect Social Security, but I was coming up on the time I could receive my pension from the city. Coupled with the income from the oil and gas leases I'd inherited from my folks, paying the bills wouldn't be an issue. As long as we stick to driving Fords instead of Maseratis, or don't become degenerate gamblers, Karen and I should be comfortable in our golden years.

I was confident the town government would let me choose my successor; the trick was who to choose. I had two quality people on the force, equally well-trained and qualified (three, if you count Karen, but she wants to retire when I do). I knew either Kenny or Bernard would do a great job. I couldn't imagine choosing one over the other. You don't ask a father which of his kids he loves the most, right? Fortunately, the problem solved itself when Bernard got the job with the county. Kenny became next in line by default.

I wanted to leave myself room to change my mind, so other than telling Karen, I kept my retirement plans to myself. But the more I thought about it, the more I wanted to do it. For a while, I thought I'd bow out on my 50th birthday, June 5th, 1977. However, all the hoopla in the lead-up to America's 200th birthday made me think I should move it up a year, to July 4th, 1976. I liked the idea of going out with a bang.

Of course, you know what they say: If you want to make God laugh, tell him your plans. I didn't, but someone must have.

Things started going sideways in '74. The oil-producing countries in the Middle East decided to teach the US a lesson for backing Israel in the latest war over there and stopped selling us their oil. That was bad for most of the country, but it was good for Burr, since we had an ocean of the stuff right under our feet. Lots of new drilling commenced. People flocked here, looking for jobs in the oil field. The town ballooned in size like a pan of Jiffy-Pop.

Unfortunately, all that growth led to a drastic increase in crime. Suddenly, my services were more in-demand than ever. Retiring in '76 would put the town in a bind. I didn't want to leave a rookie in charge, even one as capable as Kenny. I understood I'd have to tweak my plan.

In the end, my plan needed more than a tweak. It had to be changed entirely.

Kenny was shot to death.

It's a long story and I don't want to tell it again. You can read about it elsewhere if you're so inclined. I'll just say this: Kenny died in a large part because of bad decisions I made.

I made those decisions because I was a stone-cold drunk.

They should've fired me, but, for whatever reason, the town council and mayor let me stay. One council member even told me that, after all my years of service, I deserved the benefit of the doubt.

I don't know what that fella was smoking, but I appreciated the sentiment.

For a while after Kenny was killed, Karen and I were the thinnest blue line in the state. If anything positive came out of the experience of losing Kenny, it's that I stopped drinking—for good this time, I hoped. Eventually, we hired Pat part-time, but I needed someone like Kenny, someone whose shoulder I wouldn't have to be looking over all the time.

For the little money I could offer, hiring an experienced hand was out of the question. Not that it really mattered. I wanted someone I could train to do things and understand the town in the same ways that I did. I wanted a smart young guy right out of college, possessed of a burning desire to work a million miles from where anything interesting ever happened. I'd given up on my original plan of retiring in '76, but with any luck, I might find someone I could train to eventually run this place.

While I couldn't bring back Kenny, I could pay tribute to him by hiring someone like him. I don't mean to say I was looking for a rocket scientist who clothes the needy and feeds the hungry in his downtime. Kenny Harjo wasn't a genius and he wasn't a saint; he was just a good man, and as Bessie Smith used to sing, a good man is hard to find. As the first Indian on the Burr police force, Kenny broke down a barrier. I thought it might be good to break down another when I hired his replacement.

I'd honor Kenny's memory by hiring a Black man.

Now, before you go accusing me of being prejudiced against whites, as some people later did, I'd like to point out: There had never been a Black cop in Burr or any other law enforcement entity in Tilghman County. Before—and even after—I hired Kenny, every officer in this area was as white as the sheet of paper I'm typing this on. Furthermore, don't tell me that, by narrowing my focus, I wouldn't be hiring the best person. There must be thousands of men and women of all different colors and creeds who'd do a fine job as Burr's police chief-in-training.

Out of all those, I aimed to hire one who was Black.

Kenny was a full-blooded Indian cop in an all-white town, which was a hard enough row to hoe. In the beginning, he got called names and was subjected to the worst types of disrespect. He kept at it, though, and by the time he died, he'd won over a lot of people. I'm not saying he inspired every white person to love all Indians. Hell, I wasn't born yesterday. I know how whites twist themselves into pretzels trying to rationalize their prejudice. *Now that Kenny Harjo's one of the good ones*, they'll say. Still, there's no doubt he touched many people. His memorial service was packed to overflowing. Most of the faces were white.

Kenny made a difference. I couldn't replace him with just anybody.

I'd considered hiring a Black officer long before, thinking it would shake things up around here, hopefully in a good way. People I know and might otherwise respect throw around that ugly word that starts with "n" without ever having met a Black person. I'd always hoped hiring a Black officer would open some of those people's eyes. Maybe saying I'd considered hiring a Black officer is giving myself too much credit. To be honest, it was more like an idle daydream, something I never acted on for essentially chickenshit reasons.

Now, with Kenny dead, the time for chickenshittery was over.

If they'd known what I had in mind, the town government would undoubtedly have found an excuse to butt in, so I kept my plan to myself. The only person I shared it with was Red, and she wasn't about to tell anyone.

In a way, the entire interview process was a sham. I ended up interviewing lots of people I knew from the jump didn't have a shot.

At first, I didn't get any Black applicants at all, then Red suggested we send flyers to big city colleges with criminal justice programs. I didn't come right out and say I was looking for a Black fella, but I did state in big, bold type we were an Equal Opportunity Employer. We started getting more inquiries. As with most job applications, ours had a little box asking for the applicant's race. Before long we started getting some from Black fellas.

One school where we mailed a flier was the John Jay College of Criminal Justice in New York City. One recent graduate saw it, called us, and asked about the job. His name was Joel Carter.

I got goosebumps just talking to him on the phone. He seemed to be exactly who I was looking for. We talked a bit. I wanted to be clear about what he'd be up against if he got the job. He said he understood and still wanted to interview. We set up a date and time. He lived in New York City and couldn't afford to fly to Oklahoma. I couldn't buy him a plane ticket, so I raided petty cash and fronted him bus fare.

The interview was on one of those late-February days when winter can't decide if it's time to come or go. Joel was already at the station when I got to work. Red introduced him. She said I should be nice to him because he rode a bus all night to get here. We shook hands, and I thanked him for coming.

If my decision had been based on appearances alone, I'd have hired him on the spot. Unlike most of the fellas I'd interviewed who'd shown up dressed in jeans and cowboy boots or ill-fitting polyester shirts and slacks, Joel dressed like 007. He wore a dark suit with narrow lapels and a narrow tie. Everything was narrow, in fact, including the pants, which fit perfectly over a pair of low-cut black boots. He was just as good-looking as James Bond, although I'm not exactly an authority on what women consider attractive. One time Karen told me she thought William Powell—the actor who played Nick Charles in the old *Thin Man* pictures—was sexy. I said I thought he looked like a possum with a moustache. She couldn't watch his movies after that. Said I ruined him for her.

I know this: Standing beside Joel Carter would've had William Powell looking for a rock to crawl under.

I started the interview by grilling Joel on his attitude towards law enforcement. He gave good answers. In short, he viewed the profession as a public service, not as an us-versus-them death struggle, like so many cops do these days. A few times I thought he was being overly careful in the way he answered my questions, but after all, you'd expect a young man interviewing for his first job to be a little edgy. And I liked the fact that he listened to what I had to say. I'd already interviewed too many fellas who treated my half of the conversation as a chance to catch their breath before going on to blab some more about themselves. Joel didn't do that.

I asked about his background. He said he'd grown up in New York City. When I asked him why a young man who'd grown up in New York City would want to move to Oklahoma, he said his birth mother was from Lawton and his birth father had been an artilleryman stationed at Ft. Sill. Joel himself had been born in Lawton.

"You say, 'birth mother' and 'birth father.' I take it you were adopted?"

"Yes sir," he said. "As an infant. My dad was deployed to Korea in 1950. He was killed in action a week before I was born. My birth mother was killed in a hit-and-run accident a year later."

He was taken in by his mother's sister and her husband. Technically, the two women were half-sisters. Their daddy was a Pullman porter with a girlfriend at every stop from New York to San Francisco—which explains why one sister grew up in New York and the other in Oklahoma. When Joel's mother died, the Lawton police tracked down the half-sister as next of kin. She and her husband adopted and raised him in New York City.

"What neighborhood?" I asked.

"Lower East Side," he said. "East 10th and Avenue B."

I said I was familiar with the neighborhood, having lived on East 3rd Street for a time after being discharged from the Marines. "You never know, I might've seen you building a snowman in Tompkins Square."

He smiled. "Could be. I lived right next door. It's funny. I wouldn't have pegged you as a New Yorker."

I chuckled. "I wasn't. That's why I came back here."

We talked about his experience at John Jay. I asked him about a young woman of my acquaintance who'd gone there, but he didn't know her. I explained the racial situation here. I didn't hold back. If anything, I probably made it sound worse than it was. It didn't faze him.

"I don't have any illusions about what I'd be dealing with," he said. "I've been paying attention to what's going on in this country, particularly in the south. I want to do this."

I asked him what first made him want to get into law enforcement.

He gave me another of his shy grins. "Movies."

"Oh yeh? Which ones?"

"Oh, there were a lot of them, but I guess two in particular. *High Noon* was one."

"A favorite of mine, as well. What's the other?"

"*In the Heat of the Night.*"

I should've guessed. "That's a good one, too."

"*In the Heat of the Night* made me feel that what I wanted to do was possible."

"What is it you want to do?"

He leaned forward and said, with so much sincerity it almost made my heart hurt: "Make a difference."

"Well, young man," I said, "You've come to the right place."

***

We talked about his interests. He liked baseball, especially the Giants. Willie Mays was his favorite player when he was a kid. He became a San Francisco fan when the Giants moved there from New York. I was pleased to discover he had a liking for jazz. In fact, he was a jazz drummer. "I'm not very good," he said. "I'm a not-very-good saxophone player," I replied. "Maybe we could start our own not-very-good band." He seemed to get a kick out of that.

After we covered about all there was to cover, I asked him if there was anything he'd like to ask me.

He took a deep breath. "There is," he said. "Why are you doing this?"

"You mean why am I hiring a Black man?"

"That's right."

I paused to formulate my answer. "You know how you said you want to make a difference?"

He nodded.

"Well, I reckon I do, too."

"Alright," he said after thinking about it for a second. "I'll buy that."

I felt like I'd passed an important test.

Then he said, "I need to be sure of one thing."

I asked him what that was.

"Ever since we first spoke on the phone, all I've thought about is what working here would mean."

"I get that," I said. "And since we're being honest with each other, I'll come out and say that you've impressed the heck out of me."

"I appreciate that," he said. "I'm a little worried you haven't thought it through. You say you want to change things, that you want to make things better. I want to believe you, but I guess what I'm saying is: If I'm going to leave behind everything I've ever known to move here and face what you say I'm going to face, I need to be convinced you're not going to pull the rug out from under me if all of a sudden having me around becomes inconvenient."

I took a moment to consider my answer. I thought briefly about explaining what had happened to the Youngers, but I didn't. I'm not sure why. Maybe I thought that if I did, he wouldn't want the job.

"I'll be the first to admit, this town has a sad history when it comes to the way they've treated Black folks. Furthermore, you don't know me, there's no way you can know how committed I am to making this work. I guess all you can do is say 'thanks but no thanks,' or decide to trust me and give it a try."

He nodded thoughtfully. "Is that a job offer?" he asked.

"Conditional on a background check, but yeh, I guess it is."

He looked me over. I looked him over. "Alright, but with all due respect, if I ever get the feeling this whole deal is some kind of a stunt, I'm out."

"You need time to see if my motives are pure?"

"That's one way to put it."

I laughed. "Joel, the only things pure about me are the two loves of my life: Karen Hardy—that's my wife, the red-headed woman you were talking to when I came in—and the music of Charles 'Yardbird' Parker."

His face brightened. "Charlie Parker was my neighbor when I was little. My mom used to play his records for me, and say, 'This guy used to live two doors down from us.' I got tired of hearing it until I grew up and started to appreciate his music."

I told him a story about meeting Parker at a small club in Greenwich Village. "I had dreams of being a jazz saxophonist myself, back then."

"And I wanted to be a drummer."

"Yet here we are."

"Here we are, indeed," he said. We both laughed.

I'd kept him long enough. We stood and shook hands, and I escorted him to the lobby. I asked him if we could give him a lift. He already had a ticket for the next bus back to New York. The Trailways stop was just down the street. He said he'd walk. We said our goodbyes. I told him we'd be in touch.

Karen followed me back to my office.

"How'd it go?" she asked.

"Good."

"He your fella?"

"Maybe," I said. "If he'll have us."

CHAPTER SIX

I woke up the day after the shooting feeling like someone had stuffed Brillo pads up my nose and scraped my esophagus with a rusty hacksaw blade.

Sleep and I have what you might call an adversarial relationship. Since I quit drinking, it's been something I aspire to more than something I actually do. Every night I lay there staring at the insides of my eyelids, thinking about how the night before I'd done the exact same thing. It's not like I slept that great when I was on the sauce, either. I'd drink myself stupid, sleep a little while, have terrible nightmares, then wake up and ... well, stare at the insides of my eyelids the rest of the night. But at least I usually got a couple of hours. These days, it seems the best I can hope for are those last few minutes before the alarm goes off.

Without the booze, and with my throat and sinuses all irritated from all the smoke in the air, I might as well have been trying to sleep in Dr. Rader's dentist chair.

Somehow, amidst all the excitement of the day before, Wes Harmon had managed to tow my pickup. He called and told me it needed a new starter and solenoid. He had to order parts, so he couldn't tell me when it would be ready. I'd driven one of the Javelins home, so that's what I took to work.

Agent Cruickshank was waiting for me when I got there. We went back to my office, and I offered her a chair. "No thanks, I'll only be a minute."

She began by expressing the view that Joel was unlikely to face any repercussions for the shooting. "He only did what had to be done," she said. "It's too bad he was a fraction of a second too late." She said there'd be a formal investigation ("Just ticking off the boxes," as she put it), but barring something unforeseen, Joel was in the clear.

She then confirmed something I'd been afraid of: "The shooter was pregnant. They haven't done an autopsy and I'm not sure they will, but the pathologist in Oklahoma City confirmed it."

Finally, she told me she wouldn't be working the case. "I was going to tell you yesterday but I was interrupted," she said. "I've gotten a job with the FBI. I got the word yesterday morning. I'll be moving to Virginia in a few days."

I hadn't expected it, but I wasn't surprised. I congratulated her and tried to swallow my disappointment. I told her I always knew she was meant for bigger and better things. She thanked me and said this was the fulfillment of a dream. "I'm just sorry to leave you in the lurch like this."

"Don't worry about it," I said. "You'll be running the joint before you know it."

She smiled. "We'll see."

"So, this is your last week with us?"

"Actually, today's my last day. Someone else should take over this case by the end of today. I expect whoever it is will be in touch with you by tomorrow morning."

"I don't know whether to feel good for you or bad for me," I said. "I guess I feel a little of both."

"It's been fun, Chief. Well, not fun, exactly, but ..."

"No, I wouldn't say it was fun." We both chuckled. "But it has been rewarding. I've learned a lot from you."

"I've learned from you, too, Chief."

"I can't imagine it was very much."

"A surprising amount, actually. And not just about police work."

I slid out from behind my desk. "Alright then, you get on out of here. I'm sure you've got a lot to do."

I probably should've given her a hug, but I'm not much of a hugger. I don't reckon she is, either. We shook hands. "Thanks for the memories," I said.

"You're a good man," she said.

"Well, thank you for saying so," I said. "You're a good woman." It sounded corny coming out of my mouth, but that didn't make it any less true.

She nodded in a businesslike way. "Alright, then." She turned to leave, her long blond braid swinging behind her like a bullwhip.

"Tell those boys in Oklahoma City to keep me posted on this Burt thing."

"Will do," she said. "See you later, Chief."

I doubt it, I thought with some sadness.

***

Joel came in later in the morning, after having given his official statement to one of Isabel's colleagues. I told him what had Isabel said—that she didn't think he'd done anything wrong. I suppose he was glad to hear it, but if he was, he didn't show it. Karen and I told him in a dozen different ways he'd done the right thing, but nothing we said had much of an effect. Killing someone—even if unavoidable—can be a traumatic experience.

The first time I had to kill was as a Marine fighting in Korea. A Chinese soldier surprised me, or maybe I surprised him. I shot him in the face point-blank with the same Colt .45 I carry today. Little pieces of him splattered all over my face and clothes, then instantly froze solid, thanks to the sub-zero weather. I was chipping little chunks of bones and brains off my clothes for days after. If I'd had time to brood over it, like Joel did, the experience might've stopped me in my tracks. But I didn't have time to brood. The combat was too fast and fierce.

It soon became obvious Joel was in no condition to work. We'd ask him a question and all he'd do was grunt or mutter a one-word answer. He wasn't being rude; the poor man was distraught. More than once, I suggested it might help to talk about it. He'd shake his head and mumble, "I don't know," or something similar, and that would be it. I thought if anybody could get him to open up, it would be Red, but her luck was no better than mine.

Finally, I told him to take a few days off and sent him home. He put up some zombie-like resistance but ended up giving in.

All morning, reporters from various news outlets called, including fellas from all the national TV networks. I spoke to a few before I finally recognized what kind of day it was going to be. After that I had Cindy refer further press inquiries to the OSBI.

I told Pat not to answer questions about the shooting. I'd forgotten to tell Joel, but I didn't think there was much chance he'd talk. Red knew better, and as for Cindy, a prying newsman would have as much luck trying to squeeze orange juice out of a potato.

***

I had a hellacious dream.

I was sitting at my desk. My office was my office, same as always, except everything in it—walls, floor, ceiling, stapler—was painted orange. Everything, that is, but the telephone, which glowed a bright green like it was lit from within. It rang and I picked it up. On the other end was my unrequited high school crush, a girl by the name of Denise Kinney. She told me to look in my desk drawer. I opened it and found a large glass ashtray. She told me to hang up the phone and look into the ashtray. I hung up the phone and it melted like it was made of wax. I looked into the ashtray, and it became a window into my bedroom. I saw Karen in bed, fast asleep. Suddenly, water began gushing in torrents from under the bed, steadily rising all the way to the ceiling. I yelled for Karen to wake up, but she didn't respond. Soon she was submerged. She never moved but stayed flat on her back, like she was made of stone.

I forced myself awake and reached out in the dark. She was asleep beside me.

You can guess the rest: I spent the rest of the night staring at the inside of my eyelids.

***

I was still thinking about the dream the next morning on the drive to work. Cindy snapped me out of it as soon as I walked in the door.

"There's an OSBI agent in your office."

"Did you catch his name?"

"Joe Heckscher? John Heckscher? Something like that."

Of all the cop shops in all the towns in all the world, John Joe Heckscher walks into mine.

"That's just great," I said.

"That bad?"

"Worse. How 'bout you go tell him I was kidnapped by aliens, and I'll drive around until he's gone?"

"You're kidding, right?"

"Sadly, I am."

I hadn't seen Oklahoma State Bureau of Investigation Agent John Joe Heckscher in ten years. Back then, he was Odell Jones's sidekick. Odell was Isabel Cruickshank's predecessor as the OSBI agent for our area. After a slow start, he and I ended up getting along great. Heckscher was another story.

Heckscher looked enough like the Western Swing fiddle player, Spade Cooley, to be his younger brother, and he was as slippery as a rubber worm dipped in Vaseline. He was also about as big a racist as I'd ever met, which is really saying something coming from a man who grew up in Tilghman County. I didn't like Heckscher then, and unless he'd changed his stripes, I doubted I'd like him now.

Anyway, skunks don't change their stripes.

I found Heckscher with his feet up on my desk, talking on the phone and smoking one of those cigarettes that look like little cigars. I pointed at the "NO SMOKING" sign on the wall. He smiled and winked but kept puffing away.

The lines on his face may have been deeper, but John Joe still had Spade's slicked-back hair and squint-eyed leer. His manner of dress was slightly different from before. Back in the day he wore flashy country & western-style outfits, like a bargain-basement Porter Wagoner. Now he was wearing a sky-blue polyester leisure suit, with bell-bottomed pants and a shiny flowered shirt open at the collar. On his feet were a pair of bright red, silver-toed cowboy boots with fancy white stitching along the sides; one pants leg was hiked up far enough to see the University of Oklahoma logo on the pull straps. He grinned like a shark as he kept up his end of the telephone conversation. Ten years had passed since I'd last seen him, but John Joe Heckscher still struck me as someone who'd cut your throat for a can of Coors.

The conversation finally ended. "You're in my chair," I said bluntly. Courtesy doesn't pay with guys like him.

"I'm sorry about that, Emmett," he said. "Had to make a phone call. Didn't think you'd mind."

"I'd mind a lot less if you'd get your feet off my desk."

"Well, of course," he said, that depraved leer still glued to his face. He slowly lifted his feet down off my desk, got up, and walked over to the water cooler. He put his cigarette out under the spout and tossed the butt into the trash. I sat behind my desk and brushed away pieces of dried mud.

"Sit," I said, motioning to the chair in front of my desk.

He sat.

"I take it you're Agent Cruikshank's replacement."

"That's right," he said.

He shook another little brown cigarette out of the pack. I told him I'd appreciate it if he didn't smoke. He made a face but didn't light it.

I said, "What can I do for you?"

He held the unlit cigarette in front of his face like a woman admiring a new manicure. "Nothing really," he said, "unless you discovered the name of that little gal who shot Murray."

"Can't help you there."

"Still a Jane Doe, then. Well, don't worry. We'll get it squared away."

"What about you?" I asked. "Any progress?"

He smirked. "Not yet. I do find it hard to believe she did it on her own." He crossed his legs and blew imaginary smoke rings. "But we shall see what we shall see."

Neither of us said anything for a moment. From the front of the station I heard Red exclaim, "Heckscher's here?!"

Heckscher chuckled. "I reckon your wife must've missed me. You did marry that little dispatcher, right?"

I ignored the question. Instead, I gave him the universal sign the meeting was over: I stood up. "Alright then, let me know if there's anything I can do to help.

His ass stayed glued in place. "I doubt there will be, but I appreciate the offer."

I waited for him to get up. He didn't. "Anything else?" I asked.

He nodded. "There is one thing. It's about that colored fella."

I sat back down. "You mean Officer Carter?"

He flicked a speck of ash off his jacket. "Carter, that's right," he said. "I'm just wondering if he knew our Jane Doe."

"Why would you wonder that?"

"I don't reckon you asked him?"

"Are you serious?"

His smile didn't contain an ounce of good humor. "Serious as a heart attack," he said.

I don't think I've ever hated anyone more than I did John Joe Heckscher at that moment.

"I didn't ask him anything of the kind. There was no reason to."

He put the cigarette he'd been fiddling with in his mouth. "Don't be so sure," he said with a smirk. He finally got up and made to leave.

On his way out, he took out a white Bic lighter, lit up, and said in his best good ol' boy drawl: "Y'all take care now."

I got up, slammed the door, and sat back down.

Karen came in. "What was he doing here?"

"He's Isabel's replacement on the Murray case."

"Oh, Lord."

"That's what I said."

"It doesn't look like he's changed much."

"He hasn't changed at all. He asked if Joel knew the girl who shot Burt."

She laughed. "Why in the world would he ask that?"

"It's probably just something he pulled out of his rear end."

She frowned. "But still."

"Yeh. I know."

"Are you going to bring it up with Joel?"

I sighed. "Not unless I have to."

"I don't know why you would."

"Neither do I."

"Then don't."

"Alright. I won't."

Unless I have to.

CHAPTER SEVEN

Pretty Boy Floyd's funeral back in the '30s was the biggest Oklahoma has ever seen. Press accounts at the time estimated that up to 40,000 people showed up to pay their respects. Many of them treated it like a big going-away party. There was lots of song-singing, picnicking on tombstones, and trampling on graves, not to mention fights over the best vantage point for watching the casket lowered into the ground. Evidently, a bang-up time was had by all. Except for Charlie Floyd, of course.

Burt Murray's funeral wasn't as big as Pretty Boy's, but it was plenty impressive, especially when you consider the guest of honor's two most notable accomplishments were being the crooked sheriff of a backwater county for 20-plus years, and killing an entire family because their skin was the wrong color.

At least Pretty Boy Floyd spent some time as Public Enemy Number 1.

Burt's memorial service was held at the biggest church in Tilghman County, the First Baptist in Temple City, where Burt Murray pretended to worship a few times every four years in the run-up to being reelected sheriff. His widow wanted the burial kept private, so the church service was folks' only chance to publicly express their sorrow. The expected collection of political bigwigs and VIPs showed up, unwilling to pass up a chance to get their faces on TV. You couldn't take a step without bumping up against someone holding a camera or a microphone.

Hundreds of Burt's devoted followers also attended—the little people he claimed to love but really didn't give a damn about. Hordes of them gathered on the lawn outside the church before the funeral, praying for Burt and chanting his catchphrase: "Oklahoma for Oklahomans." A pair of pimple-faced, plaid-suited, jumbo-sized identical twin brothers nailed the chant's real not-so-hidden meaning by carrying a hand-painted sign that read: "O-KKK-LAHOMA for O-KKK-LAHOMANS."

I went in part because it would've looked bad if I didn't. Wes had fixed my truck, so Karen and I took it to Temple City.

I felt bad that Burt's death happened on my watch, although I must say, it chapped my rear end that some folks were blaming it on me and my department. The town had only agreed to issue a permit for the rally on the condition the campaign would provide their own security. They didn't. Now their boy was dead and we're the ones made to look bad.

I sure as hell didn't go to mourn. I hadn't wished Burt dead, but I didn't shed any tears over his demise. Not-so-deep down, I thought he got what was coming to him.

The main reason I attended this clown show was because I halfway thought I might see something or someone that would help get at the truth. I don't know what I expected, exactly, but I felt a powerful urge to know why that bedraggled young woman did what she did.

I realized as soon as I got there that unless I all-of-a-sudden developed psychic abilities, there was little chance I'd uncover any clues. There were simply too many people and too many unfamiliar faces crowded into the First Baptist Church of Temple City that day.

Some attendees were more notable than others. John Joe Heckscher was there, with his trademark smirk and shifty little eyes, more than likely on the same hopeless mission as me. The mayors of every town in the district, members of the county and state government, and sundry other men of note were present. I couldn't help but notice that the three men most responsible for getting Burt out of jail—Chester Hooks, his lawyer; Judge Samuel Zimmerman, who overturned the conviction; and District Attorney Harry "Hopalong" Hawpe, who declined to retry the case—sat together in the front pew, across the aisle from the Burt's widow and the rest of the Murray family.

Karen's reasons for going were nobler than mine. She didn't like Burt any more than I did, but she's more religious and all about saving souls and whatnot. She also felt bad for Kath Murray, Burt's widow, and wanted to help her if she could.

Since she was with me, however, I thought it best for us to keep a low profile. We sat in the last pew next to a young mother with a fidgety five-year-old in a Halloween mask. I asked him who he was supposed to be. He said Ringo Starr. I would've guessed Moe from the Stooges.

The service took turns being as bland as Cream of Wheat and as nutty as an episode of *Hee-Haw*. The preacher's name was Reverend Faust. Listening to him, you'd think Burt was saintlier than Jesus and Moses combined. He spent the better part of an hour recounting suspicious-sounding tales of Burt giving succor to the afflicted and battling for the rights of the oppressed.

If you ask me, the only rights Burt cared about belonged to the rich and influential men who helped him get elected.

Reverend Faust's eulogy was enlivened at intervals by the wails of a pretty young woman with huge, lacquered, platinum-blond hair sitting next to Hopalong Hawpe. Her name was Betsy Hill, a local hairdresser. I suspected she was one of Burt's girlfriends.

Burt had a lot of girlfriends.

As for the widow, Kath Murray: She never stopped looking stunned.

Reverend Faust's big finish was a poem he wrote in honor of Burt's passion for his beloved University of Oklahoma football team:

To thee who hath saved us from the sins of the many,
We thank you for your wise antennae.
You saved us from the curse of reason,
And prepare us for next football season.
When God reveals it's not a just rumor—
Heaven's angels really do sing Boomer Sooner.

The reverend had barely finished the last line when the organist kicked off a rousing version of the poem's namesake song. The Temple City High School cheerleading squad appeared out of nowhere, wiggling their derrieres and shaking their pom-poms. A little boy in a miniature OU football uniform rode down the aisle on a donkey led by an elderly gentleman in a tuxedo. One mourner plastered an "Oklahoma for Oklahomans" bumper sticker across the donkey's hindquarters. The crowd sang with such gusto you'd think the song was handed down by the Almighty himself.

Karen and I beat the rush and slipped out. Outside, I put on my sunglasses and pulled my hat down low to lessen the chance I'd be noticed. Burt's friends blame me for sending him to jail—which is partly fair, I suppose, since I was the one who arrested him. Of course, I only did it after he killed a bunch of people then tried the same with me, but nobody cares much about that. I wasn't in the mood to be unnecessarily excoriated, never mind physically attacked, so I camouflaged myself as best I could.

Karen, on the other hand, didn't at all care about being recognized. She doesn't need to. Everybody likes her. No one would dare give her a hard time because of the joker she's married to. On our way to the service, I asked her to be on the lookout for anything strange. She said she would, but only if it didn't get in the way of comforting folks who needed comforting. That's the kind of gal she is.

I borrowed Pat's camera. I thought it might be helpful to snap some pictures of the attendees in case they might be useful somewhere down the road. It had one of those fancy lenses that zoom-in, so you can get a close-up without actually getting close. I stationed myself behind a dark blue Lincoln Continental parked across the street from the church and snapped pictures of folks as they came out.

The group chanting pro-Murray slogans started back up again. I took several pictures of them, including Tweedle-Dum and Tweedle-Dee and their Okkklahoma sign. I doubted any of them had anything to do with Burt's death, but if I couldn't arrest them for being idiots, at least I could take pictures of them to throw darts at.

On the front steps, a small group—Hooks, Zimmerman, Hawpe, and a couple of fellas I didn't recognize—gathered around Kath Murray.

Kath and I went to high school together. We were always friendly, if not exactly friends. I remember being surprised—along with everyone else—when she and Burt got together. If you're talking odd couples, Oscar and Felix had nothing on Burt and Kath. Burt never met a man whose hand he wouldn't try to shake or whose ear he wouldn't try to bend, while Kath is quiet as a mouse and as jittery as a hen in a fox house. She was pretty in a delicate sort of way—kind of like a dried flower pressed in the pages of the family bible. As Burt's career progressed, their relationship began to make more sense. Kath turned out to be exactly the type of wife he needed: a woman who looked good on his arm, and who'd perform her wifely duties and not kick up a fuss while Burt screwed around.

Over the years, the bigger he got, the more she faded into the background. After a while, nobody thought about her much at all. Once in a while I'd see her on one of my infrequent trips to Temple City, sitting on a bench in front of the courthouse where Burt worked, sucking down cigarettes like they were chocolate milkshakes. Kath has always seemed stuck in first gear. She can't have had much of a life being married to Burt. I'd like to think that, now that he's gone, she'll take advantage of her new freedom and do something that makes her happy.

If she's going to do it, though, she'd better get a move on. She's got a bad case of asthma and spends most of the summer in Arizona. Apparently, the dry air makes it easier for her to breathe. She did come back for Burt's funeral—willingly or not, it was hard to tell; theirs wasn't exactly a marriage made in heaven. Watching her from across the street, surrounded by well-wishers or vultures or whatever they were, she looked less like a distraught widow and more like a cornered rabbit. I considered going to her rescue, but I couldn't imagine she'd be too glad to see me. I settled for snapping a few photos of her consolers.

I wasn't in much of a hurry to engage them in conversation, anyway. None were on my list of favorite people.

Judge Zimmerman and I had yet to have a one-on-one, so I can't speak to his personality or character, although the fact he let Murray out of jail did not count in his favor. As for Hooks, before he took on Burt as a client, I never had much of an opinion about him, positive or negative. His clients tend to commit rich-person crimes: tax and insurance fraud, bribery, those sorts of things. Not the kind of folks I generally arrest. Chester is considered one of the best lawyers in the state by people who can afford to hire one of the best lawyers in the state.

Harry "Hopalong" Hawpe, on the other hand, I never could stand. Hopalong has the ethics of a used car salesman, the personality of an overstimulated chihuahua, and a temperament as changeable as the weather. Why folks around here elected him to his post, I cannot explain, except that on the ballot his name had an "R" beside it, which these days is all it takes. Hawpe worked under Burt Murray in the '50s as a Tilghman County sheriff's deputy before resigning to attend the University of Oklahoma Law School. Burt paid his tuition out of his own pocket and wasn't afraid to advertise the fact. Folks at the time thought he was just helping out a deserving young man, but Burt never did anything out of the goodness of his heart. I expect that even back then he was grooming Hopalong to run for DA. Four years ago Hawpe was elected and thereby in a position to provide his benefactor a Get Out of Jail Free card. Most folks forgot how much Hopalong still owed his former boss. I did not.

The other two men in the group—a tallish fella with long sideburns, and a short guy with thinning red hair who kept his back to me so I could never see his face—I didn't recognize, but considering the company they kept, I doubted they were anyone I'd want to buddy around with.

A black limousine pulled up to the curb. Kath took a tentative step toward the car, then faltered. Hopalong groped for her hand, but she swatted it away. Karen slipped through the scrum of males and gently helped Kath into the back seat. Someone shouted my name. I looked around but couldn't see who it was. When I turned back, the limousine had driven away, and the group of men headed their separate ways. Chester and Hopalong crossed the street to where I stood. They looked like funhouse-mirror reflections of one another: Chester, skinny as a rail and tall enough to block out the sun; Hopalong, short and practically as wide as Chester is tall. Both wore black suits, white shirts, and black ties. Both wore gray, wide-brimmed felt Stetsons— Chester's, covering a full head of slicked-back salt-and-pepper hair; Hopalong's, covering not much of anything.

I nodded. "Chester. Hopalong."

Chester nodded back. Hopalong winced. He doesn't like being called Hopalong.

Chester said, "I'm a little surprised to see you here, Chief Hardy."

"Why is that?"

Hopalong leaned forward with his hands on his hips. "Well, I don't know Emmett," he said, wagging his bigger-than-normal-for-his-size head from side to side. "Maybe because you as good as killed him."

Chester patted Hopalong's shoulders, reaching a long way down to do it. "Now, now, Harry," he said, then addressed me: "My friend does have a point, however."

"I'm surprised to hear you say that, Chester."

"Why should you be, Chief Hardy? It was you who sent Sheriff Murray to jail in the first place."

I searched his face for a sign he was pulling my leg, but I couldn't find one. I guess being able to say something so stupid with a straight face is what makes him such a good lawyer.

"That's true, Emmett," chattered Hopalong. "Y'all got some nerve coming here today, that's true."

"Come on, Chester. Burt was a killer. You know that and I know that."

"Judge Zimmerman thought otherwise," said Chester. "Sheriff Murray's record was wiped clean."

"A political vendetta," said Hopalong with a little bobble-headed nod. "That's what it was."

"Hopalong," I said. "Do you even know what 'vendetta' means?"

He gave me an indignant look. "I think I do, Mr. Smartypants."

"What is it?"

His eyes got all shifty, and he scrunched up his forehead. Chester sighed. "Let's go, Harrison," he said and guided him away gently. After only a few steps, Hopalong stopped and turned around. "By the way, Emmett," he said smugly. "What's this I hear about that colored boy of yours being in on this?"

"He's a man, not a boy, and I don't have the slightest idea what you're talking about."

Of course, after my talk with Heckscher, I did, but I didn't want to give Hopalong the satisfaction.

Hooks whispered violently in Hopalong's ear, then smiled at me half-heartedly. "I'm sorry, Chief Hardy," he said while pulling Hopalong away.

***

The burial itself was private, so no one seemed to be in a rush to leave. The churchyard was still fairly packed with folks standing around in little groups, talking. I used up a second roll of film and set off in search of Karen. The sun was as hot as it was going to get, and I didn't want to spend the entire day sweating my tail off in a monkey suit. I reckoned the best plan was to track down Karen and head back to Burr.

Karen was nowhere to be found. I thought she might've ridden out to the cemetery with Kath, after all, so I set out for my truck parked a few blocks away. I was wondering if I should go out to the cemetery after all and pick up Red there when I heard the clatter of high heels running up behind me. I turned around. It was her.

"Don't run in those things," I said. "You'll break an ankle."

"Were you leaving without me?"

"I couldn't find you anywhere. Last I saw, you were helping Kath into the limo. I was afraid you'd gone out to the cemetery with her."

"No, she didn't want company." She paused to catch her breath. "So, what'd those two dunderheads have to say?"

"Apparently, Heckscher told them he's got something on Joel."

She laughed incredulously. "Is he still on that?"

"Well, they didn't come right and say it was Heckscher who told them."

"But you inferred it."

"I think it was more like they implied it."

"That's essentially the same thing."

"Is it?" I said. "Maybe it is, I don't know. The important thing is that it sounds like Joel is being looked at for conspiracy to murder."

Red stopped in her tracks. "What evidence could he possibly have?" she said. "Joel never saw that girl before the day of the shooting."

"Probably nothing, but apparently Heckscher thinks he's onto something."

We got back to walking. The only sounds were the rhythmic click of her heels and the hum of traffic on Main Street, a block over.

We arrived at my truck. I started it up and cranked up the air-conditioning. We drove a while without saying a word.

"You know," Karen said, "it's not too big of a jump to go from blaming Joel to blaming you."

"My conscience is clear. They can blame me if they want. I can handle it. What I can't handle is them coming up with some ridiculous conspiracy theory tying together Joel and that girl."

She shook her head. "We can't let that happen," she said.

"We won't."

CHAPTER EIGHT

About the only thing I did the next day regarding the Murray shooting was drop off the rolls of exposed film at Miller's Drug. Other than that, I attended to the usual day-to-day concerns. Agent Heckscher's comments about Joel stuck with me, but I hadn't heard anything else about it. That should've made me feel better, but as optimists go, I make a pretty good prophet of doom.

Joel showed up, wanting to work. He said he was better, but I only had to look at his bloodshot eyes to know that was a fib. I think more than anything, it was the idea of killing a woman that bothered him. Especially a pregnant woman. That he'd killed her too late to save Burt made it worse. Maybe the memory of her crooked little smile kept him up at night. It sure did weigh on me.

I wasn't surprised that I didn't hear anything from Heckscher. He'd want to keep me at a distance, knowing I'd push back if I disagreed with him. He'd have been right. Any attempt to tie Joel into a conspiracy would certainly inspire my heated opposition.

I was also worried about what DA Hawpe said. The way he phrased it: "What's this I hear about that colored boy of yours being in on this?"—had to mean he got the information from someone else. Probably John Joe. I hoped that's how it was. It would've been bad for Joel if Hawpe had independently discovered a reason to suspect him.

Hopalong did call that morning, a few minutes before Joel showed up. He advised me to take Joel's gun away and put him on desk duty. I asked, "Is that all?" He said, "That's all," and hung up.

I disregarded his suggestion that I confiscate Joel's gun. For one thing, I knew he had a back-up at home, so taking his service weapon made little sense. I also thought that, given the circumstances, taking his gun might feel a little like twisting the knife. Confining him to desk duty would've made sense if there'd been anything for him to do. But there really wasn't. Red does all the administrative stuff, and she keeps the hows and whys and wherefores close to her vest. Not even I know how to do most of it, and I'm happy to keep it that way. I could've had her train Joel, but with him confined to the office, I needed her to do actual police work, not hang around the station showing him how to fill out forms.

In the end, I told Joel it was our "long-established procedure" to temporarily suspend an officer who'd been involved in a shooting. Big cities probably have such "long-established procedures," but I can't honestly say we do. It's just something I'd seen on a TV show. I thought it made sense in Joel's case.

Telling him that depressed him even more. I tried to cheer him up by suggesting we get together to play some music later in the week. Joel's a better drummer than he let on when we first met. Before this fiasco, we'd been getting together once or twice a week to work on Charlie Parker tunes. "Alright," he said, brightening a bit. "We still haven't gotten *Ornithology* up to tempo."

"That's my fault," I said. "I'll work on it on my own. We'll get it where it needs to be."

That got a smile out of him, which I thought was a good sign. He left without making a fuss.

I couldn't think of anything more I could do for the young man except to keep apprised of the situation and be ready to act if they came down on him. If or when that time came, I reckoned I'd wing it like I always do and hope everything works out.

I've had some success with that approach over the years.

I've also had a few failures.

73

***

Things got more or less back to normal over the next few days. With Joel out, I had to juggle my personnel, bringing in my part-timer when he was available and coordinating a schedule with Sheriff Belcher to make sure we had coverage overnight. The latter wasn't a problem. Bernard always makes his way to Burr in the course of his shift, even when we have one of our own on the schedule.

Using Pat was a little trickier. He usually works on weekends, with an occasional Friday thrown in, like on the day of Burt's rally. During the week, he commutes to Woodward to work as an insurance claims adjuster. If Joel were to be out for too long, I'd have to try to convince Pat's boss to let him have some time off, which was no sure thing.

That left it to me and Red to handle everything ourselves, which left me almost no time at all for doing what I really wanted to do: work on identifying the fella who'd burnt himself to death the day before Burt was killed. It seemed like nobody but Red and I were much concerned about him. Unfortunately, as shorthanded as we were, any progress on that front would have to wait.

Instead, I spent most of my time doing the things I did when I was a one-man police force. I parked in front of the elementary school when the kids were getting out to make sure they could cross the street ok. I clocked a few speeders and accompanied the fire department to a couple of minor grass fires. I made myself a conspicuous presence in town, to discourage misbehavior. I caught a guy from Amarillo sitting in a red Camaro in the TG&Y parking lot smoking a joint. I weighed the cost/benefit ratio and let him go with a warning.

Things ran pretty smoothly until the weekend. Both Red and I were exhausted from working 12-to-16-hour days. We were really looking forward to handing things off to Pat and maybe taking Saturday afternoon off. That was the plan, anyway.

You know what they say about plans.

On Friday afternoon, Pat's wife went into labor, meaning Pat wouldn't be able to work over the weekend.

Saturday turned out to be a train wreck. Literally. A freight pulling a line of tank cars jumped the tracks about a mile outside town. One of the tanks ruptured and began leaking a white, milky liquid. We were afraid it could be some kind of dangerous chemical, so we called in the highway patrol, who began evacuation procedures. We eventually discovered the white, milky liquid was in fact milk, but not before we'd spent half the day moving people out of what we thought was harm's way. Karen and I spent most of the day helping the highway patrol direct traffic around the crash site so the railroad people could clean up the mess. It was well after nightfall before things calmed down.

As soon as I could get away, I went to Joel's place. I hadn't seen him since the day after Burt's funeral.

He answered the door and looked at my empty hands. "Where's your horn?"

"I didn't bring it."

"I assumed you were here to play."

"Nope. I'm here to see if you're ready to go back to work."

"Sure," he said.

"You sure you're sure?"

He grinned. "I'm sure."

"Then welcome back."

***

It wasn't as easy as all that. He invited me in, and we talked. He was still sad, but I got the sense he'd started to come to grips with what had happened. Red was a little upset when I told her I was letting him return, but after being around him even she had to admit he was mostly back to being the same old Joel.

Things were a little antsy for him at first. Almost immediately, he found himself on the receiving end of unkind comments by Burt Murray supporters. He handled each instance gracefully. He might have been unsure of himself for a day or two, but before long, he settled back in like he'd never been away.

Meanwhile, I was afraid Heckscher was going to show up at any time with some phony excuse to arrest him. When he hadn't by mid-week, I started thinking it wasn't going to happen.

I finally felt able to do more than just keep my head above water. For the first time since Bernard had called me out to Indian Valley, I had time to look into the identity of our John Doe. About all we'd done heretofore was check missing persons reports across the state, without success. I called Keith Belcher and asked him for the latest. Instead of answering right away, he asked me about my tooth.

"It's fine," I said. "It doesn't hurt."

"That's why you need to—"

"I know, that's why I should get it taken care of now," I said. "I will. So what's the latest on our John Doe?"

"There is no latest," he said. "The body's still on ice at the morgue. 'Death by misadventure,' says Dr. Morston."

Max Morston is the county medical examiner, the boss of the woman on the scene at Indian Valley, Dr. Childers.

"Does that mean Morston has done an autopsy?"

"Yup. The fella burned to death. No foul play. Just an accident."

"No ID, though."

"No ID. Haven't had the time to look."

"What about that ring he was wearing? You might be able to trace his identity through that."

"*You* might be able to. I'm too busy. I'm still trying to get the county to hire me a detective. Until they do, things like this are low on my list of priorities. Hopefully, the OSBI's on it."

If by OSBI, he meant John Joe Heckscher, I wouldn't hold my breath.

I asked if I could take a look at that ring.

"I don't have it," he said. "It's still with the M.E. You should give them a call."

I did that, but instead of calling Morston, I called Dr. Childers. I reckoned since she was the one who showed up at the scene, she'd be best positioned to help me.

First thing I did after we said our hellos was ask if she still had that ring.

"Yes, I've got it," she said. "Why do you ask?"

"I finally have some time, and I thought I'd try to track down the identity of that fella. It was a fella, right?"

"Yes, it was," she said, then lowered her voice. "Actually, Chief, I've been wanting to talk to you about this. There's something fishy about the way this man's death is being handled."

"Fishy? In what way?"

"Hold on a minute," she said. There were muffled voices, like she was holding her hand over the mouthpiece, then she came back. "Listen," she said. "Can we meet? In private?"

"How about lunch?"

"I can do that."

I told her about the greasy spoon in Watie Junction I've used over the years for all my secret meetings, of which there have been more than one but fewer than a dozen—probably a lot fewer; my memory is not what it used to be. The sign out front says "Café," so that's what I told her it was called. I gave her directions and said I'd meet her at 1:00.

I got there early, sat in a booth, and waited. Dr. Childers showed up right on time.

"Nice place," she said.

"Nah, it's a dump, but I like it." I didn't, but it was my choice to meet there, so I felt like I should defend it.

She asked me about my tooth.

"How did you know about that?"

"I'm not sure," she said. "In line at Safeway, maybe?"

I told her it was fine.

The waitress brought over menus and ice water. I asked Dr. Childers how she was enjoying her job.

"I'm not," she said. "The entire department's a mess. I knew it was understaffed and under-equipped when I took the job, but I thought at least I'd be working with professionals."

"Dr. Morston not living up to your expectations?"

She sighed. "He's a joke. No one cares how or why anybody dies. Everything's always 'unspecified natural causes,' unless it's something obvious, like a gunshot or someone getting run over by a tractor-trailer, in which case they just write 'shot in the head' or 'run over by a truck.' This John Doe is the only autopsy I've done since I've been there. I only did that because I naturally assumed, given the circumstances, one was needed. Morston hit the roof when he found out. I don't think I'm long for the Tilghman County ME's office, I'll tell you that."

"You think they're going to fire you?"

"Probably not. They're already understaffed, and qualified people aren't exactly breaking down the doors to work there. But I am looking for another job."

"Why did Morston hit the roof? Weren't you just doing your job?"

"That's the thing. At first, I thought he was laying a power trip on me. I did something without authorization, so now he was going to show me who's boss."

"*At first* you thought that. Not anymore?"

"Let's say I'm beginning to think there's something else going on."

"What?"

She looked around to make sure nobody else was listening. "John Doe didn't burn to death," she said softly. "He died of a gunshot to the back of the head from a small caliber handgun, probably a .22 or .25."

"Keith Belcher told me Dr. Morston ruled it 'death by misadventure,'" I said.

"Is that what Morston is calling it? Ok." She smiled grimly. "Listen. This is what happened: I do the autopsy. Morston blows his top when he finds out. I apologize, but I tell him, 'This is a homicide, it needs to be looked into.' He tells me he'll handle it and warns me never to do something like this again. I figure, 'Ok, I got in trouble, but it was worth it because I discovered this was a murder, and surely there'll be further investigation.' So I wait. Nothing happens. It's like I never found that bullet."

"You think someone shot John Doe, then staged it to look like he burned to death?"

"Yes I do. The fire was set to cover up the murder. Somebody shot him, either where we found him or somewhere else, and then set it all on fire, thinking the victim would be burnt beyond recognition."

"Interesting."

"That's not all," she said. "The victim had been doused in alcohol."

"How can you tell?"

"Trust me, I can. Sterno is jellied alcohol. My guess is, the killer bought a couple of jugs of denatured alcohol, poured it over the body to make sure it burnt to a crisp, then spread it around and set the fire. The perp must've figured that leaving that Sterno can lying around would lead the investigators to think it was an accident."

I could almost feel my face growing red. I said, "I'm a little embarrassed that I was fooled like that."

She waved dismissively. "It happens. What I don't understand is why Morston wouldn't want to get to the truth of this."

"I expect he's covering for someone."

"Who? And why?"

"Maybe he knows who killed John Doe and is covering for them. As for who, it could be anyone, although I'd place my money on an elected official."

"Why is that?"

I shrugged. "It's the way things run around here. Some bigwig does something wrong and tries to cover it up. Maybe John Doe got in the way of someone's political ambition. Maybe he had a hand in some rich guy's wallet. Our county government's been rotten for so long, we don't notice the stink anymore."

"But why would Morston put himself on the line like that? If he gets caught, not only is his career over, but he'll go to prison."

"Why don't you ask him?"

"Because he's disappeared."

"What? Disappeared?"

"The day after he bawled me out about the autopsy, he told the staff he was going on vacation. He didn't say where he was going or when he'd be back."

"Isn't that kind of suspicious?"

"Well, yeh. It is. But don't ask me. I only work there."

She asked again why I thought he'd be covering for somebody. I thought for a second. "Two possible reasons: One, he's being blackmailed. Two, the person behind this is paying him off. Either someone's got dirt on him, or someone's stuffing his pockets."

The waitress came by to take our order. When she'd left, Dr. Childers said, "Let me play devil's advocate for a moment: It could be that Morston was just being lazy and didn't want to do the extra work that would be involved if this was a murder."

"Yeh, but how much extra work is it, really?"

She waggled her hand. "Some. Not a lot, though. The post-mortem is the hard part, and I'd already done that. Listen, don't get me wrong. I think this stinks to high heaven."

"Maybe it does, but so far, all we know is that Morston told Sheriff Belcher that John Doe's death was an accident. Is that official? Have you seen the death certificate?"

"I filled out the autopsy report and handed it over to Morston for his signature. The death certificate is a different thing. The death certificate confirms the death. It has a cause on it, but it's approximate. Sometimes it's wrong."

"So the official cause of death is what it says on the autopsy report."

"Basically, yeh."

"And you said in the report that John Doe died from a gunshot wound to the head."

She nodded. "That's right."

"What do you want to bet it's been falsified to say, 'death by misadventure'?"

"As will the death certificate, in all likelihood," she said. "But it's the autopsy report that counts. And I'd say you're probably right."

"Can you look into that?"

"What? Look at the official report? Sure. I'll do it this afternoon."

"That'd be a help," I said. I felt a sudden need to enlighten the newcomer about the ways of this strange new world she'd found herself a part of. "Listen," I said, "a cover-up like this is business as usual around here. Look up 'good ol' boy' in the encyclopedia and it'll say 'See Tilghman County, Oklahoma.' If I were you, I'd keep my head down and not make waves. I'll look into it. I've dealt with this type of thing before." I paused. "Of course, you might think you don't know me well enough to trust me."

"I know what Burt Murray did, and I know you're the one who put him away," she said. "That counts for a lot."

"Actions speak louder than words. Let me see what I can find out, and we'll talk again."

The waitress brought our meal. I don't remember what I had. I do remember it gave me indigestion. I also remember Dr. Childers was smart and only had coffee.

That's why she's a doctor and I'm just a cop.

We chatted while I ate. She told me this was her second job. The first had been in a small town in Minnesota. She got tired of the cold and came here. It turned out to be less than she'd bargained for.

"Maybe the third time will be the charm," she said wistfully.

I asked if there was anything else she could tell me about our John Doe.

"Like what?"

"You said he'd been shot there or somewhere else. Is there any way to tell?"

"I went back to the scene and looked. I couldn't find evidence either way."

"Could you tell if he had been drinking?"

"The body was too far gone. I couldn't tell."

"No fingerprints either, I assume."

"Again, the body was too far gone. Basically just ash and charcoal."

"No wallet, I guess."

"Nope."

"Just the ring, then."

"Oh, that's right," she said and began rummaging through her purse. She pulled out a small clear plastic bag containing the class ring. The char had been cleaned off, revealing the silver underneath. The words "University of Oklahoma" circled a red stone. On the side was a year—1971.

"Look inside," she said. "There's an inscription."

I took the ring out of the bag and held it up to the light. Something was inscribed inside the band, too tiny for me to read. "What's it say?" I asked.

She said, "Yeh, I had to use a magnifying glass. It says, 'Fill the world with bellowing.'"

"Huh," I said. "I wonder what that means." "It sounded kind of familiar to me, like maybe it's something I heard in medical school. I haven't been able to nail it down, though." She spread her hands on the table. "Other than that, there's nothing I can tell you."

"One more thing," I said. "Would it be ok if I told Sheriff Belcher about all this? I trust him. He's an honorable man, and I'm sure I'll need his help at some point."

She nodded. "I was going to myself, eventually." She slumped back in her chair like she was exhausted. "You know, at first I thought I'd be a good soldier and keep my mouth shut. I'd only been working there a week when this whole thing happened. I wanted to keep my job. I tried to give Morston the benefit of the doubt. But I can't anymore." She downed the dregs of her coffee. "Anyway," she said, sounding more hopeful, "it won't be my problem for very long. I'm out of here as soon as I find something else. I hear you've got a McDonalds in your town. Maybe I'll try flipping burgers for a change."

"Don't do that yet. I'm going to need you where you are if we're going to get to the bottom of this."

She smiled. "I'm just kidding about flipping burgers. I think. I've already sent out resumes, though. I'm looking for something else. I'll hold out as long as I can, but if I get another job, I'm gone. I'll help you all I can until then. To hell with this place. I know it's your home, but I'm afraid I don't fit in."

I felt like saying: *You think I do?*

I walked her to her car, a light blue Volkswagen Beetle with big flower stickers all over it. Another thought popped into my head. "By the way, Dr. Childers, was there an autopsy done on that little gal who shot Burt?"

"If there was, it wasn't by us. From what I understand in a situation like this, it would be the responsibility of the state's Chief Medical Examiner. I know they determined she was pregnant, but they could've done that without a postmortem. I haven't heard anything about it, though."

Something else for me to think about—whether John Joe Heckscher liked it or not.

CHAPTER NINE

My truck almost didn't start. It took three tries. On the last one, it sounded like the battery was about dead. When I got back, I called Wes and told him I thought that the new starter he'd put on was a lemon. He said he'd used a rebuilt starter, not a new one. "Rebuilt or salvage?" I asked. "I told the guy I bought it from that I wanted a rebuilt one. Let me check with him and make sure." He called back a few minutes later and apologized. The guy took it off a wrecked Ford 150, the same model and vintage as my own. He told me to bring it back, and he'd get it squared away.

Red followed me to Wes's in her Falcon. I dropped off my truck and rode back with her. On the way, I told her about my visit with Dr. Childers. She thought I should tell Keith right away. I said I thought she was right.

Joel was at the front desk talking to Cindy when we got back to the station. I asked him to come with Karen and me back to my office. I began by telling him what I'd told Red.

"Wow," he said. "That's ... well, I don't know what. You mean to say the county medical examiner purposely issued a false autopsy report to cover up a murder?"

"Dr. Childers isn't certain her original report has been falsified," I said, "but given what we know, it makes sense that it would be. She's going to check on it this afternoon."

The phone rang. It was Dr. Childers. "Chief Hardy," she said, "I checked that death certificate. It says John Doe died from his burns."

I thanked her and hung up. I told Karen and Joel what she'd said. We were all silent for a moment.

"Who would benefit from a falsified autopsy report?" asked Karen.

"The person who killed John Doe," I said.

"Obviously," she said, "but who would that be?"

No one had an answer to that.

Joel said, "Knowing who John Doe was would make things a lot easier."

"I expect we'll run into some resistance," said Karen. "Someone doesn't want anyone to know."

"Who could that be?" asked Joel.

"Someone higher on the food chain than this guy," Karen said, meaning me.

Joel smiled. "You mean someone around here's got more clout than Chief Hardy?"

I replied, "Pretty near every county and local employee, from the janitor at Burr Elementary on up."

Joel laughed. It was good to see. "No, but seriously—"

"Seriously, it could be anybody. Anybody with something to lose." I told him what I'd told Dr. Childers—that the first people I'd suspect are the folks in a position of authority. "It almost has to be someone with enough influence to convince Dr. Morston to falsify that autopsy report."

"How many county officials are there?"

"Well, let's see. There's a county clerk, county assessor, county treasurer, court clerk, district attorney, and a sheriff. I think we can safely discount the sheriff, so that leaves five."

"Don't forget the county commissioners," said Karen.

"Oh, that's right. They're the ones with their fingers in the most pies. There are three of them, so that makes eight."

"What about judges?" said Joel.

"I forgot that, too. There's one elected judge in Tilghman County. Sam Zimmerman."

"Yes," said Karen, "but he wasn't elected."

"That's right," I said. "He was appointed by the governor when the former judge retired."

"Zimmerman's the one who overturned Burt Murray's conviction, right?" said Joel.

I nodded. "Yup. And he's running for reelection this year."

"So you've got the clerks, county and court; the assessor, the treasurer, DA, three county commissioners and a judge," said Joel. "Any killers in the bunch?"

"Definitely some crooks, although I'm not sure about them being killers. I wouldn't put anything past Hopalong Hawpe, that's for sure, although I can't see him actually pulling the trigger. The little you-know-what is scared of his own shadow. That doesn't mean he couldn't be involved in some way, of course."

"You know," said Karen dryly, "if Burt Murray wasn't dead, I'd suspect him to be involved in something like this."

"Burt was still alive when John Doe was killed," I said. "There's no reason it couldn't have been him."

"But there's no evidence, is there?"

"No," I said, "but we haven't really looked."

Karen said, "Let's look, then."

Joel said, "We've got to start somewhere."

I thought about it. "I'm not sure I want to jump down that rabbit hole yet. I think identifying the dead man is more likely to lead us to the killer than if we start by focusing on Burt. What if it turns out he didn't or couldn't have done it? We would have wasted all that time."

"Cast a wide net, then," said Joel.

"As far as finding the killer, yes. Hopefully, once we find out who John Doe was, things will narrow down."

"So what's this about a ring?" asked Joel.

"The one actual clue to John Doe's identity is that OU class ring he was wearing and the inscription inside: *Fill the world with bellowing.*"

"What in heck does that mean?" he asked.

"Dr. Childers said it sounded kind of familiar, like something she might've heard in medical school, although she couldn't swear to it."

"At least we have the year he graduated," said Karen. "What was it? 1970?"

"1971, I think."

Cindy knocked, said she was busy out front and needed a hand. Joel and Karen went to help. Meanwhile, I called Keith, described my conversation with Dr. Childers, and I told him we aimed to do some research into John Doe's identity. After asking about my tooth—I told him it was fine—he said, "Go for it. I wish I could help. I don't know if I told you, but we've had a rash of car thefts in Temple City, which is bad enough, but this guy running against me is just going to town on it. Between trying to catch car thieves and running my reelection campaign, I don't have time to do anything else." He paused, then added: "While I'm thinking about it, I should warn you: Heckscher has some crazy ideas about who might be involved in the Murray shooting."

"What kind of crazy ideas?" I asked.

"A 'Lyndon Johnson killed JFK' level of crazy."

"I don't suppose you can tell me."

"Trust me, buddy. You don't want to know."

"I think I already do."

***

Fill the world with bellowing.

I can't begin to tell you exactly how many people attend the University of Oklahoma during any given year. 20 or 30 thousand, at least. Erring on the low side, you've got to reckon at least a few thousand students graduate every year.

I bring this up as a way of saying: Just knowing the year this fella graduated didn't narrow it down a whole lot.

Looking at it that way, the inscription was a gift. You can be sure not every 1971 OU graduate had that written on the inside of their ring. This fella might've been the only one.

We'd already checked for missing persons reports and come up empty. We could put out a public appeal through the press. Tell folks we're trying to identify an unknown deceased male and give a description of the ring. Have it reported far and wide. See if anyone comes forward with information.

That's what an on-the-level D.A. would've done. Hopalong still hadn't done diddly-squat to determine John Doe's identity. I supposed it was possible he was unaware of the actual cause of death, but I thought that was unlikely. Where there's smoke, there's usually fire, and those cowboy suits Hopalong Hawpe wears are lined with asbestos.

I could go to the press myself, ask the public for information, pretending not to know the true cause of death. However, I was afraid that would cause more problems than it would solve. I'd be going over too many heads. At the moment, this would have to be a small-scale search.

Karen and I put our heads together, trying to glean what *Fill the world with bellowing* meant.

"What bellows?" she wondered. "Elephants?" She paused. "Politicians?"

"Politicians are blowhards," I said hopefully.

"The ring's from '71, right?"

"Correct."

"What was going on in 1971? Vietnam? Protests? Nixon was president. College students hated him. Maybe it had something to do with that."

"I guess." It still didn't sound right. "Did you have anything engraved on your high school class ring?"

"Did *you*?" she asked.

"I didn't get a class ring."

"No, I don't expect you did."

"So, did you? Have it engraved? Or inscribed, I guess I should say?"

"You know," she said. "You've seen it."

"I've never seen your high school ring."

"Oh, sure you have."

"I have not. Was it inscribed?"

"It might've been."

"What did it say?"

"I didn't say it *was* inscribed. I said it might have been."

"Which is the same as saying it was."

She frowned. "Well, yes, I guess in this case that's true."

"So what did it say?"

"None of your business."

"C'mon, Red. I'm trying to get into that fella's mind."

"That's fine. Just stay out of mine."

"Knowing why you picked what you did might help understand why he picked what *he* did."

She glared at me for a moment. "Alright, it said *Emmett & Karen*." She blushed. "I was a dumb kid."

"I'd say you possessed rare foresight at such a tender age."

"Oh, shut up," she said, blushing and trying not to smile.

Her revelation was fun to hear, but it didn't help. Unless John Doe had a crush on an elephant, it seemed apparent the inspiration for John Doe's inscription differed mightily from Karen's. We brainstormed a while longer but got nowhere.

The next step was calling OU and asking for a list of 1971 graduates and information on where they were now. I called the registrar and told them what I was looking for. They said they'd be happy to mail the information, but that might take a week or more to get here. I asked them if I could come by and get it tomorrow. They said they'd have it ready.

The next day's drive to Norman was unremarkable. My truck was still in the shop, so I had to take Karen's Falcon. It's a little underpowered for my taste, but I'd recently had the air conditioner recharged, so at least I kept nice and cool.

Over the years, Norman has spread north, while Oklahoma City inches south. Moore—the town in between—oozes everywhere, like a bottle of spilled ketchup. The stretch of Interstate 35 linking the three cities is nothing but an uninterrupted succession of strip malls, car dealerships, and chain restaurants.

To be fair, I reckon Norman's probably not a bad place to raise kids—unless you don't want to raise them to be football fans, in which case you'd be better off living anywhere else.

Finding the OU campus was easy. Wes Harmon dragged me to a few Sooner games over the years. Just this spring, Red talked me into accompanying her to a concert in the university's new basketball arena. The band was called—let me make sure I spell this right—L-Y-N-Y-R-D S-K-Y-N-Y-R-D. The only way I could've hated it more is if I hadn't been wearing earplugs. The missus and I have divergent tastes when it comes to music.

While it was easy to find the campus, it wasn't so easy to find the right building, and when I finally did—or thought I did—I couldn't find any place to park. If life was a TV show and I was the star of that TV show, there would've been a parking spot right in front. Unfortunately, life isn't a TV show. I was just a fish-out-of-water redneck cop on a visit to the big city. Who'd make a TV show about that?

I finally found a space near the football stadium. I walked the rest of the way, while all around me clusters of students hurried to get to wherever they were going. My uniform made me stick out like a sore thumb. I felt stupid like I always do when I'm around college kids. I could've gone to OU out of high school. I went into the Marines instead. I could've gone after I got out of the Marines, too, but I didn't.

I missed the boat. Now I'm resigned to feeling intellectually inferior for the rest of my life.

I climbed the steps and navigated the warren of offices and corridors until I found who I thought was the right person. I began my spiel. Before I could finish, the woman behind the counter said, without once looking up from the crossword puzzle she was working on, "You have to go to The Office of the Registrar." I said I thought this *was* the registrar's office. She said this was the Financial Aid office. I asked her for directions, but she enunciated like her mouth was full of mashed potatoes and I couldn't understand a word she said.

I left the building and searched for one of those "You Are Here" maps, or at least someone with a kind face who I'd feel comfortable asking for directions. I finally stopped a young man wearing the whitest sneakers I'd ever seen and asked him where the registrar's office was. His detailed instructions only got me more confused. My wild goose chase finally ended when I found a campus cop who took pity on a fellow officer and walked me to a different floor in the same building.

Before I could tell the woman behind the desk why I was there, she said she'd been expecting me and handed me a fat manila envelope with my name written on it in magic marker. Inside was a two-inch stack of paper with holes along the edges. "That's a computer printout of everyone who graduated in 1971," the gracious lady said. "We needed some help from the Office of Alumni Affairs to get their current addresses and phone numbers. Unfortunately, they didn't have them all, but we gave you what they had."

I thumbed through it. It looked like they only had contact information for about one out of every three. Still, it was a start.

I thanked her and went on my way.

I got back to Burr around 6:30. Red and I had a late dinner, then started calling folks. Or, I should say, Red did. I got so tongue-tied after the first couple, she told me to sit down and listen.

She seemed to have it down to a science. First, she'd introduce herself and explain that she was working on a case involving the death of a member of their graduating class. If she was talking to a man, they'd usually make a bad joke: "It's not me!" or "I'm still alive!" She'd give a polite laugh, then ask if the phrase *Fill the world with bellowing* meant anything to them. They'd say no. She'd thank them for their time and move on to the next. Not one person she dialed had ever heard the phrase. She stopped around 9:00, figuring it'd be rude to call any later than that.

She started up again the next morning at the station, this time with Cindy's help. Each took half the remaining names. After an hour, they hadn't found anybody who'd heard of the inscription. They had, however, incurred lots of long-distance charges. I suggested that, for the time being, we limit our calls to within the state. I didn't want the town council giving me grief about our phone bill.

Red was starting to get frustrated. She said, "At least when you're looking for a needle in a haystack, you know you're looking for a needle." She decided she needed a break. Cindy kept dialing; she used to be a telephone operator, so I reckon she's got more stamina. Red and I went back to my office.

"Listen," she said. "That inscription sounds kind of literary, don't you think?"

"You mean, like something from Shakespeare?"

"Right."

"You know, that hadn't occurred to me, but it does."

"Right? So who knows the most about literature in this town?" She answered before I could. "Your girlfriend." Meaning Kate Hennessey.

Red's been teasing me about Kate for years. She's the town librarian and probably the only person in town who reads more than me. One time we had a competition to see who could read the most books in a year. By December, she was so far ahead, I had resorted to reading 200-page Perry Mason novels trying to catch up, and I don't particularly enjoy Perry Mason novels. Meanwhile, Kate read 800-page books by Russian writers whose names I can't pronounce and still beat me by a mile.

Red thinks Kate has a crush on me. I disagree. We're nothing more than reading buddies.

"I should've thought of Kate myself," I said.

"That's what you've got me for," Karen said. "To be your brain."

I ran over to the library, but it was Kate's day off. I asked the woman behind the counter if she'd ever heard the phrase, *Fill the world with bellowing.* "Does it have something to do with *The Honeymooners*?" I thought she was kidding, seeing that Ralph Kramden has such a big mouth and all, but she was serious. I thanked her and said I'd drop by and see Kate tomorrow.

CHAPTER TEN

There used to be a time when I could put myself to sleep simply by thinking happy thoughts. I once told Red that, and she said, "I didn't know you had any happy thoughts." I think she was kidding, but maybe she wasn't.

Anyway, happy thoughts have been hard to come by lately. That night, I finally dozed off and had a dream that ended with me in the electric chair at McAlester with my old dog Dizzy jumping all over me, trying to lick my face. I kept pushing her away, saying, "No Diz, bad dog," worrying that when they flipped the switch, she'd get electrocuted, too. I woke up in the nick of time, but that was it, sleep-wise.

I lay awake until six, then got up and turned on the TV. The weatherman on the Today Show predicted the temperature in western Oklahoma to reach 105. I stuck my head out the door. It was hot, but nowhere near as hot as it was going to get. I grabbed a couple of doughnuts and a cold Tab then plopped down in a folding chair on the back porch, wearing nothing but the t-shirt I slept in and my BVDs.

Being able to do that is one luxury of not having any neighbors behind me.

Grasshoppers and cicadas chirred in the weeds out past the edge of where I keep the lawn mowed. Wind rustled through the leaves of the gnarly blackjacks growing along the edge of our property. Yellowjackets flew in wide, drunken circles, some of them swooping too close for comfort. A column of black ants filed in and out of a crack in the concrete. I reminded myself to patch that up.

There was a skunky smell in the air. A pair of teenagers two doors down were engaging in their daily before-school pot-smoking. Their family recently moved here from Amarillo. The house has an old tool shed, tailor-made for such illicit activities. Living practically next door to the chief of police apparently doesn't deter them. Kids are getting awfully bold these days. I've seen them smoke the stuff as they walk down the street. In fact, I wouldn't be surprised if strutting past the police chief's house with a lit marijuana cigarette has become some kind of game young folks play, like Truth or Dare. I've nabbed a few. Most times, I've just confiscated it and told them not to do it again.

I finished my donuts and Tab. Even in the shade, the sun was making its presence felt. Beads of sweat were forming on my forehead. Time to get dressed and go to work.

***

I got there a few minutes past 7:00. I wanted to talk to Kate Hennessey about that inscription, but the library didn't open until 9:00 so I'd have to wait.

I shuffled papers for a while, then started thinking about that dream. For some reason, it brought to mind Burt Murray's killing, which in my mind had taken a backseat to John Doe. The last thing I'd heard about it was Keith's comment about Agent Heckscher's crazy ideas. Based on Heckscher's comments in my office and Hopalong's outburst at Burt's funeral, I had a more than sneaking suspicion that those crazy ideas involved Joel. I suddenly felt a burning need to be sure one way or the other, so I dialed Heckscher, hoping to hear him say Joel wasn't being fitted up for conspiracy to murder. I couldn't get through to him, however, so I left a message on his answering machine asking him to call me back.

Joel came in soon after that. I called him back to my office.

"You seem to be feeling better," I said.

He nodded. "That's fair to say."

"I hope what I'm about to tell you won't set you back." I shut the door and drew the blinds on the window that looks out over the squad room.

"I've got a question," I said, "but I want you to understand: It's only something I have to ask. It doesn't mean I suspect you of anything."

He stiffened. "What's the question?"

I paused a moment to prepare. "Is there any reason for Agent Heckscher—or anyone else, for that matter—to suspect you might've known that girl who shot Burt Murray?"

"No," he said emphatically.

"You never saw her before that day?"

"Never saw her before that day."

"Never spoke to her on the phone or anything like that?"

"Never spoke to her phone or anything like that."

He held my gaze.

"Is there any reason—any reason at all—for Agent Heckscher or anyone else to suspect you might have conspired with that girl to kill Burt Murray?"

He hesitated ever so slightly, then said, "No reason that wasn't made up out of whole cloth."

I tried on what I hoped was a reassuring smile. "No offense, son, but Heckscher's been making noises about you being in his crosshairs. I just wanted to hear you deny it."

"Any evidence purporting to tie me to Murray's killing would have to be fabricated." The more he said, the faster he said it. "I had nothing to do with it except that I didn't get off that shot in time. That's bad enough. I promise, something like that will never happen again."

I believed him, although I didn't really need much convincing. "I had to ask you before Heckscher does. You understand?"

He gave an almost invisible nod. "I understand," he said quietly.

We stood. I held out my hand. "Friends?"

We shook. "Sure," he said.

But he didn't smile.

***

9:00 came around. I grabbed one of the Javelins and drove downtown to the library.

My mama took me to the library all the time when I was little. Back then, it was in a single room in the back of city hall. These days it's in a remodeled storefront downtown. I still go every chance I get.

And yes, sometimes I go there to talk to Kate, but only about books—although, to be honest, if I weren't already hitched to the woman of my dreams, I'd probably be attracted to Kate. She's like one of those librarians you see in movies, the kind who you think are kind of frumpy until they let down their hair and take off their glasses and all of a sudden you realize Miss Plain Jane is actually a thinly disguised bombshell like Dorothy Malone or Donna Reed.

Sometimes I go here looking for something to read, other times just to browse. I'm always glad to be around all those books. Reading's something I can't live without. I can't visit every corner of the world in person, but I can within the pages of a book. Reading is food for the little fella on the hamster wheel that powers my brain.

During the summer, the Burr Public Library is especially popular among those who don't have air-conditioners in their houses, or enough money to spend the day drinking root beer floats down the street at Miller's. For those folks, Kate keeps it cold enough to deep freeze a side of beef. When I got there, it had only been open a few minutes, and already most of the tables were occupied.

The woman who thought *Fill the world with bellowing* might have something to do with *The Honeymooners* was at the check-out desk when I came in. She told me I could find Kate in the stacks. I passed a circle of elderly folks in easy chairs, reading newspapers, and a small boy with his head shoved inside a microfilm viewer. I found Kate standing on a stepstool in the non-fiction aisle, shelving books about animal husbandry. I tapped her on the shoulder. She jumped like I'd goosed her with a cattle prod.

"Oh, Chief Hardy, you about scared me to death," she said.

"Sorry about that."

"Oh, that's fine," she said, breathing heavily. "Read any good books lately?"

"Actually, I have, but that's not why I'm here. I wanted to ask you a question."

"Fire away," she said, pushing a stray lock of hair out of her face.

"This might sound strange, but I came upon this phrase in this case I'm working on. I'm stuck and I thought it might ring a bell with you. *Fill the world with bellowing.*"

"Fill the world with bellowing," she repeated. "Hmmm. I do think I've read that somewhere, but I couldn't tell you for sure off the top of my head. Do you need to know right now?"

"The sooner the better, but of course, take all the time you need."

"I'll have to look around."

"I'd appreciate it."

"Ok, let me write that down," she said and reached for a pencil behind her ear. It wasn't there. She came down off the stepladder. I followed her to her desk. She found a scratch pad and scribbled down the phrase. "Let me do some looking and I'll get back to you."

I thanked her and turned to leave. "So," she said before I was out the door. "What are you reading these days?"

"The new book by that Albert Speer fella. Hitler's architect."

She chuckled. "You and your World War Two books."

I confess to having a near insatiable appetite for books about that conflict—maybe because I barely missed fighting in it. Korea was my war.

"Yeh, I know," I said. "How about you?"

"*1876*, Gore Vidal's latest. It's a sequel to his last one. You read that, right?"

Vidal's previous book was about Aaron Burr, who, while he was Thomas Jefferson's vice president, played a political dirty trick that would put Richard Nixon to shame: He killed his rival Alexander Hamilton in a duel.

"Yeh, I reckoned I had an obligation to read it since it was about the guy our town was named after."

"I think you'll like this one, too," she said.

I didn't like the first one, but I didn't say so. "I'll read it when you're done."

"I'll save it for you."

***

From the library, I drove out to the Sinclair station to see how close my truck was to getting fixed. Not too close, but Wes promised he'd have it done by the end of the day. I managed to extricate myself from his company before he could draw me too deep into a conversation about football, which, except for cars, is all he talks about. I then took a drive out to Butcherville and stopped by the Butcherville Store. It's under new ownership again. The dang thing changes hands at least once a year. Folks stopped going there after the new Safeway opened in Burr. I went in and realized I'd forgotten the name of the fella running it now. We had a pleasant talk, anyway.

Back at the station, I found Red chatting with Kate, getting along so well that you'd never know one pretended to think the other was trying to steal her husband. They saw me coming and laughed.

"What's so funny?" I asked.

"Wouldn't you like to know?" said Karen.

"I'm not sure I would, to be honest."

"I found the source of your quote," said Kate.

"That was fast," I said.

"After you left, I remembered where I'd read it," she said. "It's from a book called *The Age of Belief* by an English woman named Anne Jackson Fremantle."

"Do you have it?" I asked.

"Believe it or not, we do," said Kate. "Ms. Fremantle is one of my heroes. She ran for British Parliament, drove an ambulance in London during World War Two and was a broadcaster for the BBC at a time when proper ladies didn't do those things. We've got all her books." She grinned. "Nobody checks them out, but we've got 'em."

"What did you find?"

"Ms. Fremantle attributes the quote to St. Albertus Magnus."

"I'm afraid I don't know who that is," I said.

"No reason you would unless you were a scholar in medieval studies. He died 700 years ago."

"Who was he?" asked Karen.

"The patron saint of science."

"Science, eh?" I said. "That gives us something to go on, wouldn't you say, Mrs. Hardy?"

"I assume you mean *Ms.* Hardy," Karen said, "but yes, I think it does."

Kate's head bobbed back and forth, looking first at Karen, then at me. "Would you mind telling me what this is about?" she asked.

I said, "I can't right now, Kate. I will when I can, but there's no telling when that'll be."

"That's fine," she said. "I'm just glad to help."

Red asked if she knew what the quote meant. Kate reached into her purse and pulled out a scrap of paper. "It's actually an abridged version of the full quote. Apparently, one of Albertus's students called Thomas Aquinas a 'dumb ox' because he was so quiet. Albertus said, 'This dumb ox will fill the world with his bellowing.'" She smiled. "He was certainly right about that."

I had no idea who Thomas Aquinas was or what he was famous for, but I nodded like I did.

"Well, that's all I had to say," she said. "I'd better be getting back to work."

"Alright then," I said. "Thanks for your help."

"My pleasure."

As soon as she was out the door, Karen said, "*She likes you,*" in a sing-song voice.

"Oh, stop it."

"I'm sorry, I'm only joshin' with ya. So, are you thinking what I'm thinking?"

"That John Doe was a science major at OU?" She nodded. "Yeh, I am. That might narrow down that list of ours a little."

It did, but not by a lot. She and Cindy had already spent the morning making calls. Now we sat down and culled the list to include only those graduating with a science degree. There were dozens, if not hundreds.

"Still lots of work to do," I said.

"Yeh, but now it should only take weeks instead of months."

"I'd say you were being overly optimistic."

"I'd say you were being overly *pess*imistic. As usual."

CHAPTER ELEVEN

One good thing about being a pessimist is that you're always braced for something to go wrong. I tend to expect the worst, so when events take a turn in that direction, I'm unsurprised.

Of course, being unsurprised isn't the same as being ready—emotionally and otherwise. There's probably not another person on the face of the earth less surprised than I am when things go wrong. Yet when they do, it can still smart.

***

Red took the list of science majors to her desk and began making calls. I sat at my desk awhile, signing papers that, according to the State of Oklahoma, needed to be signed right away or the earth would explode.

Before I got halfway through the stack, Cindy buzzed me on the intercom. Evelyn Purdys at Granny's Gifts had caught a 10-year-old boy trying to steal a Hershey's bar and demanded we send someone over. I did it myself, figuring the sight of the town police chief would be more than enough to scare the kid straight. He gave me some lip, so I'm not sure it did.

When I got back to the station, my *Reserved for Chief Hardy* parking space was occupied by a black Dodge Coronet. I recognized it as an unmarked OSBI vehicle. Taking up the spots next to it was a pair of Highway Patrol cruisers. I hurried in to see what was going on.

I got there in time to see Agent Heckscher flash his badge at Cindy and push his way past the front desk. Behind him was a pair of state troopers in their Smokey the Bear hats. Both wore short-sleeved shirts rolled up further to show off tree-trunk-sized biceps. I yelled, "What in hell is going on here?" but Heckscher and the troopers ignored me. Cindy said, "They said they're here to arrest Joel," which is precisely what I was afraid of.

Heckscher and his boys barged into the squad room like they were late for a hanging. I overtook them and blocked their path. "We're here for Joel Carter," said Heckscher. "Where is he?"

I started to say he wasn't there because I didn't think he was, but then the restroom door opened and Joel walked out. He stood with hands on hips and a defiant look on his face. "Here I am," he said.

Heckscher elbowed his way past me. "Joel Carter," he said, "I'm arresting you for conspiracy to commit murder."

Joel slowly raised his hands. Any ordinary idiot could've seen he was trying to surrender peacefully, but apparently the two state troopers were idiots on a whole different level. They drew their weapons and started yelling for him to get on the ground. Joel kept calm, a faint, bemused smile on his face, as if part of him couldn't believe what was happening, while another part had expected it all along.

He bent to kneel, too slowly for the lead trooper, who kicked his feet out from underneath him and knocked him to the floor face-down. The trooper then jerked Joel's hands behind his back and cuffed him before snatching his gun from its holster and handing it to Heckscher. Rather than help Joel to his feet, he ground his knee into his back and pushed his face into the floor. By now I'd had enough. I tried to pull the trooper off. The other fella took me down in much the same way, then snapped on a pair of cuffs.

Through it all, they never stopped shouting, cross-talking so much I couldn't tell what either was saying. I don't think they cared. The only word I could make out clearly was one I don't use. Not even when I'm telling a story like this.

It starts with "n."

The trooper had his hand on the back of my head, grinding it into the floor, so I couldn't see much. I heard something like a bat hitting a baseball, which I expected was the sound of a billy club bouncing off Joel's noggin. I tried to raise up to see, and someone hit a line drive off my own head. I blacked out.

When I came to, I was on my back. Heckscher was standing over me, smiling that evil little grin of his and shaking his head.

"See? That's what you get, Hardy."

***

Sometimes I'll be reading a book and I'll come across a phrase that reads something like, "the next few (seconds, minutes, hours, days) were a blur." I used to think that was just a way for the author to avoid filling in pesky details. Maybe it is sometimes, but in this case it was warranted. What happened next whizzed by so fast, my befogged mind almost couldn't keep up.

At first, Heckscher wanted to lock us up in our own jail, probably to humiliate us. Karen put paid to that mighty quick, however, so they marched us out of the building and loaded us into separate Highway Patrol cruisers, laughing and joking and taking their time so anyone driving by could see what was going on. The better to embarrass the hell out of us.

It soon became clear that the second trooper was taking me to Watie Junction. I asked why he was taking me there and not to the county lockup, or even Oklahoma City, but he wouldn't answer. The only reason I could come up with was that Heckscher knew Keith Belcher was a friend and wouldn't be too happy about having us locked up in his jail under false pretenses. Watie Junction's police chief, Melvin Pratt, doesn't like me and would be happy to take me in. How

Heckscher could've known that. I have no idea. Sneaky is like sneaky does, I guess.

Melvin only smirked at me but welcomed the trooper like a long-lost brother. While they were locking me up, I could see there was no sign of Joel. I asked where he'd been taken, but I might as well have been talking to myself.

Instead of bars, the Watie Junction cell had strips of rusted iron woven together like a basket. The room itself was about four-by-seven feet, only long and wide enough to accommodate a toilet and a cot hung by a couple of chains fastened to the wall on either end. Someone had evidently taken a hammer to the toilet bowl. One side was gone. All that was left was a jagged porcelain semicircle to sit on if you had to do your business that way. It was hard enough to do standing up. Your aim had to be near perfect or else you'd wind up spraying all over the floor. I held it for as long as I could before I finally went. I made the mistake of trying to flush. The toilet expelled its contents and then some. I spent the rest of my time sitting on the cot with my legs up.

My vision was blurred, and I had a big knot on my head from the whack with the billy club. I shouted to Melvin Pratt in the other room that I thought I had a concussion. He hollered back: "Walk it off!" At some point, a different state trooper from the one who drove me came in and said I was being charged with criminal obstruction. He came back a couple of hours later, cuffed me and led me to his cruiser.

This fella was no more talkative than the last one. He wouldn't tell me where we were going, but soon enough, I could tell we were headed to Temple City. We pulled around to the back of the courthouse where the jail is. I expected I'd be taken inside to be booked. Instead, he went in by himself, leaving me in the car with the windows rolled up. It was hot enough to bake a turtle in its shell. A half-hour later, he came out, removed my cuffs, and said I was free to go. I didn't ask any questions.

I went into the courthouse and asked the lady at the front desk if I could use her phone, then I called Burr and told Karen I'd been released without charges. She told me she'd called Keith and told him what was going on. He said he'd fix it. I guess he did.

I went up to Keith's office.

"How's your tooth?" he asked.

"Why's everyone so interested in my tooth? It doesn't even hurt."

"Not yet, but it will if—"

"Yeh, I know. If I don't get it fixed, it'll hurt. Don't worry. I got it." He made a 'calm down' gesture. "Sorry," I said, "but I'm getting sick of everybody asking about my tooth."

"I promise I won't ask again."

I said I'd appreciate that, then changed the subject. "I presume you're the reason they let me go."

"One of them, maybe. I made a few calls. Low friends in high places. You know the drill."

"So it was like that, huh?"

"Yup."

"Any idea what they did with Joel?"

"Took him to Oklahoma City, I imagine." He leaned back and clasped his hands behind his head. "So how 'bout you give me your side of this cluster-you-know-what?"

I told him.

"Pretty ill-mannered of them not to let me in on it," he said.

"Probably afraid you'd throw a wrench in their plans."

"Probably. I take it you don't think Joel had anything to do with Burt's killing."

"I know he didn't."

"Well, even if he's innocent, he's going to need help. Does he have a lawyer?"

"I sincerely doubt it. That's probably what I need to do now. Find him one."

"Who are you going to call?"

"I was thinking about the NAACP in Oklahoma City."

"Makes sense. Listen, I got a campaign event in a few minutes. How about I get one of my guys to give you a ride back to Burr?"

"I have always depended on the kindness of strangers."

"I'm not a stranger."

"No, but you're pretty strange."

He chuckled. "Look who's talking."

Bernard gave me a ride. He spent most of it cursing John Joe Heckscher, except Bernard doesn't curse, so he used words like *darn* and *shoot* and *son of a gun*. I appreciated the sentiment, but it was kind of funny to listen to.

He dropped me off at the station a few minutes past 8:00. The only person there was Dennis Foley, our most recent in a long line of relief dispatchers. Apparently, a good relief dispatcher is as hard to find as a good man. He pestered me about what had happened. I gave him a heavily redacted version. I picked up the phone intending to call someone who could tell me where Joel was being held. I then realized I had no earthly idea who that might be. A month ago it would've been Isabel Cruickshank, but she was in Virginia now.

I called her replacement, Agent Heckscher. No answer. I called District Attorney Hawpe. Nobody home. I called the OSBI and got a recording that told me to call back during office hours. I finally called the NAACP in Oklahoma City and got through to a real live human being. She gave me the number of a lawyer who might be able to help. Howard Kepner was his name. I called him and related the situation. He told me he'd look into it right away.

I then called Karen, told her I'd made it back to town and would be home shortly. I had one more stop to make.

***

The Javelin I'd been driving earlier was still parked where I'd left it. I got in and headed for Joel's house, which was really my father Everett Hardy's house. He moved there after my mother passed away. I was in the Marines fighting in Korea at the time, so I never lived there. After my dad died, it passed down to me.

I let Joel stay there rent-free as a kind of penance for something Dad did. Or something he didn't do.

On the morning after the Youngers' house burned down, back in 1940, Dad had a chance to help them. He'd helped them before when the stakes were much lower, but this time he refused. Hours later, although we didn't know it at the time, they were murdered.

As reparations go, letting Joel stay there wasn't much—he didn't even know the reason why—but I felt it was something my dad would've wanted me to do.

A streetlamp by the driveway lit up the front of the house as light as day. I expected to find the door sealed with yellow police tape, but it wasn't. I turned the knob. The door was unlocked.

I opened the door and hit the light switch. I expected a mess— cops executing a search warrant rarely put things back where they find them—but what I saw was beyond the pale.

The living room looked like a bomb had gone off. Anything that had been on a table or shelf now lay on the floor: books, papers, lamps. A typewriter. The couch and easy chairs had been taken apart, the cushions torn from the upholstery, the backs and arms cut open and the stuffing pulled out.

The place stunk something horrible. I propped the front door open and opened the sliding glass doors in the back to air the place out. It was stiflingly hot. I checked the thermostat. Someone had turned up the heat as far as it would go on a day when the outside temperature reached over 90 degrees. I shut it off and cranked up the air conditioner.

I opened the door to the kitchen and discovered where the foul smell was coming from. Someone had taken every piece of food that had been in the refrigerator, thrown it on the floor and poured milk over it; the meat was starting to rot, and the milk had already gone sour. Every dish and glass had been taken from the cupboards, thrown to the floor, and shattered into a million pieces, including the set of Desert Rose china my mother had always been so proud of. An antique wooden clock sat on the counter with its guts pulled out. That had been hers, too.

In the garage, Dad's tools had been strewn all over the place. A claw hammer was lodged in the drywall. Someone had emptied a half-dozen cans of motor oil onto the floor.

When Joel moved in, I helped him clear the guest bedroom so he could set up his drums. Now the drumheads had been sliced to ribbons and the drums themselves splintered to pieces.

I made my way to the backyard. It had been left alone. I sat in a lawn chair and collected my thoughts.

Whatever Heckscher, or whoever had done this, were looking for, I reckon they considered finding it secondary to destroying everything they could get their hands on. Most of the stuff wasn't Joel's. It was mine, left to me by my folks. The furniture, the dishes, the books, the tools, the family photographs that now lay torn and shattered on the floor. A big reason I didn't sell the house after my dad died was that I couldn't bear to part with that stuff. I never even told Red that, although I'm sure she suspected it. Until and even after Joel moved in, the place had been my own private museum.

Now everything was smashed to pieces.

I felt rage coupled with a powerful urge to drink myself stupid. In the short term, both things would have made me feel better. Not so much in the long term, though. It took me a few minutes to get myself together. I went back in the house. I still hadn't checked Joel's bedroom.

It was as bad as, or maybe even worse than, the rest. The bed had been stripped, the mattress slashed and the stuffing strewn about. Clothes were torn in strips and scattered. Shreds of paper covered everything. In the adjoining bathroom, I found the bedsheets wadded up in a ball, stuffed in the toilet, and urinated upon.

My foot came down on one of Joel's uniform shirts. I felt something crack. I lifted the shirt to see. I'd stepped on a framed photograph of a young Black man in an old-style army uniform. He stood in front of a clapboard house, smiling self-consciously. On his shoulders were sergeant's stripes, and on his head was one of those silly little field caps they used to wear.

The fella's face was eerily familiar. I flipped it over. A name was scrawled in pencil on the back. It had faded with time, but I could still make it out.

Sgt. Gabriel Younger.

CHAPTER TWELVE

Gabe Younger was the son of Clarence and Eunice Younger, and the big brother of Ethyl Younger. We'd known for years that Clarence, Eunice, and Ethyl were killed by Burt Murray and Frank Sallee in 1940. We found their skeletal remains after dragging Burr Lake in 1967. The only family member we didn't find was Gabe. Since he disappeared at the same time as the rest of his family, we thought it probable that Murray and Sallee had disposed of his body elsewhere.

I cleared a place on the bed, sat down, and stared at the photo. It was Gabe, alright. He was older, of course. His face had fleshed out. But it was him.

My head swam. What the hell? Gabe had survived that night, and Joel had his picture. I looked at it again and summoned the image of Joel in my mind's eye. Was there a resemblance? Yes. No. Maybe. Not sure.

Could they be related?

They could be. But wait.

Joel never told me his birth father's name, but he did say he died in Korea. He was adopted by his mother's sister and her husband.

I looked at the picture. It could well have been taken in the early '50s. Probably was, in fact. If Joel was telling the truth about his father dying in the war, then Gabe was long gone—killed in Korea a decade after the rest of his family had been murdered by Frank Sallee and Burt Murray.

Now Burt was dead, shot to death by a young woman who herself died before anyone had a chance to question her.

Shot to death by Joel Carter.

My Lord, I thought. *Could John Joe Heckscher be onto something?* I could hardly bring myself to believe it, but if Joel was somehow connected to Gabe Younger, as now appeared likely, then I couldn't dismiss it out of hand. If Joel was Gabe's son—and the dates did line up—it seemed even more possible that Gabe came here to avenge the deaths of his kin.

If you'd told me that an hour ago, I'd have said you were crazy. Now it was something I had to consider.

I still believed in Joel and wanted to help him in any way I could. The best thing to do, I thought, was to reserve judgment. I knew immediately that this photograph could do him harm, even if he was innocent. Fortunately, whoever trashed the house—presumably Heckscher and his boys—was obviously more interested in tearing things up than discovering evidence. They would've found the picture if they'd been more careful, and that would've made Joel's situation even worse. It was bad enough that I'd seen it.

I put it in my shirt pocket, got up, and finished my tour of the house.

I went from room to room, picking up what few of my parents' things were salvageable and stuffing them into a pillowcase. There wasn't much—a couple of plastic coffee cups, a few knick knacks that reminded me of my folks. None of it was worth anything, but they had sentimental value. My mother's silverware remained mostly intact, although it was strewn everywhere. I had to pluck most of it from pools of sour milk.

I loaded what I'd saved into the Javelin and drove home.

Red fussed over me when I got home. I assured her I was fine, but it took some convincing. I told her the story—about getting carted to the Watie Junction jail before being driven to Temple City, where I was finally released from custody. She asked me where they'd taken Joel. I had to tell her I didn't know.

Then I told her about the house.

"Are you *kidding me!*" she said. I thought she might spit, she was so mad. "There's executing a search warrant and there's—"

"I know, I know. I'll complain to his boss, but hold on for one second. There's something else. Something big."

She looked at me expectantly. "Ok, what?"

"Apparently Gabe Younger wasn't killed with the rest of his family."

She gave me a blank stare. "Why do you say that?" Red had never known Gabe, but she knew his family's history.

I told her about finding the photograph.

She said, "That's good news, isn't it?"

"Yes and no. I'm happy to hear Gabe got away that night, and that he was able to make a life for himself, but the fact Joel has his picture opens up another can of worms."

"I guess it does, doesn't it? Why would Joel have a picture of Gabe?"

"Because they're related."

"You think?"

"I can't think of another explanation. What's more, I think Gabe was Joel's father."

"Let me see it." I handed her the photo. She took a long look at it, turned it over and read the signature, then gave it back. "There might be a resemblance."

"I don't think there's any doubt. They may not look like twins, but I definitely see similarities."

"Why do you think Gabe is his father? He could be an uncle. Or a cousin."

"When Joel interviewed with me, he told me he was adopted. He said his birth father was a gunnery sergeant in the Army who died in Korea before he was born. Gabe's wearing an Army uniform in this picture. And he's a sergeant."

"Has Joel ever mentioned his birth father's name?"

"No. I didn't ask. I should have, but I didn't. Anyway, it doesn't matter that much whether Gabe was his father or his uncle or his cousin. What matters is that Gabe's a relative. Heckscher figured that out and suspects Joel came here to get his revenge."

We were quiet for a moment.

Karen asked, "Could this mean Gabe is still alive?"

I shrugged. "Maybe, but I don't think so."

"Well, that's too bad. It would've been nice to have tracked him down."

I nodded.

"So what now?" asked Red.

"Talk to Joel as soon as possible. I've got to find where they have him stowed. Keith thought it likely that they took him to Oklahoma City, which probably means the Oklahoma County jail. I'll drive to OSBI headquarters in the morning, talk to Heckscher, and sort this out."

"Can Heckscher keep you from seeing him?"

I unleashed several epithets, none of which I will repeat, the sum total of which amounted to: "He'd better not."

CHAPTER THIRTEEN

A newsreel of the day's events played on a continuous loop inside my head. Red went to bed. I stayed up to think.

It's not only that I didn't *want* to believe Joel had anything to do with Burt's death. It's that I *couldn't*. My mind couldn't wrap itself around it. Even if Joel was related to Gabe—heck, even if Gabe was his father—I couldn't conceive of him doing something like that.

Joel said he'd never seen that little gal before that day. I believed him.

That would likely mean she acted alone, or if she had help, it didn't come from Joel.

I found a legal pad and sat down at the kitchen table. I scribbled, *Reasons for Jane Doe to kill Burt*. Underneath I wrote:

Sexual Assault.

Jane Doe was pregnant. Could Burt be responsible? If he was, it would almost certainly have been the result of rape. He'd never done anything like that before, at least not to my knowledge, but I have no doubt he was capable of it. Burt felt entitled to anything and everything he laid his eyes on. I could see him using her then throwing her away like a piece of trash.

I wrote *Revenge for* in front of *Sexual Assault* and underlined it.

Then I wrote down *Greed*.

Did Burt have something Jane Doe wanted? He had more than she did, that's for sure. Yet there appeared to be no material benefit for her to kill him. She's dead now, so we might never know. But she didn't try to rob him; she killed him in front of God and the world.

I thought we could safely rule out greed.

Jealousy.

I tried to imagine her falling in love with Burt and being angry that he wouldn't leave his wife, but that was too far-fetched to consider for even a millionth of a second. She could have been jealous of his wealth, I suppose, but there are plenty of rich folks in the world not named Burt Murray she could have gone after. Granted, Burt had a higher public profile than most, so maybe that put a target on his back. Then again, this didn't seem like the murder of some random rich guy. There was a personal component. Somehow, she'd been wronged.

I moved on to the next thing: *Revenge.*

Another realistic possibility. There are as many reasons for seeking revenge as there are people on the planet. Not all inspire murder. You might want to get even for being robbed, but I don't imagine getting your purse snatched or your pocket picked would inspire you to kill. Nah, it would have to be something big. Sexual assault qualifies. I can't imagine Jane Doe had anything of monetary value for Burt to steal, but sexual assault can steal a person's soul, and you can't put a price on that.

I scrawled another line: *Revenge for Sexual Assault.*

What if Burt hurt someone she loved? I know if anyone ever hurt Karen, I'd be out for justice, and not necessarily the kind you get in a court of law.

In smaller letters, I wrote down *revenge for hurting a loved one.*

Of course, it's possible the girl was simply out of her mind. I never knew her and had yet to find anyone who did. Shooting someone in broad daylight in front of hundreds of people doesn't seem like the act of a rational person.

I wrote down *insanity* and underlined it.

Revenge or insanity. It had to be one or the other.

***

I was out of the house by 6:30 the next morning. I drove the Javelin I'd driven home the night before and got Joel to take me to Wes Harmon's Sinclair so I could pick up my truck. I filled the tank while I was there. It cost me 14 bucks for 23 gallons of regular. Gas prices have gone through the roof lately. We settled up and I hit the road.

About the only thing the state of Oklahoma has in common with New York City is the way the roads are set up. Like Manhattan, Most Oklahoma highways run on a north/south-east/west grid. Oklahoma City is a bit south, but mostly east of Burr, meaning I spent the first half-hour of the trip driving into the sunrise—a horizon of gold and orange giving way to blue and purple clouds that looked like mountains in the distance. The glare was pretty bad, but with my sunglasses on I could enjoy it somewhat. It was hot in the car but kind of cool outside, so I tried rolling down the windows. I had to roll them right back up because of all the bugs flying into the cab. I turned on the air-conditioner.

State roads might remind me of New York, but Oklahoma City streets sure don't. Some don't even line up with themselves; you'll be driving along and all of a sudden you reach a crooked intersection where you have to jog over on a diagonal. Fortunately, I made my way to the OSBI headquarters without hitting another car or having another car hit me, which I considered a victory.

I arrived a few minutes past 9:00. The woman at the front desk was talking on the phone and refused to acknowledge my presence. After a minute or so, another line rang. She put the first person on hold and talked to the second one for a while—still without smiling at me or giving the one-finger "I'll-be-with-you-in-a-moment" sign or anything else.

I noticed on the counter in front of her there was a stack of informational pamphlets. I picked one up, walked over to a pay phone in the lobby, put a dime in the slot and dialed the number on the pamphlet. The phone behind the desk rang again. She put the person she was talking to on hold and picked up. "Oklahoma State Bureau of Investigation," she said. "Could you please hold?"

Before she could hang up, I said, "Uh, no I can't. See, I'm the handsome fella who's been standing in front of you for the last ten minutes. I'm over here by the pay phone." She looked. I waved. "I don't want to be a bother, ma'am, but I do need to see Agent John Joe Heckscher about a case."

With an aggrieved look, she motioned me over and punched some keys on her telephone. "Is Agent Heckscher available?" she asked the person on the other end, then she said, "Hold on a sec," and asked me my name. I told her. "Emmett Hardy," she said. "Uh-huh. Ok. Thank you." She hung up and said, "He's not in."

"Any idea where I could find him?"

"He's going to be out all day."

I'll bet he is, I thought. "I'm the police chief up in Burr. Agent Heckscher was in our town yesterday. He arrested a guy named Joel Carter and I need to talk to him about it."

She nervously eyed the blinking lights on her phone. "I'm sorry, but he's out for the day."

"Would you have any idea where they've stashed Carter, then?"

"I assume the county jail. Unless they shipped him out to McAlester."

"Why would they do that?"

"Overcrowding. Too many crooks, not enough cells. Now, if you'll excuse me, I have to get back to these calls." She gave me a phony smile and picked up the phone. "Thank you for holding—"

***

From the outside, the Oklahoma County Jail resembles a big-city high school—one with bars on the windows, and where every teacher packs a gun.

It would be much better if Joel were here than if they'd moved him to McAlester. If that happened, it might be days before I could cut through the red tape to see him.

The county jail folks were much more helpful than the woman at the OSBI. I told a lady in a guard's uniform sitting behind the front desk who I was and why I was there. She checked my credentials, saw they were in order, then clicked some buttons on her computer. Yes, they had a Joel Carter and yes, I could see him. She buzzed me into a small room, where a guard took my gun and placed it in a locker.

He told me to come with him, then led me down a series of corridors into a large, dimly lit room. The white paint on the walls had chipped away to reveal the gray cinder blocks beneath. Time and neglect had decorated the concrete floor with a spiderweb of cracks. The cloying smell of disinfectant almost but not quite covered the smell of something vile. There were two doors—the one I came through, and one directly opposite. A small table sat in the middle of the room, with two chairs facing each other on either side. The table and chairs were all made of metal and bolted to the floor. In one corner, a video camera was mounted from the ceiling. A clock hung on the wall facing me.

The guard had me sit in one of the chairs, then left the same way we'd come in. A minute later, the door across from me opened. Another guard escorted Joel into the room. Joel had on a pair of handcuffs and an orange prison jumpsuit. The guard sat him down, undid one cuff, and locked it onto a bar attached to the table. "Give us a shout when you're done," he said, then left the room.

To all outward appearances, Joel seemed fine, but who could tell? He'd been through the wringer. We squirmed in our seats for a minute and joked about how uncomfortable the chairs were. They were obviously made to accommodate rear-ends more well-padded than ours.

He smiled faintly. "Thanks for coming, Chief."

"Glad to do it. Wish I didn't have to." I nodded toward the camera. "Keep in mind we're probably being monitored and recorded."

"I figured."

I asked if his lawyer had been in to see him.

"First thing this morning. He told me he spoke to you last night. Thanks for that."

"Glad to do it."

For an uncomfortable moment, neither of us said anything, then we both opened our mouths to talk at the same time. I motioned for him to go ahead.

"Alright then," he said quietly, "I've got something to tell you that you're not going to like."

"You sure you want to talk about this now?" I lifted my chin at the camera.

He shook his head. "They already know. Don't ask me how, but they do."

"Ok, then. I'm all ears."

He twisted the cuff around his wrist, almost like he was trying to loosen it. "I didn't exactly tell the whole truth when I interviewed for this job."

"That so?"

"I left something out when I was telling you about myself."

"What was that?"

"It's a long story."

"I've got time.

He stared down at the table, then said, "Do you remember a guy named Gabe Younger?"

"Gabe was a childhood friend of mine." He raised his eyes.

"You're not going to believe this, but Gabe Younger was my father."

"I believe it," I said.

These days, there's no end to what I'll believe.

CHAPTER FOURTEEN

As I've mentioned, at one point in Burr's history—from 1929 until the late '30s—we had a few Black families living here. Not many, but a few. Most of them moved here so the men could work in the oil fields. Beginning in 1928, there were major gas and oil strikes all over Tilghman County. The oil companies needed workers, and they didn't care what their skin color was. Not for a while, at least. When I was little, I saw Black folks around town all the time. In fact, I saw a lot more Black folks in my everyday life than I see Asian folks around here today. I didn't think anything of it.

Eventually, however, I saw certain things that made me wonder why things were the way they were. One day I asked my mama why all the Black families lived in one neighborhood. She said, "Because there are some ignorant white people in this town who won't let them live anywhere else." To this day, whenever I think of racism, the word that comes to mind is "ignorant." Of course, there are plenty of other words that fit. Hateful and stupid work, but to me, that one word—ignorant—says it all.

I began to notice how Burr's Black citizens had a harder time than we white folks did. Like the Southeast Asians working at Little Piggy, who today live almost totally separately from the rest of us in a company-run trailer park, Burr's black folks had a ghetto of their own. It was called Jackson Corners, and it was literally on the other side of the railroad tracks. The Black people weren't allowed to shop in the same stores as us. They took their trade to a small general store that catered only to them. At the Santa Fe station, they had their own water fountains. The only restaurant in town, Edna's Eats, had a sign on the door that said, "Whites Only."

The only place whites and Blacks regularly rubbed elbows was at the last place you'd expect. School. In Oklahoma, it was against the law back then for whites and Blacks to attend school together. The law was enforced in most places in the state, but not here. Burr's school board didn't want to build a separate school for the handful of Black kids who'd recently moved to town, so they said to hell with it and let the Black kids attend ours.

I don't want to make it sound like the situation was great for the Black kids, because it wasn't. For one thing, not every white person in town was on board with having their children attend school with their Black brothers and sisters. They made their displeasure felt in numerous ways, some of them violent and all of them repellant. In addition, Black students weren't allowed to do all the things white kids could do, like play sports or be in the band.

I met Gabe Younger in elementary school. We weren't bosom pals, but we were friends. Both of us had other, closer buddies. Mine were white, his were Black. A love of fishing brought us together. Gabe and I would hitch a ride out to Burr Lake, or pester my dad to drive us out to a tank on his property. We didn't exactly flaunt our friendship. There were plenty of folks in town who wouldn't like it if they knew. But my family was fine with it and so was his. Our friendship was a highlight of what I mostly remember as a happy childhood.

Gabe's childhood, on the other hand, was less than happy, and it came to an end one night in 1940.

***

When things are as bad as they were during the '30s, folks don't have much time or inclination to beat up on one another. Everybody's in the same boat, trying to do the same thing: survive. You don't worry about losing when you've got nothing to lose. It's only when you have something that you can relax and start looking around for people to hate.

That's my theory, anyway.

When things started to get better economically, they got worse in other ways. To be specific: Certain white folks in Burr decided they wanted the Black folks gone and they didn't say pretty please. They spit on them in the street, burnt crosses on their lawns, threw rocks through their windows. Most of the Black people got the message and left town.

The Youngers were the last holdouts.

Clarence Younger was gainfully employed and a popular figure in the community, even among whites. He was cheerful and hard-working. If you found yourself shirtless, Clarence was happy to give you the one off his back. Even the rednecks liked him. I didn't know him very well; I'd see him when I went by to pick up Gabe, but that's about it. He was always friendly to me, as he was to pretty much everybody. Clarence was smart, too. Dad used to say he could've been a doctor or lawyer if he'd been able to go to college. Instead, Clarence made a living sweeping out the Santa Fe depot and giving white folks rides to and from the station in his old Model T. I expect Clarence must've thought being well-liked was enough to protect him and his family.

He was wrong.

One night, a carful of night-riders firebombed the Younger home. The family initially escaped, but their house burnt to the ground.

Clarence came by our place the next day and asked my father for help. My dad was always the type to stand up to bullies, but this time he refused. I never asked why, and he never volunteered a reason. If I were being generous, I'd say he didn't want to put his family in the crosshairs of the bigots who ran the town back then. If I were being not-so-generous, I'd attribute it to moral cowardice. I'll say this: I never saw Dad in the same light again.

The Youngers drove off, and that was it. I missed Gabe, and was sad and disgusted by how his family had been treated, but like most people in town, I figured they'd simply up and moved away.

Turns out, they never got the chance.

25 years later, we dragged Burr Lake and discovered the skeletal remains of Clarence, his wife, and his daughter. I arrested Burt. He and Frank Sallee were convicted of murder and sent to prison.

Gabe's body was never found. I hoped that meant he'd gotten away, but we couldn't know. Neither killer was going to tell us. More than once over the years I dreamed Gabe escaped and lived a rewarding life somewhere far away in a place less hostile to the color of his skin than Burr, Oklahoma.

Now here was his son telling me that's exactly what happened.

***

Joel told it to me the way his adopted parents told it to him:

After leaving our house the day after the fire, Clarence drove his family out to Burr Lake. In those days, there was a long fishing pier stretching out over the water about 20 yards, ending a few feet before the water suddenly got really deep. Clarence parked a few yards away from the pier and sent Gabe out to find some firewood while the rest of the family set up camp. The area around the lake was barren of trees. To get wood, Gabe had to walk a long way. It was dark by the time he started back. He stopped by the lake's worm shop, about 100 yards away from the pier. It was closed, but he wanted to buy a Coke out of the machine. Before he could, he saw that a police car had parked next to his family's tent. Two men in uniforms were shouting and cursing at his father. One pulled a gun and shot him in the head. The other opened the tent flap and fired multiple times. Gabe cried out. The two men gave chase. Gabe ran. The dark gave him cover. Gabe pressed himself flat on the slope behind the lake's earthen dam, a few hundred yards away from the campsite. The men searched on foot, then got in their cruiser—Gabe saw it was a sheriff's department vehicle—and circled the lake. Once he thought it was safe, he peered over the berm. He recognized the fella driving the car. Burt Murray. Round and round they went. Their searchlight passed over his hiding place several times. They called out, saying they weren't going to hurt him, they only wanted to talk. After what must've seemed to Gabe like a lifetime, they finally drove away. Gabe ran to the campsite and found the bodies of his family.

Within minutes, the men returned. Gabe took cover again. He watched them load the bodies of his family into Clarence's Model T. One man opened the driver's side door and steered. The other pushed the car down the pier and into the lake. They got back in their cruiser and circled the lake a couple more times, calling for Gabe. They gave up and drove away. Gabe didn't wait for them to come back. He ran.

"He was only thirteen years-old," Joel said. "Can you imagine? Going through something like that at that age? When I was thirteen, I was playing basketball in Central Park. Gabe was running for his life from a couple of redneck cops. Jesus."

Of course, he ran. What else could he do?

"What happened next?"

Joel laughed sardonically. "He got as far away from Burr as possible. He had no money, no family. His grandparents on both sides were dead. He had aunts and uncles, but he'd lost track of them. He didn't feel safe here, obviously. He walked along the highway, jumping into the weeds on the side of the road whenever he heard a car coming. He hopped a freight train in Alva. That took him to Kansas City. From there, he caught another freight to Chicago, then another one to Detroit. That's where he finally settled. For over a year, he survived on the streets as best he could. When the Japanese bombed Pearl Harbor, he went to the recruiting office to enlist in the Army. He was only 14, but he told the recruiters he was 18. He was big for his age, so they bought it."

At 14, I was playing junior varsity football and mooning over a girl who had no use for me. A few years later, I joined the Marines to teach her a lesson.

Joel continued. "At the time, Black soldiers weren't allowed to fight. He was sent to the Pacific and worked as a tank mechanic. Towards the end of the war, they began letting Blacks serve in combat. Gabe volunteered. He was trained as an artilleryman with an all-Black unit. He fought in Iwo Jima and Okinawa and was preparing for an invasion of the Japanese mainland when the atomic bombs were dropped on Hiroshima and Nagasaki. He won a Purple Heart on Iwo Jima, and a Bronze Star on Okinawa. I've got 'em both."

I shook my head. "That's quite a story. I take it he stayed in the Army after the war?"

"He went into the Reserve and moved back to Detroit. He worked at General Motors until the Korean War broke out, then he was called back up. They sent him to Ft. Sill to train artillerymen. That's where he met my mom. You know the rest. They sent him to Korea, and he was killed in combat not long before I was born. A year later, my mom died in a hit-and-run accident. I was sent to live with my aunt and uncle. They adopted me." He shrugged. "That's about it."

Gabe and I had probably been in Korea at the same time. I was a Marine, he was in the Army, but we might've crossed paths. Would I have even recognized him if I saw him?

"Did your folks ever mention whether he ever intended to come back to Burr to see justice was done?"

"You know, they never did," he answered. "I like to think he would have, when the time was right."

"But he didn't live long enough."

He shook his head. "No, he didn't."

I was sympathetic to Joel for the mess he was in, but I couldn't help being disappointed he hadn't told me the whole story from the beginning. I then asked what had to be asked:

"Did you come here to avenge the killing of your father's family?"

He tensed. "Chief, I swear to God, revenge isn't why I wanted this job. I was telling the truth when I said I wanted to make a difference. When I saw that flier on the bulletin board at John Jay, I couldn't believe it. I'd already decided to try for a job in a small southern town, probably in Oklahoma, since I had a connection to the state, but it could've been somewhere else. When I saw that flier on the bulletin board at John Jay, it almost seemed like a sign from God—a chance to reclaim for my family what had been taken from them. When I interviewed, I didn't even know my family's killers had finally been caught. I only discovered that after I got the job."

I reached into my shirt pocket, pulled out the picture of Gabe, and slid it across the table. "I found this in your bedroom after they searched the place."

He looked at it and slid it back. "So you knew."

"I guessed."

"That's the only picture I have of him."

I put it back in my pocket. "I'll take good care of it."

"I'll bet the place is a mess, huh?"

I nodded. "Yeh, pretty much." I didn't see any reason to go any further than that. He had enough problems.

"I can't believe they didn't find that. It was out in the open, on my dresser."

"It's a good thing they didn't."

The guard stuck his head in the door and tapped his watch. I tried to think of any other questions I needed to ask.

"Does Heckscher have any other reason to believe you conspired with Jane Doe?"

"Not that I know of," he said. "Somehow, he found out Gabe was my father. Don't ask me how, but that's all he grilled me about. He's not going to find evidence of me conspiring with Jane Doe because none exists. I never saw her before that morning. I can't imagine they'll be able to hold me for very long."

I didn't want to discourage him, but I knew guys like Heckscher could get creative in situations like this. "What's your lawyer think?" I said.

"He's 100 percent confident I won't be charged, never mind convicted. As far as getting out of here, he'll be asking the judge for a writ of Habeas Corpus. Hopefully that'll work."

"Listen," I said, "I know you're innocent, but Agent Heckscher's not going to let this go. Motive is important, and he thinks he's found one. I don't know what other evidence he has—"

"He has no other evidence because none exists," he said. "Heckscher sees I'm related to the people Murray killed and right away assumes I helped kill him in revenge." He cursed. "That's not how it is, Chief. That's not how it is."

I gave him a second to cool down. "Listen," I said. "I believe you. But it's not impossible that he's found something else—something that can be misinterpreted—that he can use against you. He thinks he's got a motive. That's a powerful incentive to dig up something to support his theory. He seems to think you teamed up with that girl to have her kill him, and that you killed her to cover up your role. I don't believe that's what happened. I'm not even saying Heckscher does. But if Heckscher *wants* to believe it bad enough, he'll beat every last bush to find something that'll put you away."

"Even if I had a motive, what was the girl's? Was I supposed to have paid her? She didn't have a penny on her when she died."

"See, now you're talking sense. Sometimes things don't make any sense."

"But if we found her motive, that would clear me, wouldn't it?"

"I expect it would."

The guard reentered the room. "Time's up," he said. He undid the cuff holding Joel to the table, then locked it around his wrist. Joel got to his feet and the guard led him to the door—rougher this time, like he was being watched and wanted to make a good impression on whoever was doing the watching. I looked up at the camera and imagined John Joe Heckscher on the other end. Watching and listening.

"You hang in there, Joel."

He managed to say, "Thanks, Chief," before the door closed on him.

CHAPTER FIFTEEN

Ever think what life would be like if you didn't give a damn? About anything?

Coast. Ignore. Get a job that pays the bills but doesn't keep you up at night.

Plenty of people wake up in the morning, go to work, come home, chug a six-pack in front of the TV, and go to bed. Day after day. Year after year. No worries. No ambition.

Sometimes that sounds really good.

Sure wish I could make myself do it.

Oh well.

***

Before starting home, I stopped by the State Medical Examiner's office to see if they'd done a post-mortem on Jane Doe. The young woman tasked with helping me was nice, but it was her first day on the job and she didn't have a firm grasp of things. She collared a young gentleman in a white doctor's smock who appeared to know a little more about how the place was run. He wrested control of the receptionist's computer terminal, tapped a few keys, and told me our

Jane Doe was indeed in their morgue, but they had not done an autopsy. I asked him why. He said, "No idea."

"And you're absolutely sure she was pregnant?" I was still having trouble wrapping my head around that fact. He glanced at the screen, then answered, "Yes."

"Has she been identified?"

"Presumably not," he said, kind of snotty-like, "since they're still calling her Jane Doe." I asked if I could talk to the Chief Medical Examiner. "He's in Paris for an air show." I almost asked why the state's chief medical examiner would be in Paris for an air show, but I thought it best to cut my losses.

That was enough of the city for one day. I stopped at a Sonic on the way home and ended up spilling my hamburger all over my lap by trying to eat and drive at the same time. I pulled over at a small playground and found a drinking fountain, which I used to wash the gunk off my hands. I found a relatively clean grease rag under the seat in my pickup and tried to use it to wipe it off my clothes, but mostly all I did was smear the mess around.

After asking about my tooth—I told her it was fine—the first thing Karen said when I walked into the station was, "What have I told you about playing with your food?"

"Funny lady."

"I'll be here all week, ladies and gentlemen."

We went back to my office and shut the door. She asked if I'd accomplished anything besides smearing mustard and ketchup all over my clothes. I said I'd seen Joel, then told her what he told me.

"Wow," she said. "That's some story."

"It is. I believe it, too. I just wish he'd told me about it before I hired him."

"Would you have hired him if you knew?"

"Absolutely."

She gave me a side-eye. "Really?"

"Really, but I can't blame him for not knowing that."

"I guess that makes sense. Did you talk to Heckscher?"

"Nah. He was my first stop, but the receptionist said he was out for the day. I got the feeling she was lying, that someone told her to say that, but whatever."

"Heck, all he's got is a suspicion based on Joel's relationship to Gabe. That's a motive, but he's got to do better than that."

"Yeh, Joel says his lawyer is confident the judge will kick them out of court, but who knows when that'll happen."

She asked what else I did in the city. I told her about trying to see the Chief Medical Examiner regarding Jane Doe, and that I couldn't because he was in Paris for an air show, which got a big sarcastic laugh out of her. "They did tell me they've still got her body in their morgue and they still don't know who she was."

"Did they do an autopsy?"

"They didn't, and if you ask me, that's a mistake. Testing for drugs or alcohol might tell us something. Who the hell knows what they're thinking? What I'd like to know is who she was and what was she doing in Burr."

"And why did she kill Burt."

"Exactly."

"You know, it's a shame your friend Gabe never came back here. Times have changed. Maybe he could've come back, told his story, and gotten justice for his family."

"Gabe died in 1951. That was well before times had changed."

"True."

"What bothers me is that Joel kept this from us. I understand why he didn't mention it in the interview—"

"You didn't either."

"What do you mean?"

"You could've told him what happened to the Youngers. But you didn't."

I felt a surge of self-disgust. "You know what?" I said. "You're right. I've got no right to criticize him." I called myself a few choice names.

"Oh, stop it," she said. "What's done is done. We just need to do what we can to keep him from being railroaded."

My phone buzzed. Red picked it up, said a few words, and hung up. "I'm needed out front."

"Alright, then. Thanks for listening."

"That's why I get the big money."

On her way out, I asked if she'd made any progress with our list of OU graduates. She said they'd called a few more. "No luck. We'll get back to it when we can."

***

She reappeared at my office door later in the afternoon. "Emmett, there's someone on the phone you need to talk to. I think he might be able to help with our John Doe."

"What's his name?"

"Rob Richards."

I put the call on the loudspeaker. "Hello, Mr. Richards, this is Chief Hardy. I understand you have some information for us."

"Uh, yeh," he said. "I graduated from OU in 1972 with a bachelor's degree in biology. Now I teach seventh graders at a junior high school in Pawhuska. That lady I was just talking to asked me if I knew anything about the phrase, 'Fill the world with bellowing.' I told her that was the motto of the Unholy Trinity Society."

"What is that, exactly?"

"It was a club for physics majors at OU. I was a biology major, so I didn't have anything to do with them, but I remember the club. It was pretty famous. Or maybe I should say infamous."

"Judging by the name, it sounds like some kind of anti-religious group."

He chuckled. "I doubt any of those guys were religious, but that's not where the name came from. I'm sure you've heard of the Manhattan Project. You know: the guys who built the first atomic bomb? Trinity was the name they gave the first A-bomb test. It's a play on that. I guess the point was, there wasn't anything holy about building a bomb that could eventually lead to the end of the world.

Know what I mean? Those Unholy Trinity guys were the smartest of the smart—and nuts, boy, let me tell you. The stunts they used to pull! I dated the only female member, a girl named Eva Benefiel."

"Can you tell us how to get in touch with her?"

"Well sure, let me—" There were rustling sounds from the other end of the line. "Here it is." He spelled out her name and gave me her phone number. "I haven't spoken to her in years. I think she still lives in Norman, though. I believe she's working on her PhD at OU."

I said I was much obliged. He told me to give Eva his regards. I said I would and ended the call.

Karen had been standing by, listening. "Paydirt," she said.

I said, "Let's hope so."

I got through to Eva Benefiel and put her on speaker. I told her who I was and said that Rob Richards told us she might be able to help with a problem we had. She asked what the problem was. I told her.

"I've got 'Fill the world with bellowing' inscribed on my class ring," she said. "We all did. It was a tradition with the members of Unholy Trinity."

I asked if she had a picture of the group.

"There should be one in my yearbook. Hold on a sec, me check." She came back a minute later. "Yup," she said. "I'm looking at it as we speak. You're welcome to come by and take a look if you want."

We arranged for me to visit the next day.

"I guess you're heading back to Norman tomorrow," said Karen. "With all this driving you're doing, I hope you're saving your receipts. Gas prices are getting crazy."

"Tell me about it," I said, and told what it cost me to fill up my truck.

She said, "It's going to be over a dollar a gallon before you know it."

"The day gas costs a dollar a gallon is the day I start riding a bicycle."

"I hope that doesn't happen before tomorrow. I'd hate for you to have to ride a bike all the way to Norman."

By the time I left the next afternoon, gas at the Sinclair had actually gone down a penny.

***

Eva Benefiel lived in a small rundown apartment complex a few blocks from the OU campus. She apologized for the state of the place. "I'm only a lowly graduate assistant. I'm lucky I can even afford this."

She had the page bookmarked. There were two photographs—one of the entire club, and one of only the graduating seniors. There were about 20 total members. Six were seniors.

She pointed herself out in the larger group. "That's me, the only girl. I was a junior that year."

"But you knew the seniors, right?"

"Oh sure. We all hung out together."

A caption under the photo listed the seniors' names. I asked if she knew where they were now.

"I work with these guys," she said, pointing out three of the men, "so I know they're not dead. At least not as of 3:30 yesterday afternoon." She pointed out a fourth. "This guy's working on his doctorate at MIT. He couldn't get out of Oklahoma fast enough. I seriously doubt he's the one you're looking for."

That left two. Their names were John Smith and Leon Qualls.

She pointed at Smith. "It can't be John. I just saw him last night. He works the graveyard shift at a convenience store near the campus."

"What about Leon Qualls?"

"You know," she said thoughtfully, "he may be the one." She paused. "My God. Leon was a mess. Brilliant mind, but severe emotional problems. He had a breakdown a few years ago and ended up living on the streets. I used to see him around occasionally. Very sad."

"Have you seen him lately?"

"Not for months. In fact, the last time I saw him was at John's store. You know the Sunshine Store, right? On Campus Corner?"

"Not really."

"You should talk to John. He works the overnight shift. 11:00 to 7:00. He might be able to help."

I noticed she was wearing her class ring. I asked to see the inscription. She took it off and showed me. It was the same as Leon's. "It's so small," I said. "How did the jeweler fit all those words in?"

"I've asked myself the same thing," she said. "The guy was good."

I handed it back and asked if I could borrow the yearbook.

"Take it," she said. "It's for a good cause. Bring it back when you're done."

She offered me a cup of coffee, but I saw a roach nibbling on an open packet of sugar lying on the coffee table and decided I'd best be getting along. On my way out, I said it must've been hard being the only woman in a club full of men. "I understand it was a pretty crazy bunch."

She laughed. "It depends on what you mean by crazy. Most of their pranks were kind of silly. Complicated, but silly. I remember, one weekend they took apart a professor's car and reassembled it in his classroom."

"How'd they manage that?"

"Oh, it wasn't hard. It was just a little Volkswagen. I'll tell you this: That professor sure was surprised on Monday morning."

The thought of going to all that trouble simply to mess with a professor was intriguing and I could have asked a million more questions about it, but I decided to save them for the next time I saw Eva Benefiel.

CHAPTER SIXTEEN

I've heard it said that Norman is Oklahoma's version of Austin, Texas. I've also heard people say that Austin is Texas's version of Greenwich Village—a place I've actually been—which to me suggests any comparison between Austin and Norman is purely aspirational on the latter's part.

Campus Corner is the only part of Norman that's the tiniest bit bohemian. It's a several-block section of town adjacent to the university, comprising a multitude of bars and restaurants and assorted businesses catering to college students. Its biggest draw is a strip club named Walter Mitty's. Many Norman-ites consider the very existence of Walter Mitty's a sign of the coming end times. My personal beef with Mitty's is that it's too cheap to hire live musicians for the gals to gyrate to. They use a jukebox.

The Sunshine Store sits on the northwest corner of Campus Corner, across the street from an Italian restaurant and a TV repair store. It was well before 11:00, but I thought I'd drop by anyway, hoping I might get lucky and find John Smith working an earlier shift.

The store's most notable feature was an enormous collection of pornographic books and magazines lined across its back wall. Maybe they worked some kind of deal with Walter Mitty's, I don't know. I was almost embarrassed to be in the same room with such a cornucopia of smut, especially while in uniform. I averted my eyes and bought a Norman paper. The guy working the register said if I wanted to see John Smith, I'd have to come back after 11:00.

That gave me a couple of hours to kill. I crossed the street to the aforementioned Italian restaurant. It looked nice enough, at first, anyway. A waitress took my order. I read the paper and waited for my food. Before long, the owner—a short, thickly muscled fella with a strong Italian accent—approached and told me in no uncertain terms to keep it down. I found this strange, since I hadn't said a word or coughed or sneezed or done anything except read my newspaper. He came back again a few minutes later and told me once again that I was being too noisy. Normally I would've got in the fella's face, but as a stranger in a strange land, I reckoned the best thing to do was eat my pizza and drink my Tab as quietly as I could then get the hell out of Dodge. I left a ten on the table for an eight-dollar check. Muscly Guy gave me a dirty look on my way out.

I heard the song "Mustang Sally" playing somewhere in the vicinity and took it upon myself to investigate. I tracked it to a biker bar a couple of doors down from the Sunshine Store. I stood on the sidewalk outside and listened for a while. The band's saxophone player had me feeling a little jealous, wishing I could play like that. At one point the bouncer came out and asked if there was a problem. Maybe my uniform unnerved him, I don't know. I explained I was waiting for somebody and he left me alone.

When I got back to the Sunshine Store, there was a different fella working the register. I assumed it was John Smith, but he was too busy to talk. I walked over to the magazine racks and read a copy of Time with the cover conspicuously displayed so no one would mistake me for a sex fiend. A pimply-faced kid wearing a red polo shirt with a tiny alligator on the chest had his face stuck as far as it could go into a magazine called *Big Boobs*. He looked up and saw me, saw my badge, then decided there was somewhere else he had to be.

The cash register was set behind a circular counter in the center of the store. A line of what appeared to be college kids waited in line all the way down one aisle and halfway up the next. Most clutched a six-pack or two of beer. A fella with the body of an NFL linebacker and the face of a twelve-year-old waited to pay for a single can of Budweiser. He kept looking at me nervously from the corner of his eye. When it came his turn, he hesitated before putting his beer on the counter. The cashier said, "Need to see some ID, bud." The kid handed him a card. The cashier examined it and said, "This isn't yours." Then he opened the register, dropped the license in, and closed the drawer.

The kid said, "Hey, you can't do that!"

"I just did."

The kid turned to me. "Can he do that?"

Doing my best not to smile I said, "He just did."

"Oh man, cut me some slack!" the kid said, almost in tears. "That's my brother's driver's license. He's going to kill me!" The cashier pulled out an eighteen-inch length of thick insulated cable and smacked it on the counter hard enough to make everyone in the place jump. "Not my problem," he said. "Next!"

The kid cursed, handed me the beer, and walked out. A few other underage beer purchasers took the hint and followed him.

The cashier smiled and said, "I'll take that off your hands." I handed him the beer. He placed it on the floor beside his feet and recommenced ringing people up.

I said, "Excuse me, I can see you're busy, but could you tell me if your name is John Smith?"

"That depends," he said, ringing up the next customer. "Is John Smith in trouble?"

"Not that I know of. I just want to ask a question about one of his friends."

"John Smith is always glad to cooperate with the authorities," he said. "I'll be with you as soon as I can."

I waited. The last person in line was a cute little gal in a halter top and excruciatingly short cut-offs. Smith tried to flirt, but she wasn't having any of it and walked out without saying a word. "Her loss," he said in a fake-cheerful way. He turned to me. "What can I do you for?"

"I was wondering if maybe you could help me with a case I'm working on."

He made a show out of looking at my "Burr, OK Police Dept." shoulder patch.

"You're not Norman PD."

"No, I'm from a little town called Burr in the western part of the state."

A large group of rowdy young men entered the store and went straight for the beer cooler.

"Burr, huh?" said Smith. "Weren't you folks in the news about a month back? This have something to do with that?"

"No, this is about something else."

"Yeh, well, I'm John Smith." The group approached the register and paid.

"Busy night, huh?" I asked once they'd all left.

"Every night is busy around here."

I told him my name and said I was trying to identify the victim of a shooting out my way. I mentioned I'd gotten his name from Eva Benefiel and said I thought it was possible the person I was looking to ID was a 1971 graduate of OU and a fellow member of the Unholy Trinity Society. "I've got the OU yearbook from 1971," I said. "Maybe if I show you a picture—"

"No need," he said, a distressed look on his face. "I know who you're looking for. Leon Qualls."

"How can you be sure?"

"Because I haven't seen him in over a month."

"You and Leon are friends?"

"Not really. I tried to be, but I don't think Leon ever had any real friends. Except for one, maybe." He made a give-it-here gesture. I handed over the yearbook. He took it and looked at the picture.

"Poor Leon." He lifted his chin toward a small table with two chairs in the front of the store. "He and his girlfriend hang around all night, every night, drinking coffee at that table over there." He lifted his chin toward a small booth by the front window. "I usually charge them for the first cup, then give them free refills. Sometimes I don't charge them at all. If they're hungry, I'll give 'em a hot dog and write it down as spoilage. Or at least that's how it was until about a month ago."

"He has a girlfriend?"

"Yeh. I guess you could call her that. She's pregnant, and I suspect the kid is Leon's. Talk about an odd couple. She's very, very slow, while, in some ways, Leon's the most brilliant person I ever met."

"One of those 'opposites attract' situations, huh?"

"Yeh, well, in some ways, they aren't that opposite. Both had serious problems. Leon's are emotional. Hers are cognitive. Actually, his might be worse."

I asked him what he meant by that.

"Leon is schizophrenic."

"You mean he has multiple personalities?" My scant knowledge of mental illnesses begins and ends with clinical depression, which is what I was diagnosed with at the VA hospital a few years ago.

"That's a popular misconception," said Smith. "Schizophrenia is a chemical imbalance in the brain. The wiring goes all out of whack. It distorts a person's sense of reality. Schizophrenics think strange thoughts. They hallucinate, get paranoid. They get delusions like the government's out to get them, or someone's monitoring their thoughts. Stuff like that. It messes with their emotions, too."

I said that sounded even worse than multiple personalities. Smith said that in a way it was.

"It screwed him up pretty bad," he continued. "In school, Leon kept to himself almost completely. He wouldn't look anyone in the eye. The only time you could get him to talk was in class. Even then, the professors had to pry answers out of him. But his insights were incredible. He made connections no one else could have made. When it came to physics, Leon could focus like a laser, but good luck getting him to talk about the weather."

"How is it that Leon got into that club?"

"Because he was brilliant," he said like I'd asked a stupid question. "Unholy Trinity was merit-based. It wasn't necessarily the people who got the highest grades; it was those who thought most creatively. If they didn't invite Leon, they might as well not have a club."

"It sounds to me like it was a miracle he got through four years of school."

"It didn't take Leon four years. He did it in two, even though he was older than the rest of us. His parents hadn't let him go to college when he graduated from high school because of his problems." He shook his head. "Poor guy, I think school was all that was holding him together. The summer after graduation, he barged into the emergency room one night in a panic. From what I've been told, he insisted the CIA had implanted a device in his brain to spy on his thoughts. He claimed to have evidence Richard Nixon was running a prostitution ring out of the Oval Office and wanted to have Leon killed to keep it quiet."

"That sounds pretty crazy."

"Yeh, Nixon was an evil genius, but that was during Watergate. I'm pretty sure he had other things on his mind."

The guy who'd been reading *Big Boobs* came back. Smith said, "This isn't a library, friend." The guy turned on his heel and walked out.

"Anyway," Smith said, "Leon begged the doctors and nurses to remove the device. Of course, there wasn't any device and they tried to tell him that, but he wouldn't listen. Apparently, he lost control. They called the cops, who took him to Central State."

Central State Hospital is a mental institution located in Norman. It has a fancier moniker these days, but most folks still call it by its original name.

"They kept him there for a while," Smith said. "I don't know exactly how long, but it couldn't have been more than a year before they turned him loose. I'd started grad school when I started seeing him around dressed like a hobo, walking fast like he was late for something but not really having any place to go. He took to wearing heavy gloves all the time, all year round."

"Did you ever try talking to him?"

He nodded. "Many times. I'd see him on the street and pull over, ask him if he needed a ride. He wouldn't even stop—just walked with his head down, mumbling to himself. He did that a lot. Talked to himself." He paused. "More likely he was talking to the voices in his head. He liked to go to the movies. I followed him into a theater one night. I said 'hi,' but he looked right past me. We were the only ones in the auditorium. I sat somewhere in the middle. He stood in the back row by the door. At first he was quiet, but after a while he started talking to his invisible friend. He kept getting louder and louder, like he was arguing with someone. After the movie, I asked the manager about Leon. He said, 'Oh, he's no trouble. He comes once a week, holds up the line a little while he's counting out change to pay for his ticket. The only problem is that sometimes he talks to his invisible friend.' Sometimes people would complain. He'd go in and ask Leon to be quiet. Leon would apologize and keep it down for a few minutes, then start back up again. The manager didn't seem to mind very much. He felt sorry for Leon."

"You say Leon always wears gloves?"

"Yeh. Thick, heavy work gloves. Blue and white, with a very distinctive pattern. Paisley-like. Oh, and the tips of the fingers were cut off so he could count out his change."

"There weren't any gloves on the fella we found."

He shrugged. "I don't know what to tell you. Leon always wore those gloves. Maybe this guy isn't Leon."

"Maybe not," I said, although at this point I was certain he was. "So what about this girlfriend?"

"Oh, Carrie." He sighed. "She's another sad case. When I started here, the regulars used to call her 'The Dog Lady.' Apparently, she'd steal dogs out of people's yards and bring them around here. That was before she met Leon. Hold on a sec," he said, as if struck by an idea. "I'll be right back." He disappeared into the cooler, then came back with a large cardboard box, taped shut like it was prepared to be shipped, only there was no address, just the name "Leon Qualls" written in thick magic maker. Smith sat it on the counter.

"Leon's parents come in here once a month. They give me a box and ask me to give it to Leon. I've never looked inside, but I assume it's some kind of care package."

"Is there some reason it needs to be refrigerated?"

"Not that I know of. My manager here hates Leon and Carrie. If he knew I was keeping things here for them, I'd probably get canned, so I hide Leon's boxes in the cooler. The manager never goes back there. Too much like actual work. He's called the cops on Leon and Carrie more than once. I'm supposed to do the same whenever I see them, but to hell with that."

A drunk man wearing pink Bermuda shorts and a Hawaiian shirt and leading a bald poodle on a leash came in and asked for a pack of Camels. Smith rang it up. The guy left, practically dragging the dog behind him. Smith called after him, "Hey, be careful with that dog!" The fella vanished. Smith mumbled under his breath, "People don't deserve dogs."

I asked him if he knew how to get in touch with Leon's parents. He shook his head. "Nah. They gave me their phone number one time, but I lost it. I probably threw it away by accident." He pushed the box across the counter. "Here. Maybe you should take it with you."

"Maybe I should." I picked it up. It was surprisingly light. "Any idea where I could find Carrie?"

"Carrie's with Leon."

"She wasn't when we found his body."

"Maybe you didn't see her, but she was there. I guarantee it. Those two went everywhere together."

I was struck by a terrible thought. I showed him a picture of Jane Doe taken on the day of her death.

"Oh, man," he said, his voice catching. "That's Carrie. She's dead, too, isn't she?"

"She is, I'm sorry to say."

For a moment, he seemed unable to speak.

"Was she shot?"

"One of my officers shot her in the line of duty."

"Is she the one who shot that politician?"

I nodded.

"So this *does* have something to do with that thing I saw on the news."

"I didn't think so until now. But yeh, that's what it looks like."

"Wow," he said quietly. "Carrie shot that redneck running for Congress. Unbelievable."

An older fella wearing a white windbreaker brought a bag of Cheetos and a can of Budweiser to the register. I listened while he and Smith talked about baseball for a minute and the guy left.

"You know, Carrie might've shot that guy because he hurt Leon. She was very protective of him. One time I saw her go after a drunk fraternity boy who'd been hassling Leon. Scratched the hell out of him. You'd have thought the guy was going to bleed to death. Carrie never cut her fingernails. They were like talons."

I noticed that when I examined her body.

"You wouldn't know her last name, would you?"

"Sorry."

"Know anyone who might?"

"Nah, I really don't. As far as I know, she didn't have any friends other than Leon. I never saw her with anyone but him."

It was after midnight and well past time to hit the road. I'd already gotten more than I'd bargained for. I thanked him and asked for his phone number. He wrote it down on a beer-can-sized brown paper bag, which I stuck in my pants pocket. I wrote mine down on a different bag. "Call me if you come across his folks' phone number, or if you hear from them again."

"Will do."

I picked up Leon's box and started for the door. "Do you mind if I ask you a personal question?" I asked.

"As long as it's not, 'What's a guy like you doing in a place like this?'"

I chuckled. "Actually, that's exactly what I was going to ask."

He shrugged. "Who knows? I guess maybe Leon and I have a lot in common. Neither of us is very good at doing what's necessary to get ahead. Obviously, Leon's problems are worse than mine. But I've got my own issues."

"Like?"

"Sometimes I'm kind of a scaredy cat."

"You didn't seem too scared when you took the ID off that fella."

"He was just a big kid. He wasn't going to hurt anybody. Anyway, that's a different kind of not being scared, if you know what I mean." He shrugged. "Whatever. Mitty's closes at two. It gets quiet after that. Gives me time to read."

***

Karen was asleep on the couch when I got home. I woke her up. "Go to bed."

She yawned. "I want to hear about your trip."

I settled into my ancient La-Z-Boy, too bone-weary to make it recline. I told her what I'd discovered. She rubbed her eyes and sat up.

"So Jane and John Doe were a couple," she said. "Who would've thought?"

"Smith says if Carrie shot Burt, it must be because he hurt Leon in some way."

"I'd say killing him would qualify."

"But why would he? Where would those two have even crossed paths?"

"I'd say that's for God to know and you to find out."

I told her about the care package from his parents.

"Think we should open it?" she said.

"I think we should. If nothing else, it might help us find his folks."

Karen agreed. I got a steak knife from a drawer in the kitchen and cut open the box. Inside were clean clothes, some homemade beef jerky, an envelope with five 20-dollar bills stuffed inside, and a box of

Hostess Ding Dongs. On top was a note: "Leon, we love you with all our hearts. Please come home!" It was signed simply, "Mom and Dad."

"That doesn't tell us much," I said.

"Except that his folks love him," said Karen quietly.

I gathered my last ounce of strength and got to my feet. Red sank deep into the couch and closed her eyes. "Maybe Leon was visiting family around here," she said, almost like she was talking in her sleep.

"I don't know anyone with the last name Qualls, do you?"

"No, but they could be on his mother's side."

"How would we find that out?"

"Beats me. Ask me in the morning after my brain starts working."

We stopped talking while a jet flew overhead.

"We need to find out," I said when it had passed.

"But not tonight," she said with a yawn.

I yawned right back. "No, not tonight. I'm too tired to think."

She got to her feet and stretched. "You and me both."

CHAPTER SEVENTEEN

With Joel being detained, I needed help. I called Pat and asked if he could somehow wrangle a day off from his real job and give us a hand. He said he had his hands full with the new baby and all, but he'd see what he could do. He called back a few minutes later and said both his boss and his wife had given him a thumbs up, but not before noon.

I'd have to perform patrol duties until then.

It was a good day for driving with the windows rolled down. The temperature was in the mid 70s and wasn't expected to go much over 80 in the afternoon, which is about as cool as you're going to get in Oklahoma this time of year—unless of course a tornado is imminent, and that's not something you wish for.

I cruised in one of the Javelins with the air-conditioner turned off for the first time in a couple of months. The good citizens of Burr were on their best behavior, so there wasn't much for me to do. I sat behind the billboard outside of town that serves as our speed trap and pointed my radar gun at a few cars. Every single one was at or below the limit. Our speed trap isn't much of a trap anymore. Too many people know about it.

I thought a lot about John Doe, or, as I now knew him, Leon Qualls. In the beginning, I wanted to identify him because it was the right thing to do. Now I knew his name, knew he was a murder victim, and that he was directly connected to the young woman who shot Burt Murray. Suddenly, the two cases were connected.

Cindy radioed me around lunchtime and told me Pat had reported in. I made one last stop at Miller's to pick up the pictures I took at Burt's funeral. I tossed the photos in the glove compartment and headed back to the station.

Red checked with the OSBI again to see if anyone had filed a missing persons report on Leon since the last time she'd checked. No one had, so she called OU, trying to get a fix on where he was from, and who his parents were. After being put on hold a half-dozen times, she finally discovered Leon was from Weatherford, and that his parents were science professors at Southwestern Oklahoma State University located there.

Weatherford isn't a heck of a long drive from Burr. I didn't particularly want to be the one to tell his folks their son had died, but I didn't want to leave it to John Joe Heckscher, either. In fact, I wasn't sure I even wanted Heckscher to know I'd uncovered Leon's name, never mind that he'd been murdered. After the stunt he pulled on me and especially Joel, I didn't have an ounce of trust in him. Of course, I never did, but he'd now sunk even lower in my estimation. I didn't trust DA Hawpe, either. He'd just muck it up, like he does everything else.

All things considered, I thought the best path forward would be for me to tell Leon's parents myself. At some point, I'd have to share the information with someone in a position to do something about it, but I thought I should be picky about who that was. Karen understood my misgivings about letting Heckscher and Hopalong in on the deal but thought I should go to Keith and let him handle it. "He's in a better position to do something about it," she said. "You do it, you're digging a hole for yourself." I expressed my disagreement and said I was going to do it anyway. She said she understood my motivation but added: "Don't come to me later and say I didn't warn you."

I said, "I've been in trouble before."

"And you will be again."

***

I checked the Qualls' house first, but nobody was home, so I drove to the campus. Fortunately, SWOSU is a lot smaller than OU. I was able to find the science building without much trouble. I even found a good parking spot.

I stuck my head in the first office I came to and asked where I could find Mr. Qualls. A young man who looked barely old enough to shave directed me to a room on the second floor.

The door was open. A man sat at his desk, gazing out a window with his back to me. I knocked and he swiveled his chair around. "Can I help you?" he asked. I asked if he was Mr. Qualls. He said he was. Right away he seemed nervous. A cop uniform often has that effect on people. I introduced myself and we shook hands. "Call me Jim," he said. I told him I needed to speak to him and Mrs. Qualls about their son. He picked up his phone and pressed a couple of buttons. "Freda?" he said in a shaky voice. "There's a policeman here who wants to talk to us about Leon." She walked through the door within seconds.

Jim Qualls was a short, thin, pale man about my age. His hair was waxed into a flattop and white-walled on the back and sides. On his face was a pair of thick horned-rim glasses. He wore a plain white short-sleeved dress shirt and a bow tie. Freda Qualls was about the same age as her husband, stout and slightly taller. Her face was ruddy, her reddish-brown hair thick and frizzy. Her dress was as colorful as her husband's outfit was drab—multicolored, in what I guess you'd call a psychedelic pattern. It ended several inches above her knees.

Both looked fearful, like they knew what I was about to tell them. I wished I didn't have to.

I started by telling them, as gently as I could, that Leon had been found dead in the burnt remains of an abandoned building outside Burr. I didn't want to start by telling them he'd been murdered. It was enough of a blow hearing their son had died. They seemed sad but not surprised—like they'd been living with a sword hanging over their head.

They asked how I knew it was him. I told them about the ring and my talks with Eva Benefiel and John Smith. They asked to see a picture of the ring. I showed it to them. They recognized it immediately. Mrs. Qualls began to cry. Mr. Qualls slumped in his chair, looking dazed. "We haven't had much contact with Leon the last couple of years," he said. "We wanted to bring him home when they released him from the hospital, but he wanted to stay in Norman."

I didn't say anything for a bit, wanting to let them get the worst out of their systems. "We fought to bring him home," Mrs. Qualls finally said in an anguished voice. "But he got so upset, we were afraid he'd have a relapse. We compromised and found a place for him in a group home there in Norman."

I asked what a group home was. She said it was a kind of halfway house for people with problems like Leon's—a place they could stay and be looked after, yet still have a measure of independence.

Leon was there only a short time before leaving on his own account, crawling out a window in the middle of the night. The folks at the group home called the Quallses the next morning when his absence was discovered. They drove to Norman to search for him and eventually found him sleeping on an old couch in a derelict building. They begged him to either go back to the group home or come back to Weatherford. He refused.

"He actually sounded quite cogent," said Mrs. Qualls, like she was trying to convince us all of something she really didn't believe.

"He did make a pretty good argument for himself," added Mr. Qualls. "He said he only planned to stay in that old building until he got a job and could save enough to get an apartment. I said if he went back to the group home, he could do the same thing and still have a decent roof over his head, but he wouldn't listen."

"He hated being locked up," said Mrs. Qualls. "'I want to be free,' he said. I could understand that. And he promised to take his medication." She shrugged miserably. "What can I say? We gave in."

But Leon couldn't or wouldn't keep his promise. "The owner of the building discovered Leon living there," Mrs. Qualls continued. "He called the cops and had him kicked out. They tried to direct him to a shelter, but he wouldn't go. After that, he never slept in the same place twice. He went to the Salvation Army shelter to get food, but he wouldn't sleep there."

"Pretty soon he ran out of pills," said Mr. Qualls. "We gave him money to have the prescriptions refilled, but he refused to do it. We drove to Norman two or three times a week and found him walking the streets. We tried to talk him into coming home with us. He wouldn't do it. We went to the Norman Police and asked them to help. They said there was nothing they could do. Leon was an adult."

"Did you ever go before a judge and try to have Leon committed?" I asked.

"Of course we did!" Mrs. Qualls almost shouted. "The judge found Leon competent."

I asked how that was possible.

Mr. Qualls shook his head. "Mr. Hardy, there are times you wouldn't even know Leon was sick, when he can be as clear as a bell. He was like that when he went in front of that judge. The doctor who'd treated Leon in the hospital said as long as Leon took his pills, he could function. After all, he's not a kid. Leon turned 30 this year. The judge ruled Leon competent on the condition that he promise to take his medicine. Leon promised he would, but he didn't."

"He hated the medication," said Mrs. Qualls. "It made him tired all the time."

"At least it stopped the voices," said Mr. Qualls.

I remembered how Smith had said school was Leon's salvation and asked them why he didn't go back and work on his PhD.

"That's a good question," said Mr. Qualls. "We wanted him to, thinking that it would help him focus and cope. But he refused. He never would say why."

When they learned Leon was spending most nights at the Sunshine Store, they arranged with John Smith to deliver the care packages. That went on for a while, with the Quallses making the trip to Norman as often as they could, sometimes twice a week.

Occasionally they found Leon, but he seemed to have a sixth sense they were coming and avoided the store on most nights they visited. They would leave the box with Smith and drive back to Weatherford. Over time, the trips dwindled.

Mrs. Qualls said, "When we went last week, Mr. Smith said he hadn't seen Leon in a month. We drove all over Norman, but we couldn't find him." I asked why they didn't file a missing persons report. "I don't know," she sighed. "We'd gone weeks without seeing him before. I guess we didn't think there was any point."

I excused myself to get a drink of water and to give them a few moments to themselves. I came back and asked them if they knew any reason Leon would have gone to Burr. "You don't seem to think it's strange he was found there."

"Leon's grandfather lives in Burr," said Mr. Qualls.

"Really? Who's his grandfather?"

"Pete Kuhlman." Pete was the cheapskate oil millionaire whose death Bernard and I discussed on the day we found Leon's body.

"Pete Kuhlman is Leon's grandfather?"

They nodded.

"Are you Pete Kuhlman's daughter?" I asked Mrs. Qualls. "I'd always thought Pete and his wife only had one child. Janie."

"No, no, no," she said. "I'm no relation to Pete Kuhlman whatsoever. Janie Kuhlman was Leon's birth mother. He was adopted. I thought you knew."

"I didn't."

"Did you know her?" asked Mrs. Qualls.

"Janie and I went to high school together," I said. "We were the same age." I took a deep breath. "I was the first person on the scene the night she died."

***

Janie Kuhlman was the featured baton twirler in the Burr High School marching band. She wore a skimpy little red, white, and blue-sequined uniform tight enough to inspire impure thoughts in the minds of local boys and probably even a few girls. Janie also played the flute in concert band.

She had other talents, as well. Getting along with people, for instance. Janie was as friendly and outgoing as her father was grouchy and unsociable. And boy, was she smart. She probably would have been class valedictorian if she hadn't dropped out in the fall of her senior year to have a baby.

George Riley was the daddy. George was a year ahead of Janie and me in school. He was already working full-time at the natural gas processing plant in Butcherville when the child was born. They named the boy George Jr. Janie didn't graduate, but I do remember her coming to the ceremony with George and the baby, cheering us all on. Right after that, I joined the Marines. Janie and her husband settled in to raise George Jr.

The boy was seven by the time I came back to town and took this job. The first major event of my tenure—even before the situation with Burt and the drunk driver that ended months later with that little girl getting killed—was to attend to a car crash that claimed the lives of his parents.

It happened on New Year's Eve. Janie and George Sr. left their little boy with a babysitter and drove to Alva for a dance at the Elks Club. They ran into a dust storm on their way home. It was dark; the visibility was poor, and George Sr. was driving too fast. He may also have been intoxicated. A tanker truck carrying a load of gasoline broke down and stalled at an intersection in Butcherville, not far from the gas plant where George worked. The car plowed into the tanker. There was an explosion. I was cruising north of town when in the distance I saw the fireball. By the time I got there, the Rileys had burned to death. Underneath the stench of gasoline, I could smell the same nauseating odor I would encounter more than 20 years later when I came upon the body of Leon Qualls.

Back then, Leon was still George Riley, Jr. His only living relative was his grandfather, Pete Kuhlman. Pete didn't want to have anything to do with him, so the state put him up for adoption. George Jr.

bounced around from foster home to foster home. At last, he ended up Jim and Freda Qualls. He was already exhibiting behavioral problems, but the Quallses fell in love with the boy and adopted him.

Right away, they learned he hated his name. As Mrs. Qualls explained it: "His father, George, Sr., was dead, so of course that was painful for him. It got so that when we called him by his name, he'd put his hands over his ears and scream, 'George is dead, George is dead!' One day, I asked him if he'd like to have a new name to go with his new family. He liked the idea. I asked what he thought would be a good name. He immediately said, 'Leon,' like he had it in mind all along. I don't know where it came from, but it was fine with us."

Having a new name didn't solve Leon's problems. He was still a handful. The Department of Human Services had said Leon was simply a normal mischievous little boy, but his new parents soon realized something was seriously wrong. They took him to a child psychologist, who diagnosed something called dementia praecox. The doctor's suggested treatment consisted mainly of them being abnormally strict with the boy. It didn't help. By the time he was in high school, Leon was hallucinating and hearing voices.

At the end of their rope, they took Leon to another doctor. This one said the other fella was a quack. Leon didn't have dementia praecox, he had schizophrenia, which is a whole different thing. This new doctor prescribed antipsychotic drugs. They helped. The voices and hallucinations stopped. But Leon hated taking them.

"They dulled his senses," said Mrs. Qualls. "Caused him to gain weight."

"Basically," said Mr. Qualls, "it was a choice between the lesser of two evils."

Leon might not have liked the drugs, but he took them, and it paid off. He graduated at the head of his high school class. "He was supremely gifted intellectually," said Mrs. Qualls, pride piercing her veil of grief.

Science was Leon's thing. He was offered a full-ride scholarship to OU, but his parents wouldn't let him go. "He did extremely well in school, but he couldn't take care of himself on a day-to-day basis," said Mrs. Qualls. "He wouldn't take his meds if I didn't remind him. We'd go through cycles. He'd take them for a while and things would go well, then he'd start slacking off and, before you knew it, he was hearing voices again."

The Quallses wanted him to stay home and go to SWOSU so they could help take care of him, but Leon refused. "For Leon, it was OU or nothing," said Mr. Qualls. For several years, Leon did little but read physics textbooks and watch TV. He still wanted to go to OU, but as yet wasn't willing to go against his parents' wishes. That would come later. Eventually, his folks despaired of his future and, after a number of years, gave their consent. As Mr. Qualls said, "We couldn't deny him any longer."

I asked if Leon had any kind of relationship with his grandfather.

"We tried many times to get Kuhlman interested in Leon," said Mrs. Qualls, "but Kuhlman didn't want to have anything to do with him."

I asked, if that was the case, why would Leon have been visiting his grandfather?

"Leon remembered and loved the old man from when he was a little boy," said Mr. Qualls. "Maybe it's because Kuhlman reminded him of his time with his birth mother, I don't know. From the time we got him, Leon would ask us to take him to visit the old man. Kuhlman would never allow it."

"Pete Kuhlman was a mean, greedy old man who never did anything for anybody unless it filled his own pockets," said Mrs. Qualls acidly. "The more Leon tried to have a relationship with him, the more he resisted."

Jim addressed his wife. "He called the police on him that time, remember?" She shook her head in disgust.

"Called the police on him?" I said. "Why?"

"He said Leon was harassing him and he feared for his life."

"Ridiculous," said Mrs. Qualls. "It really hurt Leon. He never stopped loving that old man, no matter how mean he was treated."

"To this day, Pete Kuhlman refuses to acknowledge his relationship to Leon," said Mr. Qualls. "Which is a shame, because he's a multi-millionaire. He could help Leon get the best care if he wanted to, but he won't spend a cent."

I realized they had not heard of Kuhlman's death. I told them.

"When did this happen?" asked Mr. Qualls.

"A few days before we found Leon."

They were quiet for a moment, then Mr. Qualls asked: "Did Leon die of smoke inhalation or was his death caused by burns?"

This was what I had hoped to avoid, but knew I'd have to face, sooner or later. "I'm sorry to have to tell you this, but a post-mortem revealed that Leon died of a gunshot wound to the head."

Mr. Qualls gasped in shock. Mrs. Qualls gave a bitter chuckle. "That's it, then," she said.

"What's it?" said Mr. Qualls.

"Isn't it obvious? Leon tried to visit Kuhlman again. Kuhlman decided to end it once and for all and killed him."

"Why would you say that?" I asked.

"Kuhlman thought Leon was after his money," she said. "Which is absurd, by the way; Leon couldn't care less about money. Leon showed up wanting to see him. Somewhere in his twisted mind, Kuhlman thought Leon was trying to rob him. He shot him, then burnt the body to cover up his crime."

I inwardly questioned the plausibility of such a scenario. Pete was in no condition to kill anyone at that point. Besides, it appeared that he died before Leon. I kept my qualms to myself, however. Maybe the Quallses were too dazed to see it.

Mrs. Qualls asked, "What happened to his money?"

"I'm not sure. If he didn't have any kin to leave it to—"

"He had Leon," snapped Mrs. Qualls.

"You're right," I said. "I am sorry. I didn't know that before today."

She shook her head. "It doesn't matter. Wherever it went, it didn't go to Leon."

Very carefully, I asked, "Did Leon ever mention anyone named Carrie?"

They shook their heads. "Why do you ask?" said Mrs. Qualls.

"John Smith said Leon had a girlfriend by that name." I did not add that she was the woman who shot Burt Murray.

Mr. Qualls asked, "Could she have done it?"

Mrs. Qualls shook her head violently. "I'm telling you; it was Kuhlman."

I said, "I don't think the girl would've done that, sir. Smith says she was very protective of Leon. As for Pete Kuhlman, we'll certainly look into his possible involvement."

They were too drained to talk any longer. Mrs. Qualls asked when they could expect to receive Leon's body for burial. I told them I couldn't be sure. Mr. Qualls volunteered to identify the body. "You don't want to do that," I said. He didn't argue.

I encouraged them to call Keith Belcher at the Tilghman County Sheriff's office but asked them to wait until the next day. "You're the only ones I've told about this. I just found out myself, and I wanted to come to you first. I'll fill in the sheriff after I leave here."

They agreed. I thanked them for their time and apologized for having to deliver such bad news. Mr. Qualls saw me to the stairs, leaving Mrs. Qualls alone in the office.

Before I left, I asked Mr. Qualls if he was sure Leon knew his grandfather was wealthy.

"Oh yes, he knew," said Mr. Qualls. "Not that it mattered. Leon just wanted his grandpa."

CHAPTER EIGHTEEN

Karen warned me not to tell the Quallses before I told Keith. It wasn't until I was driving home that I thought about all the reasons she'd been right. I was in such a hurry to do the right thing, I forgot to do it in the right order.

Of course, the Quallses would want to bury their son as soon as possible.

Of course, Sheriff Belcher should know John Doe's identity as soon as I discovered it.

Of course, I should tell the investigator on the Burt Murray case that Jane Doe and John Doe were connected.

But I didn't do any of those things. Now I had to scramble to make things right.

I stopped at a phone booth at a gas station in Seiling and dialed Keith. I told him what I'd done and what I'd learned: John Doe's name was Leon Qualls and he was Pete Kuhlman's grandson, and the woman who shot Burt was Leon's girlfriend and her name was Carrie-something.

There was silence on the other end. I asked if he was still there.

"I am," he said. "It's a lot to take in, is all. You know you should've told me before you went to the family?"

"I do know that, and I'm sorry, but if I hadn't, I wouldn't have learned about the connection between Pete and Leon."

"No, you wouldn't have. I would have." He paused. "Oh well, what's done is done. So how do you feel about sharing this info with Agent Heckscher?"

"I'm against it."

"How about District Attorney Hopalong?"

"I'm against that, too."

I could almost hear him roll his eyes.

"Listen, Emmett," he said, "This is too big for you to handle on your own. You're going to have

to tell them sooner or later."

"Yeh, well, after what they pulled on Joel and me, I prefer it to be later."

He tried to talk me into telling them, but despite my realization about doing the right things in the wrong order, I didn't bend. He said I was shooting myself in the foot. I said Karen told me I was digging a hole for myself. "I defer to her judgment," he said.

I asked if there'd been any word on Dr. Morston's whereabouts. He said not that he knew of, but I should ask Annie Childers. I finished by suggesting he keep tabs on Leon's body, that whoever was behind this coverup might try to make it disappear. He said he would, but that I should bring that up with Dr. Childers as well.

I went into the gas station, got change for a dollar, then came back and called Dr. Childers. I told her what I'd told Keith, then asked her if there was any word on Dr. Morston.

"No one knows where he is," she said. "It's quite the mystery. I'm the only one in the office who suspects something's wrong."

"Because you're the only one who knows he falsified that autopsy report."

"Right," she said. "Of course, I haven't mentioned it."

"What about John Doe's—I mean, Leon Qualls's body?"

"What about it?"

"Is it intact?"

"No. It's burnt to a crisp."

"You don't mean it's been cremated?"

"No, it's in the morgue, in the same condition as the last time you saw it. Why do you ask?"

"I'm a little concerned someone might try to dispose of it as a way of covering up certain unlawful shenanigans."

"That's not going to happen."

"Probably not, but promise me you'll keep an eye on it. I want to make sure there's a body for his folks to claim when the time comes."

"Alright, I promise. Anything else?"

"Yeh," I said. "You still have that bullet?"

"I gave it to Sheriff Belcher." She paused. "What's this all about, anyway?"

"When I find out, you'll be the second to know."

***

I got back to Burr a few minutes past 5:00. I stopped at the station. Karen had gone home. Pat was on duty. He had everything under control. I left him to it.

When I got home, I found Red in the utility room sorting laundry. I snuck up from behind and wrapped my arms around her. "I'm home."

She jumped. "Oh. You scared me." She kissed me on the cheek and asked how it went.

"You were probably right when you said I should've waited to tell the Quallses about their son."

"I know I was."

"While we're at it," I added, "I'm sorry for not being around much lately."

"Yeh," she said, "I'm starting to forget what you look like. Last night I dreamed you actually worked a full shift and let me have the day off."

"Sounds like a pretty good dream."

"Oh, it was. You had Paul Newman's face."

"That must've scared you to death."

"Oh yeh, it was real scary. So scary, I'm going to try to have the same dream tonight."

She had supper waiting. Meatloaf. We sat down at the kitchen table. She asked if I'd discovered anything new by talking to the Quallses.

"A few things," I said, then recounted Leon's sad history, including Mrs. Qualls' belief that Pete had killed him.

"That's incredible," she said. "So Leon Qualls is Janie Kuhlman's son?"

"Yup."

"Weren't you on the scene of the accident the night she died?"

"I was. It's a pretty crazy coincidence."

"Especially considering the way they both died."

"You mean burned?"

"Yeh."

"Well, technically, Leon died of a bullet to his head, but you're right. It is kind of eerie the way things played out."

I bit into the meatloaf. "This is good."

"Once in a while, I get it right."

"You sure did this time."

She waved off the compliment. "So, you agree with Mrs. Qualls? You think Pete killed Leon?"

"I can see why she'd believe that, but I doubt it's true. He'd been dead for at least a week before we found Leon."

"Maybe he had help."

"Maybe," I said, not believing it.

"Seriously, Emmett. He could've killed Leon and put him in his deep freeze. Did he have a deep freeze?"

I said, "I don't know. Maybe." My feeling was that this was getting more and more far-fetched. Red will debate a point forever if she thinks she's got half a leg to stand on.

"Someone could've killed Leon for Pete," she said, "then kept him in a deep freeze somewhere. Pete dies. Whoever killed Leon retrieves the body and takes it out to Indian Valley. He leaves a wine bottle and that Sterno can lying there, then sets it on fire. You and Bernard find the Sterno can and the bottle, figure it's some hobo who got drunk and fell asleep cooking supper. Voila." She snapped her fingers. "The perfect crime."

"It's possible, I guess. But I can't think of anyone who'd do that for Pete. The only person who could stand him was Myrtle Dennis."

"Myrtle was looking in on him when he was sick, right?"

"Yeh," I said, then added: "I wouldn't be surprised if she did that, hoping to be remembered in his will."

Red seized on that. "Was she?"

"I don't know. Haven't seen it."

"Don't you think you should? See it, I mean?"

"You're not saying Myrtle had anything to do with it?"

"No, of course not. I'm just saying that if you looked at Pete's will, you might find someone who had a motive."

I hadn't thought of that. "You mean someone willing to help Pete get rid of an unwanted pest?"

"Yeh, or someone who was tired of waiting for him to die."

"It's possible."

She took a bite of meatloaf. "You don't think I used too much ketchup?" she asked.

"No, it's great," I said, although now that she mentioned it, I thought maybe it was a little too ketchup-y.

She pushed away her plate.

"So what's next, Lieutenant Columbo?"

"Good question."

"I know it is. That's why I asked."

"How about you drive to Temple City tomorrow? Look up the Court Clerk, ask her to pull Pete's will."

"Anything to get out of the office. Does that mean you'll be in tomorrow morning?"

"For a little while, at least. I want to go out to the Kuhlman place and have a look around."

"See if he had a deep freeze."

"I will."

"What exactly do you expect to find?"

"I don't know. A sign Leon had been there, maybe."

"Who's going to run the joint with us both gone?"

"Seems like it pretty much runs itself these days."

She picked up a butter knife and waved it. "Maybe it seems like that to *you*—"

"I'm kidding! Don't worry, I'll figure something out."

"Oh, that's right," she said, putting down the knife. "You jazz musicians just make it up as you go along."

"You bet," I said. "I'm the Charlie Parker of hick-town cops."

***

I went into the station the next morning while Karen drove to Temple City. I tried to make an appointment to talk to Keith, but his secretary said he'd be in court all day and that I should call tomorrow. I didn't mind so much. What I really wanted to do was have a look around Pete Kuhlman's place.

I tried and failed to get hold of Joel's lawyer, getting an answering machine instead. I decided I was getting a little sick of those. I got in a Javelin, took one last sweep around town, and found all was quiet on the western front. I came back and told Cindy where I'd be, then walked out the door. At that moment, a Tilghman County Sheriff's cruiser pulled up with Bernard Cousins behind the wheel. The passenger-side door opened. Out jumped Joel Carter.

"Lucy, I'm home!" he said with a grin. Bernard waved and drove off.

"You're out!" I said.

"Heck yeh, I'm out. The judge cut me loose."

"Judge Zimmerman?"

"No, the associate judge. Judge Cannon. That writ of habeas corpus did the trick. The judge decided that there wasn't sufficient evidence to hold me."

"You ready to go to work?"

"I am."

"Ride with me," I said. We got in my truck, and I explained where we were going.

"You been home yet?" I asked.

"Nah, I just had Bernard drop me off here," he said.

Considering the ransacked state of his house, I reckoned that was a good thing.

"Alright now," I said. "Tell me about this welcome turn of events."

He leaned back on the headrest and sighed. "Ok, about 4:00 this morning a guard came to my cell, handcuffed my hands behind my back, shoved me in the back of a highway patrol cruiser and drove me back to Temple City. Bernard took charge of me when we got to the county jail. He told me if it was up to him, he'd let me go, but of course he couldn't do that. A couple of hours later, another deputy came and told me I was due in court. My lawyer was already there, along with Heckscher and Harry Hawpe. Apparently, Judge Cannon had ordered that I be brought back to Tilghman County. Howard and Harry Hawpe presented their cases. Judge Cannon ripped into 'em and ordered me released. So here I am."

"Oh baby," I said. "That must've felt good, hearing him bawl-out Hawpe and Heckscher."

"Well, he was mostly angry at Hawpe, but yeh, it was kind of fun."

I told him what we'd discovered while he was locked up, then related the sordid details about the search of his house. After that, he didn't talk, but just stared out the window until we got to Kuhlman's.

***

Here in Oklahoma, we have basically two types of rich folks. The first are those who love to show off their money by buying fancy cars and huge mansions and valuable paintings and giving cash to their alma mater to build football stadiums and have libraries named after them. The second are the Ebenezer Scrooge-types who throw around nickels like man-hole covers.

Pete Kuhlman was of the latter persuasion.

I didn't know Pete too well and have no regrets about having kept it that way—which is not to say I had anything against him, but I do know he was a pretty miserable person. The first time I had reason to speak to him was the night his daughter and son-in-law died. He covered his grief with bluster, cussing and accusing me of doing a half-assed job trying to rescue his daughter. I didn't blame him for lashing out, but after that night, I tended to steer clear of him and, with rare exceptions, managed to do so for the next twenty-odd years.

After losing his wife and daughter, Pete basically became a hermit. You might think having a young grandson would've given him something to live for, but you'd be wrong. It could've been that raising his dead daughter's son was too much for him to contemplate. That's why he let the state put him up for adoption. It's hard to say. I didn't know him very well.

His house fit the profile of the man. If you didn't know better, you'd think it was the home of a dirt farmer barely scratching by, not an oil millionaire. There wasn't anything wrong with it, really; it was a typical one-story Oklahoma farmhouse with wood siding and a porch and trees in the front yard. Attached to the house was a homemade carport with a rusty metal roof and an unpaved driveway. Forty or fifty yards behind the house, there was a barn with fading red paint.

I parked in the carport. Joel and I walked around the outside of the house, looking for signs that might suggest Leon had been on the premises. We didn't find anything. We checked the barn. Nothing interesting there either, just hay and field mice.

A side door led to and from the carport. We knocked, not expecting anyone to be home, but you don't go barging into someone's house even if you know they're dead. No one answered. I tried the doorknob, kind of hoping it would be locked; I'd taken a course in lock-picking several months earlier and had been carrying around a little set of tools in a pouch on my gun belt but had not had occasion to use them. Sadly, the door was open. We walked in.

The house smelled like Lysol. I reckoned Myrtle Dennis had given the place a good cleaning after Pete died. The door opened into a bare-bones kitchen—stove and oven, sink and refrigerator. In one corner there was a crate of empty Coke bottles and a large plastic garbage bag of empty Coke cans waiting to be returned for their deposit. We went through all the drawers and cupboards but found nothing of particular note—a couple of plates and pans, and an empty plastic garbage container under the sink.

As per Karen's instructions, I looked around for a deep freeze. There wasn't one—just a regular freezer in the refrigerator that was too small to store a body. I looked inside anyway. It was empty except for a tray of ice covered in frost.

The rest of the house was sparsely furnished and fairly neat, considering its last occupant had been bedridden. On top of the toilet, I found a white rag wadded into a ball. I picked it up and shook it out. It was an old Ku Klux Klan hood. I reckon that cleaning a commode is about the only constructive thing it'd ever been used for.

The master bedroom was located off the living room. It had two windows; one looked out on the front of the house, the other onto the driveway. A hospital bed that had been stripped down to its mattress. I imagined Pete must've spent a great deal of time there in his last days.

Joel and I stood together and took it all in.

"I haven't seen anything suspicious," I said. "How about you?"

He shook his head. "Nope."

"Obviously, this place has been pretty well scrubbed," I said. "If there was ever any sign of Leon Qualls, it's gone now."

"We could talk to the person who did the cleaning," he said.

"That would probably be Myrtle Dennis," I said. "One last expression of her devotion."

We started to leave when I noticed something behind the open door. I closed the door and saw it was a chest built into the wall. I checked the drawers one by one. It was roughly built and without rollers, so it shrieked like a banshee every time I opened one. They were all empty until I got to the one on the bottom.

What I saw made my heart beat faster: a pair of thick, heavy work gloves—blue and white in a strange, paisley-like pattern, with the tips of the fingers cut off.

Just like the kind Leon Qualls wore.

CHAPTER NINETEEN

I called Joel over. "Look at this," I said.

He peeked in the drawer. "Gloves?" he said. "What about them?"

"The guy in Norman who knew Leon said he always wore a pair of work gloves. Blue and white with the tips of the fingers cut off."

"Doesn't everyone around here wear work gloves?"

"A lot do," I admitted, "but Pete hasn't needed them for a long time. It's odd that of all the things we *could've* found in this house, the one thing we actually *do* find is a pair of gloves that match the description of Leon's."

He nodded. "Hmmm. Well, you'd know better than me, but it seems like a rather tenuous connection."

"Maybe you're right, but I'm going to check it out."

I grabbed the gloves and closed the drawer.

***

Karen had returned from Temple City by the time Joel and I got back to the station. I gave her a minute to hug him half to death, then the three of us went back to my office. After Joel told her his story, he and I described our trip to Kuhlman's. I showed Red the gloves. Unlike Joel, she was sold on their significance.

"Those aren't just any old pair of work gloves," she said. "I've never seen a pair like them. You should call John Smith and see what he has to say."

I told her that's what I aimed to do. "What about you? Did you get a look at Pete's will?"

"Pete Kuhlman left his house, the barn, and all his worldly possessions to Myrtle Dennis. His cash holdings went to the Cowboy Hall of Fame."

"What constituted his worldly possessions?" I asked.

"Everything within the house and barn. The only things it explicitly listed were a 1957 Chevy 3100 pickup and an autographed photo of Calvin Coolidge in an Indian headdress."

"How much is Calvin Coolidge's autograph worth, I wonder?" said Joel.

"Oh, the autograph wasn't Coolidge's," said Karen. "It was Chauncey Yellow Robe's daughter's."

"Who's Chauncey Yellow Robe?" I asked.

Karen shrugged. "I assume the Indian gentleman Coolidge was posing with."

"That must've thrilled Myrtle," I said.

"Yeh," she agreed. "I doubt she would've killed Pete over that."

"Make a note to give her a call and ask if she cleaned up at Pete's after he died."

"Will do," she said. "By the way, I also pulled his death certificate."

"What did it say?"

"Natural causes."

"That's it?"

"That's it."

"But as far as the will goes, there was nothing suspicious?"

"I didn't say that."

"So there was something suspicious."

"It didn't say anything about mineral rights."

"How could that be?" I said. "Oil and gas made Pete a rich man."

"He sold them."

I shook my head and said, "No, no, that can't be. No one sells their mineral rights."

"Kuhlman did. The County Clerk had the papers on file. He sold them to something called the Southwestern Oklahoma Oil Partnership in exchange for $120,000 a month for the rest of his life."

I whistled. "Not bad, if it's on the level."

Joel laughed. "SWOOP," he said. "That's pretty good."

"What do you mean?" I said.

"SWOOP. It's an acronym. Southwestern Oklahoma Oil Partnership. As in, they *swooped* in and got Kuhlman's mineral rights."

"Very clever," I said. "So what exactly is this SWOOP?"

"I assume it is what it says," said Karen. "Some kind of business partnership having to do with oil."

"Whose names are on the documents?"

"Pete's, his lawyer's, and some fella named Jimmie Gracey, the group's managing partner."

"Was there an address and phone number for this SWOOP?"

"The address is a post office box in Waynoka, of all places. The phone number has an Enid prefix."

"Is there some way we can find out the names of the other people involved in this? If I assume there are partners besides this Gracey fella."

"I'm sure there is," she said. "I'll figure it out. But there's something else that's strange."

"Besides the fact that people just don't do this sort of thing, you mean?"

"Right," she said. "The deal was, Pete would receive $120,000 a month for as long as he lived."

"What's strange about that?" I said. "Sounds pretty good to me."

"Maybe Pete knew he was going to die and figured he'd rather have the cash in hand while he was still around," offered Joel.

"I reckon he wasn't planning on dying anytime soon," I said. Karen waved her hands trying to get us to shut up.

"But listen," she said. "Pete never received a single payment."

Joel and I both said: "What?"

"He died before getting paid. He was to receive the first payment on July 1ˢᵗ. He died two weeks before that."

Joel asked: "Who receives the payments now that he's dead?"

"That's the thing," she said. "No one. According to the documents, the payments were to cease upon his death."

"So SWOOP didn't have to pay a penny," I said.

"Surely *someone* collected," said Joel.

"Yeh," said Karen. "SWOOP. They collected."

"I can't believe Pete would sign a deal like that," I said. "Who was his lawyer?"

Karen said, "Some guy named Walter Fessler. He's also the executor of Kuhlman's will."

Joel looked like he was dragging. I asked him if he was ok. He said he was, but I didn't believe him. I told him to go home and take all the time he needed to clean up the mess Heckscher had made. He thanked me and took off.

"He hasn't been home yet?" said Karen once he'd gone.

"Nope."

"Maybe we should help him clean up."

"I think this is probably something he'd rather do by himself."

∗∗∗

Karen went out to her desk to make some calls about Walter Fessler. I made a couple of calls of my own.

The first was to Myrtle Dennis. I asked if she'd cleaned Pete's house after he'd died. She said she'd been surprised to find it clean the day she found the body. She had no idea who'd done it. "Maybe Pete did it before he died," she said.

The second call was to Bernard Cousins. On the day we found Leon's body and he told me Pete Kuhlman had passed, Bernard mentioned someone else who'd died under similar circumstances. I couldn't remember who it was. My call woke him up; dropping off Joel had been the last thing he'd done on his shift. It took him a few seconds to remember what I was talking about.

"Oh, yeh," he said after a yawn. "That was Earl Calvert."

"Right," I said. "Refresh my memory. Earl was a rancher, right?"

"Yeh, he raised Black Angus."

"Is that how he made his money?"

"You mean, is that how he got rich? Nah. Earl did all right with cattle, but he made most of his money off oil and gas."

"Just like Pete Kuhlman."

"Yeh, I reckon it was just like Pete."

I apologized for waking him up and ended the call.

Another oil and gas millionaire. Dead without anyone to give his money to.

CHAPTER TWENTY

Karen spent the next hour or two at her desk, doing what she could to solve the mystery of Walter Fessler. Once finished, she came back to my office and plopped down into the room's only comfortable chair other than my own.

"The guy's a ghost," she said. "The state bar association has never heard of him. Neither has the Attorney General's office. Neither has any of the 26 state District Attorney's offices."

"I can't wrap my brain around why Pete would've done this," I said. "I suppose he could've figured having $120,000 dollars of spending money month-to-month was better than holding on to the rights and making whatever he was making. Obviously, the royalties would've paid out more than that in the long term."

"I guess he wasn't thinking long term."

"But Kuhlman was a miser," I insisted. "He wouldn't spend the money he had."

"What can I tell you, cowboy? Maybe we'll know once we track down this Fessler guy."

"Thanks for trying," I said. "Put that aside for now. There's something else I need you to do."

She sighed. "And what would that be?"

"I need you to run back to Temple City and pull another will."

"And whose would that be?"

"Earl Calvert's."

"Ah, poor old Earl," she said. "What's suspicious about him?"

"He was a rich oilman who died without heirs."

"Like Pete."

"Like Pete."

She groaned and heaved herself to her feet. "Alright, so I assume I'm looking for the same thing."

"Right. See who ended up with Earl's money. Especially the mineral rights. Might as well get a copy of his death certificate, too."

"Will do," she said. On her way out, she said, "Are you going to cook tonight?"

"I will if you want me to,"

"I want you to."

"Alright, then," I said. As she started down the hall, I called after her: "You know what to do if there's no mention of mineral rights?"

She yelled back: "Go to the court clerk and find out if they've been sold."

"Right, and don't forget the name of Calvert's executor," I called out, but by that time she'd left the building. I wasn't worried. She'd know what to do.

I stopped by Joel's on the way home. He'd bagged up just about everything. All that was left to do was the scrubbing and cleaning. I offered to help, but he declined my offer. I loaded the bags into the back of my truck, drove them to the dump, and headed home.

I got there before Red did. Spaghetti is one of the few things I can cook that does not involve grilling a big slab of meat. We didn't have any big slabs of meat, so my decision about what to prepare for supper was made for me. I dug up a box of dry noodles and found one of those little green cardboard shakers of Parmesan cheese in the refrigerator, along with most of a jar of Chef Boyardee spaghetti sauce. I don't like Chef Boyardee sauce—it's too dang sweet—but that's all we had.

I'd just finished setting the food on the table when Karen walked in. She gave me a kiss and sat down to sample my wares.

"*Wunderbar!*" she said, kissing her fingertips.

"*Wunderbar* is German."

"What's Italian for '*wunderbar*'?"

"I don't know. *Arrivederci*?"

"No, '*arrivederci*' means 'see you later.' Something like that." She took another mouthful. "Mmm-mmm. My compliments to Chef Boyardee."

"I think you mean Chef Hard-ee."

"Oh, my! Stop, stop, stop!" she said, holding her sides and pretending to laugh.

I got a cold Tab out of the refrigerator and sat back down.

"That stuff's poison," she said, nodding at the pink can.

"I assume you're talking about the Tab and not the spaghetti."

"Hah, hah. You know what I mean. That stuff kills lab rats."

"Yeh, well, I'm not a lab rat. Anyway, it beats the alternative."

The alternative, as she knew all too well, was booze.

"You're right," she said. "I'm sorry."

"That's alright," I said. "So how was your trip? Find out anything?"

She nodded. "You might say that."

"Something good?"

"Where to start?" she said with her mouth half-full. "First thing: Earl Calvert left his ranch to Joe Ray Biby."

"That name's familiar."

"Joe Ray was Earl's ranch hand. Worked for him for years."

"That's right. Lives in Butcherville out by the gas processing plant."

I nodded. "He's a good man. Don't think we need to worry about him." I sucked up some spaghetti. "Mineral rights?"

"Sold right before he died."

"To SWOOP?"

"Give the man a cheroot."

"What's a cheroot?"

"A cigar."

"Why didn't you just say that?"

She just shook her head.

"Executor?" I asked.

"Guess."

I held an imaginary envelope to my head, Carnac-style. "Walter Fessler."

She pretended to applaud. "You are correct, sir."

"Anything else?"

"Only that Earl died before he could receive a single payment."

"Just like Pete."

"Just like Pete."

"We're onto something."

"I would have to agree."

We finished and got up to do the dishes; she washed, I dried. We talked about Joel and how glad we were that he'd been released.

"I'd like to know for sure he's out of the woods," she said. "Have you heard anything from Hawpe or Heckscher?"

"I haven't, although, the way Joel told it, the judge reamed them out pretty good."

She scoffed. "That doesn't necessarily mean they're going to drop it."

"I think they will."

We finished the dishes and retired to the living room.

"But you don't *know*," she said.

"Know what?"

"You don't know Hawpe is going to drop the charges. Why don't you call him to make sure?"

"It can wait until morning," I said, settling my aching bones deep into my La-Z-Boy.

"I'm not going to be able to sleep until I know," she said in a tone I know better than to disregard.

I jack-in-the-boxed back to my feet. "I hope Hopalong isn't an early-to-bed, early-to-rise type."

I went to the phone in the kitchen and dialed Hawpe. He wasn't thrilled to be bothered at home, especially by me, but he did tell me that unless or until other incriminating evidence arose, Joel was off the hook.

I hung up and said in a loud voice, "Hawpe says Joel's been cleared." No answer. I went back to the living room. Red wasn't there. I called out again. "I'm in here!" she said.

I followed her voice to the bedroom to find her lying in bed, decked out in a sexy black nightgown I'd almost forgotten she had. My knees almost buckled.

"Wow," I said. "Haven't seen that in a while."

"I put it away for special occasions."

"It's been a long time between special occasions."

"Oh, so you want me to take it off?"

"Um, maybe," I said. "But not just yet."

CHAPTER TWENTY ONE

Keith and I set up a meeting for lunch the next day at the same greasy spoon where I'd met Dr. Chiders a few days earlier. I was a little wary of showing my face in Watie Junction after experiencing the hospitality of its Ringling-Brothers-clown of a police chief, but I couldn't think of any place more out of the way. I roped in Dr. Childers and Karen, too. I'd have brought Joel, only I needed to leave him in charge while Karen and I were gone. I'd fill him in afterward.

This was Karen's first visit to this particular eating establishment. Upon laying eyes on it, she said, "You sure know how to pick 'em."

"It's better inside," I lied.

I've never asked the help what the place's official name is; the fifteen-foot-tall sign out front says, "Café." Not Joe's or Harry's or Nelda's Café. Just "Café." You can tell by its shape that it's a painted-over Phillips 66 sign; you can still see traces of the old orange and black logo peeking out from underneath. On the wall facing the parking lot, there's a painted mural of folks having the time of their lives eating bacon and eggs and stacks of pancakes. The person who painted it exercised a significant degree of creative license.

Karen said as we walked in: "What a dump." When she's right, she's right. On its best day, "Café" smells like the dumpster behind McDonalds. The small AC unit over the door might as well be sucking instead of blowing for all the good it does. The dining area was barely roomy enough for a half-dozen tables, each with a red-and-white-checked vinyl tablecloth and two or more mismatched chairs. The ceiling fan served mostly as a magnet for grease and as a resting spot for flies. A few old men sat drinking coffee, staring off into space, and, by the looks of things, not much caring for each other's company.

A gum-chewing teenaged girl in a white t-shirt and cut-offs greeted us with a cheery, "Y'all can sit wherever you like." We took the table farthest away from the table of grumpy old men.

"Oh look, free eggs," said Karen, scratching with her thumbnail at a yellow crust that had evidently bonded permanently with the tablecloth.

"You know, in French, 'café' means coffee," I said.

"You don't say?" she said. "In Oklahoman, it means 'greasy spoon'."

The waitress came over with two menus the approximate thickness of the Oklahoma City phone book and a glass coffeepot. She poured Red a cup, then offered to pour mine. I held my hand over the cup and asked for a Tab. She asked if Diet-Rite would be ok. I said that would be fine. Red took a swig of her coffee, then made a face like she'd swallowed razor blades and chased it with rubbing alcohol.

"No good?" I asked.

She shook her head and said in a choking voice, "Juan Valdez would not approve."

The girl arrived with my Diet-Rite and two glasses of water. Red knocked hers back in one swallow.

I looked over the menu. Karen said, "You're not really going to eat, are you?"

"Sure. Why? Aren't you?"

"Not before I personally inspect the kitchen."

"Suit yourself," I said. "A man's got to eat."

Keith and Dr. Childers walked in the door. I waved. They saw me and started back.

"Don't come crying to me if you get ptomaine," said Karen.

"Dr. Childers will save me if I do," I said.

Dr. Childers said, "Save you from what?"

"The food," I said. "It's a joke. Don't worry about it." I introduced the women to one another. We made some small talk. The waitress brought over water, more coffee, and menus. Keith opened his. "How can such a small place have such a huge menu?"

"I never look at it," I said. "I always order the cheeseburger."

He clapped it shut. "Then that's what I'll have, too."

Karen looked at us like we were a couple of hyenas trying to choose between rotten zebra carcasses.

"What'll it be?" I asked Dr. Childers. "I'm buying."

"That's very kind of you," she replied, stealing a look at Karen, "but I'm really not very hungry."

"Smart girl," said Karen.

I called the meeting to order. "There have been some new developments, but first I want to outline the big picture to make sure we're all on the same page."

I went over what we knew: from Bernard and I finding John Doe's body at the Indian Valley fire, to Burt's shooting, to Dr. Childers' discovery that John Doe died not of his burns but of a gunshot wound, along with Dr. Morston's subsequent falsification of the autopsy report. I described how I'd discovered John Doe was Leon Qualls and how he was the orphaned son of Pete Kuhlman's daughter. I told them how John Smith had identified a picture of Burt Murray's killer as Leon's girlfriend, tying the deaths of Leon and Burt together. I finished with the story of how Joel and I discovered what I thought were Leon's gloves, which suggested he'd been at Pete's house at some point before either man had died.

I took a gulp of Diet Rite, giving Keith a chance to chime in. "Judging by what you say, I'd venture to guess this Carrie person killed Burt as revenge for killing Leon."

"I'd agree with that, but there's more to it," I said and yielded the floor to Karen. She explained what she'd discovered about Earl Calvert's and Pete Kuhlman's wills: the sale of their mineral rights;

how the men had both died shortly after signing the contracts; and how the same lawyer—Walter Fessler—had not only handled both transactions but was also the executor of both men's wills.

"The thing is," I said, "we can't even be sure this Fessler guy is a lawyer. The state bar has never heard of him."

Karen said, "We can't find anyone who *has* heard of him."

"So Leon was Kuhlman's unwanted grandson?" mused Keith. "That puts Pete in the frame. Leon wants money. Kuhlman refuses. Leon insists. Kuhlman kills him."

"That might be how it was," I allowed, "but keep in mind Leon's mental problems and Pete's illness."

Karen said, "I don't think Pete did it. I think the same people who killed Pete killed Leon."

"Wait, wait, wait, wait," said Keith. He turned to Dr Childers. "Didn't Pete die of natural causes?"

She nodded. "As far as I know, he did. That's what Morston assumed. At least I *assume* that's what Morston assumed. There wasn't a post-mortem."

Keith eyed Red. "Why do you think Pete was killed?"

"Money," she said. "The rights sale said Pete was to receive his first payment on July 1st. He died two weeks before that. According to the agreement, the payments were to cease upon Pete's death, which means whoever's behind this SWOOP thing never had to pay a cent."

"Pete was sick, though, right?" said Keith.

"He was sick, but he'd been sick for years," she said. "Why'd he die so soon after signing that deal?"

"The same thing happened with Earl Calvert," I said, "except Earl hadn't really been sick. He was just old."

"What did Earl die of?" asked Keith.

"Natural causes," said Karen. "The death certificate doesn't specify."

"What about Pete?" I asked.

"Same," she said. "Pretty big coincidence, don't you think?"

"It sure is," Keith admitted. He turned to Dr. Childers. "Could they have been poisoned?"

She nodded. "Certainly. There are lethal drugs that disappear once they're introduced into the body. Of course, they don't even have to disappear if no one's looking for them."

"Which no one did," I said. "We already know Dr. Morston changed the results of the autopsy you did on Leon Qualls."

Dr. Childers added, "An adherence to truth is not a huge issue in that office, believe me."

"I'm telling you," said Karen. "This whole thing is tied together."

I said, "It's the 'how' and the 'why' we don't know."

"Which is why we need to track down this Walter Fessler," said Keith.

"And Jimmie Gracey," said Karen. "Whoever he is."

"Whoever they *both* are," said Dr. Childers.

Keith laughed. "Good Lord, Chief Hardy, what a mess. You've never heard of letting sleeping dogs lie, have you?"

"Have you?"

"Fair enough. I guess the question is, what do we do next?"

"Eventually we're going to have to kick it up the ladder, but right now that means going to the DA and/or John Joe Heckscher, and I'm not comfortable with that."

Keith tapped the table with his fingertips. "You know, I've been thinking. Heckscher's all over the Murray case, but he's shown no interest in John Doe—er, I mean Leon Qualls. I might be able to take on that case myself. The trouble is time, as in: I don't have any. This auto-theft ring in Temple City is running me ragged. Between that and running for reelection, I've hardly got time to breathe."

"Let me handle it, then."

He looked at me like that was what he was thinking all along. "That might work," he said.

"That ok with you?" I asked Karen. "You'd have to run things for a while."

"How's that any different from the way it's been the last two weeks? Sure, go ahead."

Keith said, "If anyone asks, it's probably best not to mention anything about the Murray case. Say you're trying to identify John Doe so he can get a Christian burial. Something like that."

"Easily done," I said, then added: "No one needs to know about Leon's girlfriend, either. We don't even have a last name for her."

"No one needs to know about anything we've talked about," said Karen. I added: "Until we're ready for them to know."

Keith said, "10-4 on that."

The waitress brought over our burgers. We dug in. Dr. Childers asked why I was resistant to bringing Agent Heckscher into the loop. "It seems to me that by telling him what you know, you'd be making his job easier," she said.

"You'd think," I said with my mouth full. I swallowed, then added, "Don't forget how quick he was to arrest Joel, and that's with hardly anything to go on. John Joe Heckscher is a snake."

Keith said, "I think your opinion of Heckscher might be colored by past experience."

"Correct. My past experience of him being a snake."

Dr. Childers looked confused. "I must be missing something," she said.

"Annie," I said, "John Joe Heckscher didn't arrest Joel because he had evidence Joel conspired to kill Burt Murray. He arrested him because he's a stone cold racist."

"Well, to be fair," said Karen, "there was a potential motive."

"What was it?" asked Dr. Childers.

"Those folks Burt killed back in 1940," I said. "Turns out they were Joel's grandparents and aunt."

Dr. Childers shook her head like she was trying to clear out cobwebs. "This thing gets wilder at every turn."

"Emmett," Keith said, "I don't like Heckscher any more than you do. But aside from him being a piece of crap on a personal level, he's a pretty typical cop. He wants to solve the case. Hell, he wants to be head of the bureau someday. He knows the best way to get there—along with kissing a lot of rear ends, of course—is to catch as many bad guys as he can. Especially in high-profile cases like this. Maybe we should bring him in on this."

They all looked at me, waiting for a response.

I shook my head and said, "I just don't trust him. I'm sorry. I don't."

Karen gave me an elbow to the ribs. "You don't trust anyone."

"That's not true. I trust the people at this table."

She turned to face me. "Listen, hon," she said. "I know state law enforcement agencies haven't exactly covered themselves in glory in the last few years where you're concerned. But even *you* have got to admit, most of them believe in doing the right thing. Heckscher's a pig, but he's done harassing Joel and there aren't any other Black people around here for him to frame."

"*Maybe* he's finished with Joel," I said. "Hopalong said they were, but we can't take his word for it."

"If you ask me," said Keith, "Heckscher would be less inclined to harass Joel if he had other leads."

"Y'all are ganging up on me," I said, then added: "I just can't stand that guy."

"Oh hell, Emmett," said Keith. "*No one* can."

I shrugged.

"Alright bud. It's your investigation. Hold off on telling Heckscher if you want." He smiled mischievously. "You're spoiled from working with Isabel Cruickshank these last few years."

"Isabel was good," I said, kind of sheepishly.

"Yeh, she was, but your problem is, you only like to work with women."

He was right, although I wasn't about to admit it.

Dr. Childers turned to Red and asked: "Is that true?"

Red gave me a look. "Maybe it is," she said. "There are worse ways for a man to be."

CHAPTER TWENTY TWO

After lunch, I called John Smith to ask him about the gloves we had found. I forgot he sleeps during the day, so it was the middle of the night for him. Seems like I'm always waking people up out of a sound sleep.

I placed the gloves on the desk in front of me and asked Smith to describe the gloves he remembered Leon wearing. His description matched the ones we'd found to a T. I thanked him and told him to go back to sleep.

I was beginning to feel rushed about getting to the bottom of this. I'd made a big mistake by blabbing to Leon's parents before I had my ducks in a row. It was only a matter of time before they started asking around about their son. My best hope was that they take my advice and go to Keith. He's good at calming people down and making them see things his way. I didn't want them to go to Hawpe or the OSBI. Not before I was ready.

I wore civvies to work the next morning, knowing I'd be doing detective work all day. I stuffed my badge into my shirt pocket and stowed my off-duty weapon—a nickel-plated Colt Police Special I bought at a gun show earlier in the summer—into a small holster concealed in my left boot. I don't usually carry a gun when I'm out of uniform, but I was starting to feel kind of queasy about the way things were going.

I looked through copies Red had made of the documents, hoping to find something that might shine some more light on things. The wills were clearly written, as legal papers go. They confirmed what Red had told me: Earl left his estate to his ranch hand; Pete left his to Myrtle and the Cowboy Hall of Fame.

The mineral rights documents, on the other hand, might as well have been written in Latin. In fact, I think some of it was. I skipped to the end and saw that Earl and Pete, Walter Fessler, and SWOOP's managing partner, a fella named Jimmie Gracey, had all signed on the dotted line.

There was something else. Both sets had been notarized by the same person: Betsy Hill.

I checked the wills. Betsy Hill had notarized them as well.

Betsy Hill was the woman doing all that conspicuous weeping and wailing at Burt Murray's funeral.

I asked Red if she knew anything about Betsy Hill.

"I know what you know—that she works at Jesus is Lord." Jesus is Lord is a local beauty salon, so-named by the original owner, an extremely religious person with a flair for cosmetology. The building itself was once a Pentecostal church.

"So Betsy's a notary, huh?"

"Oh yeh, she got her commission about five years ago. I've had her do work for us a few times."

"She notarized all those documents. The bills of sale, the wills. Everything."

"Did she? I should've caught that. I'll bet she can put us in touch with Fessler."

"And whoever this Gracey fella is."

I rolled up the documents and drove over to Jesus is Lord. It still looks like a church, except the stained-glass windows had long ago been removed, boarded over, and painted the same white as the rest of the building. The sign over the marquee read "Jesus is Lord

Hairdressers." Underneath was a Bible quote: *And the king will desire your beauty—Psalm 25:11.*

I hadn't been inside the place for years. It hadn't changed. It was still the same tiny sanctuary, re-jiggered to be a place for women to have their hair laminated into strange and unnatural shapes. On the walls were framed prints of women with gigantic, helmet-like hairdos.

Betsy was sitting in one of her fancy hair-styling chairs reading a copy of People magazine. You could never accuse her of not practicing what she preached; her platinum blond mane was teased and hair-sprayed into a globe-like sphere, high- and wide-enough to shame Dolly Parton.

I could see her stiffen when she saw it was me.

"Hello, Chief Hardy."

"Hey Betsy, I understand you're a notary. I see where you did some work—"

"I'm not a notary," she said.

"Really? My wife told me you were."

"Nope. She's wrong."

"If you're not, I reckon you might be in trouble for impersonating one." I showed her copies of the documents with her seal affixed.

"They made me do it," she said tightly.

"Who are 'they,' and what did they make you do?"

She jabbered: "All of them, all of them, all of them!" then stopped. "I'm sorry, Chief Hardy," she said more calmly, "but I can't speak to you without my lawyer present."

"Was one of those people you're talking about named Walter Fessler?"

One of her eyes twitched a little.

"How 'bout Jimmie Gracey?"

It twitched again.

"Who's your lawyer?" I asked.

"Chester Hooks," she blurted. "Talk to him."

Chester's got a reputation for getting unprepared lawmen on the witness stand and carving them into tiny little pieces. I preferred to postpone tangling with him until I knew more.

"Ok, I'll be going, Betsy." I started for the door, then remembered something. "There's another thing I've been curious about. I remember you sat next to District Attorney Hawpe at Burt Murray's funeral. As I recall, you were really broken up. I didn't know you and Burt were close."

Her eyes shot laser beams. "Talk to my lawyer."

I returned to the station and related to Karen what had transpired.

"That's stupid of her to lie to you, of all people," she said. "I've been taking documents to her to be notarized off and on for years."

"I think it was just reflex. I came at her out of nowhere. Her first impulse was to deny it."

"It sounds like she'd be the nut to crack."

"Yup. Unfortunately, we'll have to get past Chester to do it."

"Are you going to go talk to him?"

"Not now. Before I talk to him, I want to be armed with more information."

I asked her to run an OSBI check on Fessler to see if he had a criminal record. "While you're at it, why don't you have them check out the fella who signed the documents handing over Pete Kuhlman's and Earl Calvert's mineral rights. Jimmie Gracey."

She called the OSBI and asked about Fessler and Gracey. They said they'd get back to us. "Who knows how long that will be," she said. "In the meantime, I guess you could drive to Waynoka and stake out the post office."

"I could dawdle around his box. Confront him when he goes to check his mail."

"Of course, he may not check his mail every day. It's not his personal box, it's the company's."

"Yeh, that's a good point," I said. "It would help if I knew what he looked like."

"Did you ever get back those pictures you took at Burt's funeral? He might be in one of those. Of course, since we don't know what he looks like, we'd have no way to know which one is him."

"True," I said. "Let's look at them, anyway." The Javelin I'd driven the day I picked up the photos was right where I'd left it. I retrieved the pictures from the glove compartment and went back into the station.

Red and I sat at my desk and shuffled through the prints. Most of them were of the "Oklahoma for Oklahomans" yahoos. "There's no way to tell if he's one of these guys," she said.

We soon came upon the pictures I'd taken of the group around Kath Murray—Chester Hooks, Hopalong Hawpe, Judge Zimmerman, and two other fellas I didn't recognize. I only got a clear picture of one of them. The other guy's back was to the camera in every shot.

"Maybe it's one of these guys," I said, pointing out the two strangers.

"I don't recognize that one," she said, referring to the guy whose face was to the camera, "and the other one's got his back turned."

"Yeh, but we can see he's got red hair," I said. "We might recognize him from that."

She nodded. "Possibly. You should take these with you."

"Sounds like a plan."

All the way to Waynoka, I thought about the red-haired guy in the pictures. I'd seen a fella with red hair recently, but no matter how much I wracked my brain, I could not remember who he was or where I'd seen him.

You wouldn't guess to look at it now, but Waynoka was a major air and rail hub back in the day, by Oklahoma standards, at least. It had a Harvey House for rail passengers and an airport that Wiley Post flew in and out of with some regularity. Will Rogers and Charles Lindbergh and Amelia Earhart are all reputed to have come through town at least once. Unfortunately, the town's glory days are behind it. The only trains that come through are freights, which sometimes sit immobile for hours on the tracks bisecting the town—clogging intersections and bringing what little traffic there is to a standstill.

You can avoid the long waits by coming in from the south, so that's what I did. Just outside the town, I passed a place called Miller's Café, which is not affiliated in any way with Miller's Drug in our town. I'd been there years before and remembered the food being pretty good. I hadn't had much of a breakfast, so I dropped in for a bite.

Miller's isn't exactly the Ritz, but it's a heck of a lot nicer than "Café" in Watie Junction. On the walls were faded photos of local attractions, most notably Little Sahara State park, which is exactly what it sounds like: 1,000 acres of sand; a Disneyland for dune buggies. I walked in to find a table of old boys in farming gear—coveralls and trucker hats, mostly—drinking coffee and shooting the breeze. I walked over and introduced myself. One of them looked familiar.

"Have we met?" I asked.

"You're the police chief up in Burr, aren't you?" I said I was. He said, "You gave me a speeding ticket a few years back."

"I trust you've since reformed," I joked.

His grin lacked a full complement of teeth. "Not much," he cackled.

I asked if any of them knew Jimmie Gracey. All of them did. Apparently Gracey used to come into Miller's occasionally to eat breakfast. They hadn't seen him in a while—among the men, estimates varied from a week to a month. He was not well-liked. That much was clear. He sat at a table by himself without saying hello to anyone, which in a place like Waynoka is about the biggest social sin a man can commit.

"Plus, he talks like a Yankee," groused one of them.

I took out the best of the pictures from the funeral and pointed out the fella I thought might be Gracey. "Is this him?"

They all agreed: That was Gracey, alright. They all claimed knowledge of where he lived, but no two of them could settle on the same set of directions. Lucky for me, one of them had the address scrawled in his little black book. Gracey's place was located on a county road east of town. I reckoned that would be easy enough to find. County roads around here are numbered logically and mostly laid out on a grid. According to the men, I'd have a hard time missing it. One of them said, "It looks like a trailer house with the wheels cut off." That's something they all agreed on.

I decided that instead of eating lunch, I'd pay Mr. Gracey a visit.

As I expected, I didn't have any trouble finding the place. The men at Miller's were right about what it looked like. It was a pint-sized metal box. There was no front yard to speak of. The building itself only stood maybe four feet off the road and was surrounded by a chain-link fence. There was no more than six inches of space between the fence and the building. The front gate swung freely on its hinges. The latch was broken. There was a mailbox attached to the wall by the door. I opened and found a stack of mail addressed to Jimmie Gracey. I thumbed through it. The oldest was postmarked June 23rd.

I rang the doorbell. Nobody answered. I rang it again. Still no answer. I knocked. Nothing. I put my ear to the door. No sounds from within. Jimmie Gracey was either hiding or he wasn't there. There was no vehicle parked nearby, so I reckoned it was the latter.

I walked the periphery. There was only that one door. You couldn't have crawled in through a window even if you wanted; they were the slatted kind that only open by turning a handle on the inside. I tried to peek in, but the glass was frosted so I couldn't see a thing. In the gap between the house and the fence, weeds had grown almost as high as my waist. I wondered how a fella would cut it. There's not a mower in the world that could fit inside such a small space. The ground surrounding the building was hard-packed red dirt. The only sign of civilization was an empty oil can wedged between the house and the fence. I leaned forward to look at it and a bug flew out of the weeds and up my nose. I snorted it out.

The nearest house was fifty yards down the road. I walked over and knocked on the door, hoping that whoever lived there might give me a line on Jimmie Gracey. No one answered. I walked around to the side of the house and saw in the distance a fella unloading bales of hay from the bed of a truck. If I wanted to talk to him, I'd have to come back later.

I didn't expect Gracey to show up. It seemed apparent by the stack of unopened mail that he hadn't been around in quite some time. But I thought I should at least wait a little while, just in case. I sat in my truck and kept the engine running so I could use the air-conditioner and listen to music. I put in a tape Kenny Harjo had given me, an album by a jazz trumpet player named Chet Baker. Over the years, I've taken a personal interest in Chet's music, him being a fellow Okie and all.

After listening to the entire tape two-and-a-half times, I decided to drive back into town and stake-out the post office box. Gracey might not be living here anymore, but maybe he was still picking up his business mail. I didn't expect he'd show, but stranger things have happened. I'd come this far and hated the idea of this being a wasted trip.

I almost stopped by the Waynoka police department to tell them what I was up to, but at the last minute, I decided against it. I know from experience that cops are worse than dogs when it comes to protecting their territory. I thought it better to avoid that potential pitfall.

The air-conditioning in the post office was so strong it made me shiver. The fella behind the counter was about my age, with less hair, but a bigger belly. I said I was supposed to meet someone and asked if it would be okay if I waited inside. He said I was more than welcome.

The room with the mailboxes was small—about ten-by-ten-feet. The walls were lined with rows of mailboxes. Those on the bottom row were jumbo sized. All of them had small glass windows, so you could peek inside and see if you had any mail without opening it up. The SWOOP box was one of the big ones. I bent over and looked inside. It was full to overflowing.

I waited and tried not to look conspicuous. Every once in a while I'd look out the front window and shake my head like I couldn't believe the person I was supposed to meet was so late. I kept sneaking glances at the picture of Gracey, trying to brand it onto my brain. People trickled in and out. Each one smiled and asked how I was doing. I smiled back and said I was doing real good.

None of them were Gracey.

After a while, the clerk came in. He lit a cigarette. "Looks like your friend's pretty late, ain't he?"

"It sure does," I said. I peered out the window like I was looking for him. "Maybe you know him," I said, and showed him the picture of Gracey.

"Sure, that's Jimmie Gracey. He comes by here to pick up his mail. Used to, anyway. Haven't seen him in a while." He touched the SWOOP box with the toe of his black mailman's shoe. "That's his box, right there, number 301." He took a deep drag, then talked while he exhaled. "Technically, it isn't his, of course. It belongs to the Southwest Oklahoma Oil Partnership. But Gracey's the fella who rented the box and picks up the mail."

"I don't suppose you could take a look and tell me the last time he did that? Picked up the mail?"

He tapped an ash onto the floor. "That ain't something I'm supposed to do."

I turned over my hole card. "Would it help if I told you I was a cop?"

He gave me a side-eyed look. "Not from around here, you're not."

"You're right. I'm the police chief in Burr, over in Tilghman County." I showed him my badge.

His face showed recognition. "You must be Emmett Hardy."

I chuckled. "I reckon my reputation precedes me."

"Sure, I remember seeing you on the news when that colored girl was killed in your town a few years ago," he said. "How long ago was that, exactly?"

"It's been a while," I said, not wanting to think too hard about it.

"Well, seeing as you're a celebrity, I reckon it won't hurt to take a look. Gracey's mail's been piling up, anyway. We've about given up on him coming in to pick it up."

I followed him into the next room and waited while he retrieved the mail.

"This is it," he said, laying a six-inch-high stack of envelopes on the counter.

"It's ok if I go through it?"

He winked. "It's not ok for you to do it. You'd need a search warrant for that. But I can look at it for you."

That got a smile out of me. I said, "I reckon that'll work."

"Are you looking for anything specific?"

"Well," I said, "mainly I wanted to talk to Gracey, but seeing that he's probably not going to show up, I guess the next best thing would be figuring out when he was last here. Is that something you can help me with?"

"Heck, all I need to do is take a peek at the bottom of this stack." He put on a pair of thick reading glasses, peeled off a few envelopes, and held them close to his face. The lenses made his eyes appear as big as baseballs. "The oldest postmark is from June 25th," he said. He pulled off the glasses. Without them, he looked like Mr. Magoo. "Before then, he came by every day," he added. "I don't know what happened."

I thought I might.

June 25th was the day Burt Murray met his end.

I asked him if there was anything in the stack from or addressed to a Walter Fessler. He went through it and didn't find anything. I gave him my business card and asked him to give me a call if Jimmie Gracey showed up.

"I probably hadn't ought to," he said, crinkling his face. I waited. He un-crinkled it. "What the heck," he said, like he'd decided to do something naughty. "Sure, I'll give you a call if I see him."

I thanked him for his help and started to leave, but he wasn't done with me. "Chief Hardy, I was meaning to ask. Have you ever run into a gal over there in Burr by the name of Karen Dean?"

"I run into her every day," I said. "Her name's Karen Hardy now. She's my wife."

His jaw literally dropped. "You don't say? That's a heck of a coincidence, ain't it?"

"Why's that? You know Karen?"

"I went to junior high school with her in Edmond. Then she moved to your town for high school, and I lost track of her. Does she still have red hair?"

"Oh yeh, she's still got it. With a few grays mixed in. Tell her I said that, and I'll deny it."

He gave me a don't-that-beat-all shake of his head. "What else is she up to these days, other than being married to you?"

"She's my assistant chief."

"That's wonderful. Just wonderful." He smiled shyly. "She still as pretty as ever?"

"Prettier every day."

It was like the memory had put him in a trance. "Ain't that something," he whispered. "Well, you tell her ol' Bruce Watkins from Edmond Junior High said hello, alright? Tell her I might come up and see her one of these days."

I thanked him again and started to leave. He stopped me again. "By the way, Chief, you never told me why you're looking for this fella."

"I'm trying to get some information on a case, and I thought he might be able to help."

"It's not about that Burt Murray thing, is it? Dang, I sure hated to see that. He was a good man."

Somehow, I managed not to throw up all over his nice clean floor. "Nah, this is about something else."

***

Back at the station, I told Red about finding Gracey's place and how it looked like he hadn't been there for a while. I then described my post office visit and the information I had pried out of the clerk.

"That's got to be significant," she said, "Gracey dropping off the map the same day Burt was killed."

I expressed my agreement. "By the way, that clerk says he went to junior high with you. You remember a guy by the name of Bruce Watkins?"

She put on her thinking-hard face. "Hmmm," she said. "Barely. It's been so long."

"Well, he sure remembers you."

She smiled faintly. "Oh, that's sweet," she said, then clapped her hands and rubbed them together. "Ok, so is that all you got? Because while you were gone, I learned some things."

"About Gracey?"

"About Gracey and Betsy Hill."

"What about Betsy?"

"Get a load of this," she said, and showed me the last page of SWOOP's agreement with Pete Kuhlman.

"What am I looking at?"

"See here?" She pointed out the date it had been signed. "June 6th, 1976. Now look at this." She pointed at the expiration date on the notary stamp. "December 31st, 1975. Betsy's commission had expired when she signed off on these documents."

I shrugged. "Are you saying I should arrest her for that?"

"No, but it gives you something on her. A notary's supposed to return or destroy their stamp and get a new one when their commission expires. Obviously Betsy didn't. That's got to be a misdemeanor, at least."

"Right, so if she decides she doesn't want to talk to me voluntarily, I can hold this over her head."

"Exactly."

"Got it," I said. "What's the story on Gracey?"

"First off, I asked them about Walter Fessler. They'd never heard of him. Gracey, however, is another story." She read from a notepad: "Jimmie Gracey: white male, 36 years-old, from Bangor, Maine. Arrested in 1961 for aggravated assault. Convicted and sent to the Maine State Prison in Thomaston, where he served two years of a three-year sentence. Moved to Oklahoma when his parole expired in

1966. In 1969, he received an associate degree in accounting from Oklahoma State University. In 1972 he was convicted of embezzlement and money laundering and spent the better part of the next three years in McAlester."

"You know who else was at McAlester during that time, don't you?" I asked.

"Oh yeh, I know," she said. "Burt Murray."

"Coincidence?"

She waggled her hand: maybe-maybe-not. "Might be good to find out if they knew each other."

"How can we find that out?"

"Give me one minute," she said and dashed out of my office.

It took her fifteen.

"They were cellmates."

"So. No coincidence."

"I'd say not."

Gracey missed a scheduled meeting with his parole officer on June 28th. After repeated failed attempts to contact him, an arrest warrant was issued. He'd been missing since at least June 28th, and maybe as early as the 24th. The fact that he was Burt's cellmate pointed to something illicit. Devising a fishy scheme to con two old men out of their mineral rights isn't something you'd expect from a person with a record for assault, but it's sure enough something an embezzler might do. The fact he disappeared at almost the same time Burt was killed set off even more alarms.

"Alright," I said, "so Gracey was Burt's cellmate. He shows up in Tilghman County after his release from prison and gets involved in this SWOOP deal, which looks to be a scam designed to separate rich, elderly oilmen from their mineral rights. The two we know about—Pete and Earl—died before collecting a cent. Was that a coincidence?"

"I don't see how it could be."

"But how can we prove it?"

"We track down Gracey or Fessler." She ran her hands through her hair like she wanted to pull it out by the roots. "Lord, this is so complicated!" she said. "I don't know, Emmett. It might be time to hand this off to Heckscher. He's got the wherewithal to do things we can't."

She was right, of course. If I lived someplace normal—a place I could trust the authorities not to set a convicted killer free—I wouldn't hesitate to let someone more capable than me handle it. But I didn't live in a place like that. I live in Tilghman County, Oklahoma, where there's exactly one elected official who I trust to do the right thing.

On the other hand: What else could I do? We'd about exhausted our meager ability to get to the bottom of this.

"I'll tell you what," I said. "Let me talk to Betsy Hill and see what she has to say. I doubt she'll tell me anything useful with her lawyer sitting right there, but you never know."

"What about Dr. Morston?" she said. "He's the only one here who we know for a fact did something wrong."

"I'd talk to him if I could find him, but who knows where he is? I'll talk to Betsy for now. If I don't get anything out of her, I'll tell Heckscher what I know and wash my hands of the whole thing."

"I think that's the right thing to do."

"Is it?" I said. "I sure as hell hope so."

CHAPTER TWENTY THREE

Folks could hardly believe it when Chester Hooks moved his office from Temple City to Burr. Nobody could understand why a big shot lawyer like him would relocate from the county seat to a place like this. Chester practices all over the western half of the state, so I guess it doesn't matter where he sleeps, but it never did make sense to me why, out of all the places he could've hung his shingle, he picked Burr. I always meant to ask him about it, but never did.

His house used to belong to Edgar Bixby—a local farmer and gas tycoon who was convicted on a murder conspiracy charge back in the '60s and later died in prison. I expect that if Chester had been his lawyer, Edgar would never have gone to jail. Edgar's widow Denise couldn't wait to get rid of the house. She sold it to Chester for a fraction of what it was worth.

Denise's maiden name was Kinney. She is, by coincidence, the same Denise who broke my heart in high school by choosing Edgar Bixby over me. I guess there's no accounting for taste.

**

Karen and I decided I might as well go straight to Chester, since Betsy wasn't going to talk to us without him by her side. I tried his office first. His secretary told me he was working from home for the day, but she could relay a message. I asked if she could call him and ask if I could come out and see about a matter of some urgency. She put me on hold for a few seconds, then came back on the line and asked me what it was about. I said it was a matter involving Betsy Hill and her expired notary commission. She put me on hold again, then came back and said he'd see me in half an hour.

I had barely set foot on that property in the years since I arrested Edgar. The house itself was a cut-down version of a huge limestone mansion in Ponca City built in the '20s by the oil tycoon E.W. Marland, who based it on a palace he'd seen on his travels in Italy. Edgar copied Marland's house, albeit on a smaller scale, which was appropriate, since Edgar's fortune, as impressive as it was, never came within spitting distance of E.W. Marland's.

I rang the doorbell. A small, slim, dark-skinned woman in what looked like a white nurse's uniform answered the door. She looked like Helen Ramirez, the woman Gary Cooper character threw over for Grace Kelly in *High Noon*, I guess because Grace Kelly was blond and not a Mexican. "Chief Hardy?" she said in slightly accented English.

"That's me."

"Hello, I am Daniela," she said with a pleasant smile. "Please come with me. Mr. Hooks is expecting you."

The house had changed drastically since the last time I'd been inside. Gone was Edgar's hokey western-themed décor. Chester had redecorated the place in a modern style, with furniture made of chrome and glass and black leather, and lamps that looked like flying saucers. On the walls, instead of the pictures of cowboys and Indians that Edgar favored, there were huge, densely layered abstract paintings. The signature on one said "Pollock" which I assume referred to the person who painted it and not the fish.

Daniela led me past half a dozen bedrooms and almost as many bathrooms to Chester's office. Chester waited at the door, towering over me, his face creased with a smile that would not have been out of place on an embalmed corpse. I've always thought Chester looked like

Dracula—not Bela Lugosi's, but the guy in the '50s remake. Christopher Lee. Chester's older than Lee, but he dyes his hair black and has the same long face. When he smiles, his eye teeth are even a little bit fang-like. Today he was wearing non-Dracula garb—white pleated pants, white sneakers, and a button-down long-sleeved white shirt with a yellow cardigan tied around his neck, all of which blended nicely with his fish-belly white skin. If not Dracula, he at least looked like one of Casper the Friendly Ghost's unfriendlier cousins.

"I've only got a few minutes, Chief Hardy," he said, tapping his watch, which I'm pretty sure was not a Timex. "I'm having a friend over for tennis."

That explained why he was dressed like a 1927 Harvard undergrad.

I said, "I didn't see a tennis court outside."

He motioned for me to come in. "It's an indoor court, Chief," he said. "I converted one of the outbuildings."

The only outbuilding on the property big enough to house a tennis court was the air-conditioned pen Edgar had built to house a prize pig many years ago. I reckon Chester wasn't much of a pig fancier.

Chester motioned toward a liquor cabinet behind his desk. "Could I offer you a drink?" he asked. I declined. "Mind if I have one, then?"

"Have at it."

He poured himself a generous amount of Johnny Walker Black and took a dainty sip, then motioned for me to sit. My chair looked like it had come off the set of *Star Trek*. Fortunately, it was more comfortable than it looked.

He sat back and swiveled his fancy high-backed leather chair slowly back and forth. "So, Chief Hardy, what is this about Betsy Hill's expired notary commission?"

"I understand Miss Hill is one of your clients."

"She is."

"I'm a little surprised you'd agree to represent someone like Betty, as prominent as you are in your profession."

"Everyone deserves sound legal advice."

"I agree, but I wouldn't think a hairdresser who moonlights as a notary public could afford one of the most expensive lawyers in the state."

He stopped swiveling and crossed one leg over the other. "Even the most accomplished attorneys occasionally work pro bono," he said, "although that's not the case with Miss Hill. She assists me with some of my legal work. In return, I've offered to represent her, should the need arise."

"And now it has, I guess."

"Possibly. So tell me, what's this about? Something about notarizing without a license?"

I shifted in my chair. My jeans made an obscene sound, rubbing against the leather. Both of us pretended not to hear.

"Her commission expired several months ago," I said, "but she was still notarizing documents as recently as two or three weeks ago."

"You're not going to arrest her for that? I'm sure it was simply an oversight."

"Honestly, Chester, I'm only bringing it up because the documents in question are connected with something I'm working on. I'm looking for a fella—a couple of fellas, really—and haven't been able to find either one. I was hoping Betsy could help."

"Who are these men you're looking for?"

"Have you ever heard of an attorney named Walter Fessler?"

"Can't say that I have."

I studied his face. Either he was telling the truth, or he'd make a hell of a card player.

"How about a fella named Jimmie Gracey?"

He blinked. Maybe he's not that great a card player after all.

"I have had dealings with Mr. Gracey, yes."

"Would you mind telling me what kind of dealings?"

He smiled indulgently. "As a matter of fact, I would mind. It's a matter of attorney/client privilege. Why do you ask?"

"Oh, I see. So you're Jimmie Gracey's lawyer, too."

He made a face like I'd caught him with his hand in his drawers. "Yes, I am. Why do you ask?"

"Well, Chester, I've been looking for him. Now that I know you're not only Betsy Hill's lawyer, but his too, I'm kind of hoping you could set it up so I could talk to both of them."

He downed what was left of his Johnny Walker and poured another. "Miss Hill, maybe. Mr. Gracey is incommunicado for the time being."

"He is, huh? Any idea where he's gone off to?"

"Sadly, I don't. I've been trying to get in touch with him for several days with no success."

"In your opinion, would his disappearance have anything to do with something called Southwest Oklahoma Oil Partnership?"

"I'm sorry," he said, "I'm afraid I don't know what that is."

I studied him. He wasn't giving anything away.

"It's a business of some sort," I said. "Mr. Gracey is the managing partner. Walter Fessler is the lawyer for another party in the transaction. I haven't been able to track down either of them. I was hoping Betsy might be able to help, that's all."

It was Chester's turn to study me. "I trust you have no intent on filing charges."

"For the expired commission? Nah, I'm sure it was an oversight, like you said."

He took another sip of Johnny Walker. "As I said, I can't help you with Mr. Gracey—"

"You do know he skipped parole and there's a warrant out for his arrest, right?"

He nodded. "Obviously."

"So I reckon you're in a pretty big hurry to find him."

He hesitated. "I'm sorry, Chief, but I can't discuss Mr. Gracey's situation."

"Fair enough. But you can set me up to talk to Betsy Hill, right?"

"That depends. I need to know the details."

"What do you want to know?"

"Is this in pursuit of a criminal investigation?"

"It is."

"Involving this partnership you spoke of?"

"Yes."

"Would you mind sharing the nature of the investigation?"

"Like you, counselor, I've got things I need to keep confidential."

He downed the rest of his second drink and in the same long unhurried movement got to his feet. My time was up, apparently. I stood as well.

"It's been good to talk to you, Chief Hardy," he said. "I'll relay your request to Ms. Hill."

"Will you recommend she speak to me?"

"I'll advise that she consent to an informal interview," he said. "I'll be by her side, naturally."

"Naturally."

***

Chester's secretary called me at the station to schedule a time. We set it up for the next morning at 10:00. I'd have liked to have taken Red along as an extra set of ears, but Chester insisted I come alone. He also stipulated that no notes were to be taken. If I knew for sure I had the District Attorney on my team, I might have tried to bargain him down, but I had my doubts about that, and anyway, I wasn't ready to rope in Hopalong just yet.

He wanted to meet in his office downtown and not at the station, which suited me fine. The IGA grocery store downtown went out of business when the new Safeway opened. Chester bought it, gutted it, and turned it into the fanciest and so far only office building in town.

A pair of swinging glass doors led to another pair of swinging glass doors, which led to the outer office of Chester Hooks, Attorney at Law. A young, smartly dressed woman sat behind a desk, typing. Her fingers moved so fast I thought she must be faking. She saw me and stopped. She said hello and asked if she could help me. I told her who

I was and why I was there. She picked up the phone, announced my arrival, and told me to go right in.

I'd been in Chester's office before, so I knew what to expect. It's a pretty typical lawyer's office: paneled walls, a big wooden desk with a telephone and papers scattered about, and a couple of padded leather chairs—regular furniture like you tend to find on planet Earth, as opposed to the space-aged stuff he had at home. Chester was dressed in a black suit, white shirt, and black tie. His gray hair was slicked back, the way he always wears it. His eyes were bloodshot, which didn't surprise me, given all that expensive Scotch whiskey he'd been knocking back the day before.

The only thing different from my last visit was a big metal box with lots of switches and red lights on the front and a large freestanding typewriter next to it. Chester saw me looking at it and burst into a big, pompous song and dance. "It's a microcomputer," he said, then spent five minutes bragging about all it could do and how expensive it was. I pretended to listen, nodding when it was appropriate. When he finally ran out of things to say about it, he pulled open a door to still another room. "In here, if you please. Miss Hill is waiting."

The meeting room was larger than his office by half. Most of the space was taken up by a long, egg-shaped table, surrounded by a few chairs. Betsy Hill sat at one end. Chester took the chair next to her. In front of him was a yellow legal pad and a telephone. I sat at the opposite end of the table.

I said, "Good morning, Betsy."

She said, very politely, "Good morning, Chief Hardy."

Chester got the ball rolling. "So I understand you want to ask Miss Hill about someone named Walter Fessler."

"Don't forget Jimmie Gracey," I said. "You know, counselor, if you don't mind, I reckon I might as well show her the documents involved. It might help jog her memory." Before he could object, I removed several documents from the manila envelope I'd brought with me and pushed them down the table.

Chester put on a pair of granny glasses, which would've looked odd on just about anyone else, but seemed perfectly in character for him. "So what am I looking at here?" he said. "Ok," he continued after a minute, "two of these are wills. The others are related to the sale of certain mineral rights by the deceased." He removed the glasses, leaned back, and shrugged. "What about them?"

"I wanted to make sure she knew what I'm talking about. You remember when you notarized these, Betsy?"

She pretended to look at them good and hard. "Yeh, I think so."

"You see the fellas who signed the will? Jimmie Gracey and Walter Fessler? Could you tell me how you came to meet them?"

Chester turned to her and said in a voice dripping with fake concern, "Would you be willing to tell Chief Hardy how you met these gentlemen?"

She nodded primly. "A few months ago, Jimmie Gracey called me and asked if I could notarize some documents. I said I'd be happy to. He gave me an address and a time to meet. I went and notarized the documents. A few months later, he called and said he had another job for me. We met again, and I notarized some more documents."

I waited for her to continue. She didn't.

"That's kind of the shorthand version, though, isn't it?" I said. "I mean, first you had to notarize the sale of Earl Calvert's mineral rights to that organization Mr. Gracey represents, right? Then later on, Mr. Calvert revised his will to reflect the change in his circumstances. You didn't do all that the same day, right? The dates on the papers are different."

Her face flushed. "I went to Mr. Calvert's place twice."

Chester broke in: "What difference does it make whether she made one trip or two trips to Earl Calvert's?"

"I'm sorry, Chester," I said with a smile. "You're right. It doesn't matter much unless you're a stickler. All I really need from Betsy here is some information on how to get in touch with Mr. Gracey and this other fella, Walter Fessler."

Chester leaned back and folded his hands over his non-existent belly. "As you know, Chief, Mr. Gracey has seemingly disappeared. As his attorney, that's a concern of mine, but I doubt Miss Hill knows any more than I do about his whereabouts. Is that true, Miss Hill?"

"I don't know where he is," she said sullenly. "All I have is what's on the papers."

"In other words, his address and phone number," said Chester. He read the Waynoka post office box number out loud. "That's what you have, that's what I have, and that's what Miss Hill has. We can't tell you any more than that."

"You have his home address, don't you, Chester?"

He wavered for a second. "Well, of course I do."

"You can give it to me, then."

He paused. "Wait a moment." He buzzed his secretary and asked for Gracey's home address and phone number. He wrote them on the yellow legal pad and slammed down the phone. "Damn!" he said. "I'm sorry, I bit my tongue." He pulled a handkerchief from his jacket pocket and dabbed at a spot of blood at the corner of his mouth. Once that was taken care of, he ripped the top sheet from the pad and pushed it at me. "Here," he said. The phone number his secretary gave him was identical to the one on the sale documents; the address was the same as the one the old fellas in Miller's had given me.

I hadn't gotten anything new out of Chester, but it was fun watching him get a little bit hot and bothered.

"Now, was that so hard?" I said. "Ok, both of you: How about Walter Fessler? So far, he's only a signature on a few pieces of paper. The Oklahoma Bar Association says he isn't a member. The Attorney General's office has never heard of him, nor has any of the state's 27 District Attorneys. From what I can tell, the man's a ghost. The only other people who I know met him are Earl Calvert and Pete Kuhlman, and they're both dead. Betsy, can you tell me how to get in touch with him?"

She glanced sideways at Chester like she expected him to answer. He did not disappoint.

"Miss Hill confided to me in advance that she was concerned you'd ask about Walter Fessler. She was worried because, unfortunately, she has misplaced that information." He gave her hand a fatherly pat. "I've told her that, combined with the fact she notarized certain of these documents after her commission expired, she could be in some slight legal jeopardy—for instance, if these sales are litigated, or the wills contested. I hope whatever you're working on won't require anything along those lines."

I let my head fall back and stared at the ceiling for a moment. *Don't give up yet,* I said to myself.

"Betsy," I said, "can you at least describe Fessler's appearance?"

She gave Chester a nervous glimpse. "I don't know," she said. "I didn't get a good look at him."

"You were in the room with the fella on at least four occasions and not one time did you get a good look at him?"

"Chief, I'm going to have to ask you not to badger poor Miss Hill. She says she can't remember what he looked like, and I think you should take her at her word."

Clearly, her story about losing Fessler's information was a load of crap, but I suspected the fact she concocted it with Chester's help made it unlikely I'd ever get the truth out of her.

"Alright then, I know when I'm beat." I got up to leave, but before I did, I had one more question. "Betsy, in the beauty parlor the other day, you said, 'They made me do it.' Who are 'they,' and what did they make you do?"

She looked at Chester.

He held up a hand, as if to say, "I'll handle this."

In his best deep, dark courtroom voice, he said, "That was a complete misunderstanding, Chief Hardy. Miss Hill thought you had come on behalf of a dissatisfied customer. The day before, a woman and her husband asked Miss Hill to style the wife's hair a certain way. Miss Hill thought she had given them what they asked for, but afterwards they professed to be appalled at the results."

"She was afraid I was going to arrest her for giving someone a lousy haircut that they made her give?" I tried one last time. "I'm confused. Come on, Betsy. What's this all about?"

Chester abruptly stood. "I believe we're done here, Chief," he said in a smooth, unbothered voice. "I'm afraid I have another meeting, and Miss Hill must get to work." His smile showed off his longer-than-normal eyeteeth. I noticed the spot of blood from his chomped-on tongue had returned, and his eyes were even more bloodshot than when I'd come in.

I suddenly remembered my name wasn't Van Helsing. "Thanks for your help," I said, then beat a hasty retreat.

CHAPTER TWENTY FOUR

I'd barely begun telling Red what had transpired with Hooks and Betsy when Hopalong called, in a state of extreme agitation.

"Emmett, what is this I hear of you harassing Betsy Hill?" I could almost hear the spittle spray the mouthpiece.

"Harry, calm down. I wasn't harassing her. I only wanted to ask her a few questions."

"Chester Hooks tells me you're trying to chase down a couple of ghosts."

"Only one of them's a ghost. The other fella is by all accounts made of flesh and blood. He just hasn't been seen lately."

"Funny, Hardy, real funny," he blathered in his high-pitched Alvin and the Chipmunks voice. "If you think Betsy Hill's done something against the law, I need to know."

"I'm not saying she has, Harry. I'm trying to track down a couple of fellas and I thought she could help, that's all. They had her notarize some documents, and—"

He interrupted: "What kind of documents?"

"Wills," I said.

"Why in the world would Jimmie Gracey be signing a will?" I heard the sound of someone wrestling the phone away from him, then muffled voices. He came back after a few seconds. "You did say you were looking for Jimmie Gracey, right?"

"I didn't say, Harry, but he is one of 'em. Do you know him? Because if you do, I could really use some help finding him."

I thought he'd hung up, then realized he was holding his hand over the mouthpiece again. He came back and said, "I just got notified that someone with that name has skipped bail, is all."

That didn't explain why he brought him up in the first place, but never mind.

"The other fella I'm looking for is named Walter Fessler," I said. "Have you ever heard of him?"

"Whose wills are we talking about?"

"Are you going to answer my question?"

"Don't be a smart-ass. Whose wills?"

"Earl Calvert's and Pete Kuhlman's."

He grunted. "What's wrong with them?"

"Both Earl and Pete used someone named Walter Fessler to draw up their wills and serve as executor. The thing is, there's no one named Walter Fessler licensed to practice law in Oklahoma."

"That's ridiculous. Of course there is."

"You know him, then?"

"Um-uh-mmm," he stammered. "I mean, Mr. Calvert and Mr. Kuhlman wouldn't have hired someone to make out their wills who wasn't a lawyer."

"You wouldn't think so, but apparently they did. We made all the calls. You can check yourself if you want."

He put his hand over the mouthpiece again. More muffled voices. He came back on the line.

"I don't know what you're up to, Emmett, but I advise you to drop it right now. You're messing with something that doesn't have anything to do with you. *Comprende?*"

"Everything but *comprende.*"

The line went dead.

"What's got Hopalong's panties in a bunch?" asked Red.

"Well, Hopalong Hawpe is definitely acquainted with Jimmie Gracey and Walter Fessler," I said. "If I didn't know that before, I do now."

I described how he'd brought up Gracey out of thin air and how he'd pushed back on the idea that Walter Fessler wasn't a lawyer. "He tried to cover his tracks, but he's easier to see through than Claude Rains. I got the distinct feeling someone was there with him, telling him what to say."

"Chester, probably," she said off-handedly. "Everyone knows he's Hopalong's brain."

"Yeh, I wouldn't be surprised if Chester went to Hopalong after he was done with me."

"Seriously?" she asked. "Why? To complain?"

"Maybe to complain, or maybe Chester's involved with SWOOP somehow. We know it's a partnership, but the only partner we know is Gracey. Chester might be another."

"Maybe Hawpe is, too," she added.

"I sure wouldn't put it past him. He started by accusing me of harassing Betsy Hill, but really he seemed a lot more interested in what was going on with Earl's and Pete's wills."

"Chester being involved would explain why he's so eager to represent Betsy Hill."

"It would. Betsy was genuinely scared when I tried to question her in the salon. 'They made me do it,' she said. Is Chester part of 'they?' Is Hopalong?"

"You think she's in trouble?"

"If she helped someone cheat those old men out of their oil money, then hell yes, she's in trouble."

She nodded. "I know she'd be in trouble with the law, but I meant: Do you think whoever's behind this is liable to hurt her?"

I shrugged. "Hard to say."

"If somehow Leon Qualls' murder is tied up in all this ..." she said in a rueful manner. "I can't believe Betsy would willingly be a part of something like that."

"Maybe she had no choice. Maybe they made her an offer she couldn't refuse."

Unsmiling, she said, "Alright, godfather. Let's hope she doesn't wake up next to a bloody horse's head."

***

I drove around for a while and listened to music on my truck's cassette deck. I put in a tape called *Blue Train* by a tenor saxophone player named John Coltrane. Charlie Parker's been my favorite musician for as long as I can remember, but lately Mr. Coltrane's been coming up on the outside.

Music helps me think. Lord knows, I had some thinking to do—especially about Jimmie Gracey and whoever else might be part of this SWOOP deal. Hawpe's phone call made me think maybe he had a hand in it. If he did, maybe Chester did, too.

Like Karen said: Everyone knows Chester Hooks is Harry Hawpe's brain.

Besides being cheated, I had to reason to suspect that Earl and Pete were murdered, too. Neither was subjected to a post-mortem, and the man who signed their death certificates—the medical examiner, Dr. Morston—had left town on what was starting to look like a permanent vacation.

And what about Leon Qualls and his girlfriend? We know Dr. Morston falsified Leon's autopsy report, but to what end? There was no reason to suspect him of killing Leon. More likely he tried to cover up the murder at someone else's behest—presumably the person who pulled the trigger. The only physical evidence in the Qualls case—Leon's gloves—pointed at Pete being Leon's killer, but Pete was old and frail and unlikely to have been able to pull off such a scheme.

To my mind, Leon's killer had to have been Burt. Otherwise, why would Carrie have killed him?

On top of everything: Who in the world is Walter Fessler and where can he be found?

I hit a brick wall. Gracey was gone. His parole officer couldn't find him. Chester Hooks, his lawyer, claimed not to know where he is. As for Walter Fessler, the only person I knew who'd actually laid eyes on the man—Betsy Hill—insists she doesn't remember what he looks like. I can't be sure he even exists.

I'm up against it, I thought. *Karen was right. I don't have the resources to do what needs to be done.*

John Coltrane's music worked his magic; by the time I returned to the station, I knew what I had to do. I didn't like it—I hated it, in fact—but it could not be avoided.

I needed to talk to OSBI Agent John Joe Heckscher.

CHAPTER TWENTY FIVE

Heckscher wasn't any happier to take my call than I was to make it. I told him I had information on the Murray case. "I'm busy," he snarled. "Can't you tell me what it is over the phone?"

"Agent Heckscher, what I've got is big and involves some important people—"

"Yeh, well, I reckon your idea of who's important differs from mine."

"John Joe, this is a long story. I can't and I won't talk about it over the phone."

"Hell, we got the girl who done it. What else is there? All we need to know is her name, and we're done. I reckon we'll have that soon enough."

"There's a lot more to it than that, John Joe."

He sighed audibly. "Alright then. I'm giving the keynote speech at the OSCPA dinner tonight in Oklahoma City. If you're going to be there, I reckon we can talk afterwards."

I'd have preferred he come to me, but I was in no position to bargain. He gave me the time and location. I told him I didn't have reservations. He said I could pay at the door.

I said I'd see him after his speech.

***

OSCPA—most members pronounce it 'osk-puh'—is the Oklahoma Sheriffs and Chiefs of Police Association. Among other things, it exists to grease the gears between different law enforcement agencies in the state. I've been a dues-paying member for years. To be honest, paying dues is about the extent of my involvement. I'm not much of a joiner, but I've always figured the OSCPA was worthy of my support, even if they don't always deliver on their mission. I'd sent some of my young officers to attend its training courses, but I'd never been to one of their events. I guess there's a first time for everything.

Red made me wear my only suit. It hadn't been cleaned since Burt's funeral, but it was in pretty decent shape. The tie was another matter. I looked for it all over, then remembered I'd taken it off and stuffed it into my coat pocket after the funeral. I reached in and there it was, wadded up in a ball. Red gave it a once-ever with a steam iron. It still wasn't perfect, but it would have to do.

I don't clean up very well, but my Lord, Red sure does. She wore a dark-green, short-sleeved dress that buttoned up the front. A belt cinched at the waist emphasized her shape—which, I might say, her husband finds extremely attractive. She even wore make-up, something she doesn't normally do. It covered up her freckles, but that's ok. She's gorgeous anyway.

We took my truck. The drive to Oklahoma City takes roughly two hours. The dinner started in an hour-and-a-half, so unless we hit the road in a hurry, we'd miss the whole thing. The event was being held at the Lincoln Plaza, a fancy hotel that hosts a lot of conventions and the like. I drove faster than I should, but we still arrived a few minutes late. I pulled up at the door and gave my keys to a fella in a valet's uniform. His name tag said "Charlie." I made a joke about him being a Charlie parker. "You know? Like Charlie Parker, the saxophone player?" The valet smiled politely. I complained to Karen as he drove off. "He didn't get my joke." She said, "Oh, I think he got it. It just wasn't funny."

The event was being held in the hotel's dinner theater. It cost $25 apiece to get in. I thought for that money the valet could at least laugh at my joke. The lady at the door told us we could sit wherever we liked. The place was only half full, so we had plenty of choices. The theater was configured like a Las Vegas showroom, with three tiers of plush red-leather upholstered booths arranged in a semi-circle facing the stage. It was dimly lit and hazy with smoke. What light there was came from candles on the tables. All you could see of people were dim profiles, their faces illuminated occasionally by the flash of a cigarette lighter.

The tables nearest the stage were taken, so we took one toward the back. A cocktail waitress in a skimpy outfit took our drink order. Selling liquor by the drink is still technically illegal in Oklahoma, so you'd think with the room full of cops, they'd steer away from selling booze, but no. Apparently, whichever jurisdiction was in charge agreed to look the other way. For once, I wasn't tempted. I ordered a Tab and Red had a Coke.

We got there as Heckscher's speech ended and before food was served. The guest of honor left the stage to a big round of applause and made his way to his table, shaking hands with folks along the way.

The meal was creamed chicken over rice, with peas and pimentos and assorted vegetables. The waiter called it "chicken a la king." According to Red, that means "chicken meant for a king."

I wouldn't want to be king of any country that serves chicken like that. Give me southern fried, any day.

As we ate, an Elvis impersonator in a star-spangled white jumpsuit took the stage and sang "Blue Suede Shoes" and "Jailhouse Rock" and other of Mr. Presley's hits, backed by an eight-piece band with horns and background singers and even a couple of dancing girls in metallic gold leotards. The audience ate it up. I thought it was worse than the real Elvis, which in my book is like saying broccoli tastes even worse than asparagus. Karen thinks I'm a snob because I don't like Elvis. The way I figure, not liking him doesn't make me a snob. It's fine if others do. I just don't, is all.

Make-Believe Elvis finished his set, and we finished our meal. A friend of Red's from Temple City dropped by our table and they got to talking. I excused myself and went to find Heckscher.

He'd been joined at his table by a fella in a dark blue uniform from some dinky town on the outskirts of Tulsa. Heckscher's outfit was showy, as usual. The suit was made out of faded blue denim; the pant legs and lapels were embroidered with an elaborate design which might or might not have incorporated a peacock having sexual relations with a pelican. Underneath the jacket he wore a bright red western-style shirt with shiny metal tips on the collar. Around his neck was a bolo tie with a silver and turquoise clasp. His legs were under the table, so I couldn't see whatever boots he broke out for the occasion. I'm sure they were as tasteful as the rest of his outfit.

He saw me and said something to the guy in the uniform. The fella nodded at me, then got up and left. I scooted into the booth and sat in his place.

"I thought you OSBI types weren't supposed to draw attention to yourselves?"

"You mean the suit?" He grinned. "I only dress like this for special events."

I'd bet cash money he sleeps in sequined pajamas, but I let it pass.

"So what's this all about, Chief?" He called me 'Chief' in the same way he might have called the fella who'd just entertained us 'Elvis.'

I ignored the slight and began my story. A waitress came by and set down two pieces of chocolate cake. I let mine sit. He ate his while he listened. When I finished, he looked off into space and tapped out a disjointed rhythm with his fork. I started to think I'd made a wasted trip until he said, "I hate to admit it, Hardy, but I think you're onto something."

***

The relief I felt took me a little by surprise. "The thing is," I said, "I've taken this as far as I can on my own. I'm going to need help if I'm going to track down Jimmie Gracey and Walter Fessler."

"Don't you think, now that you've told me, tracking them two down is my responsibility?"

"Of course, but that doesn't mean I have to stop. I'm going to keep looking. I'm not telling this because I want you to take it off my hands. I'm telling you because I could use your help."

He pursed his lips. "Tell you what. Tomorrow I'll come up to your place and we'll talk about it." We shook on it.

Walking back to my own table, I realized that for the first time since I'd met John Joe Heckscher more than a decade earlier, I didn't want to kick him in his baby maker.

Karen asked me how it went. I said I'd tell her on the drive home. We ran into a few people I knew on the way out, so it took us a while to make our getaway.

Once we were on our way, I said, "The good news is, Heckscher thinks we're on to something."

"You say that like there's some bad news."

"There is. It looks like he aims to elbow me out."

"We both kind of knew that would happen. At least he's taking things seriously."

I snorted. "Maybe," I said, my newfound lack of disdain for the man ratcheting up in the opposite direction. "Maybe not. Knowing him, he'll only put as much effort into it as benefits him."

"It all benefits him. This is a big deal, especially if it's all tied together. Solving it would be a big deal for someone as ambitious as Heckscher."

I thought of something and laughed.

"What's so funny?" asked Red.

"Wouldn't it be perfect if by dropping this in Heckscher's lap I'd be setting him up for a big promotion?"

"You'd best get used to the idea. That's likely what's going to happen."

I shook my head in wonder at the strange ways of the world.

CHAPTER TWENTY SIX

The next morning I waited for Heckscher to show up or call. He did neither.

I imagined it could mean he was working on it without me. I'm not a trained investigator. He is. If he could put together all these strands better than I could, then God bless him.

That's how I should feel.

But I couldn't. I didn't trust him to do the right thing.

I didn't trust him not to cut corners.

I didn't trust him not to scapegoat an innocent man, like he tried to do with Joel.

The man's a snake, I kept thinking.

The more time that went by without him getting in touch, the more jittery I felt. I wandered out into the squad room and bugged Karen for a while. She said, "Fretting over it isn't going to make him materialize out of thin air. Why don't you go out and do something useful? I'll call you if he shows up."

Unfortunately, there wasn't much that was useful to be done. This is Burr, Oklahoma, not Chicago or New York. Even on its worst day, there's a limit to how much actual policing is required. Joel and Red had the bases covered. I'd eaten breakfast, and it was too early for lunch. For a while, I cruised up and down Main Street with John Coltrane playing "I'm Old Fashioned" on my tape deck, then I drove out to the speed trap, thinking I could direct some much-needed revenue into the town's coffers. Joel had beaten me to it. I waved. He waved back.

Red hadn't hailed me with news about Heckscher, so I radioed in, myself, to see if he'd called, or shown his face. He had not.

The noon whistle went off while I was cruising Main Street for the umpteenth time. At first, it reminded me of the day Burt was shot, then a thought popped into my mind that I could drive to Waynoka and see if there was any sign of Jimmie Gracey. A fool's errand, probably, but at least it was something constructive to do. I radioed in and told Cindy where I'd be, then headed out.

I stopped at the Waynoka Miller's on my way into town. The same old fellas as before were drinking coffee and chewing the fat. None of them had seen Jimmie Gracey since I'd been there last. At the post office, the same clerk was on duty. He told me SWOOP's box was getting fuller by the day.

My last stop was Gracey's house. I resigned myself to the fact that I was wasting time, that Jimmie Gracey was gone for good, but figured I might as well check it one last time.

My resignation lasted right up to the minute I pulled up to his house and saw a cream-colored Buick Regal sedan sitting in the car port.

My heart skipped a beat. I parked on the road and jotted down the plate number in my little black book. As I walked past the car, I noticed a hole in the passenger-side front door. It looked like it had been made by a fairly large-caliber firearm.

I got out of my truck, unholstered my .45 and made sure I had a full clip, with a bullet in the chamber. Thus reassured, I put it back in the holster but kept the strap unsnapped and my right hand resting on the grip.

As I walked down the path to the door, I noticed the padlock from before had been removed. I swung open the strange gate blocking the door and knocked. No answer. I curled my hand over the grip of the Colt and knocked again. "Mr. Gracey," I said, "this is Emmett Hardy from over in Burr. If you've got a minute, I'd like to ask you a couple of questions."

The door jerked open a couple of inches and the business end of a handgun thrust through the crack, six inches from the tip of my nose. "Sure," a raspy male voice said. "I've got time. C'mon in." I heard him cock the gun. "Take your hand off that gun, or I'll blow your head off."

I raised my hands. He opened the door wide enough to pull me in, then slammed it shut.

I looked around. Whatever this place was, it wasn't fit for someone to live in. It was a single-room workshop of some kind, stinking of motor oil, grease, and gasoline. There was no lamp, and the overhead light socket was empty; the room was lit by sunlight coming through a few frosted windows. Car parts were scattered everywhere. The only furniture was a barstool, a workbench, and a small wooden cot with a rolled-up Coleman sleeping bag on top.

"Mr. Gracey, I presume?" I said.

He relieved me of my Colt and stuck it in his belt, careful to keep his own gun jammed in face. He said: "Who the hell are you?"

"Emmett Hardy. I'm the chief of police in Burr."

"Chief of police in Burr, huh?" he drawled. "You took a wrong turn somewhere, don't you think?"

"No sir, I'm not lost. I knew you lived here in Waynoka. I wanted to ask you a few questions, is all." I cussed myself for not carrying my backup weapon, the little .38 Police Special I sometimes stuff into my boot, but I'd left it in my glove compartment. "Really," I said, trying to talk reason to a man who seemed unfamiliar with the concept, "there's no need for this."

"Yeh," he growled, "I think there is. Get on the floor." He kicked my legs out from under me. "On your stomach." He pushed me face-first to the floor and knelt beside me. "Let me have your hands," he said, grinding the gun barrel into the back of my head. I crossed them behind my back. He snapped on a pair of handcuffs. "Don't move," he said, then got to his feet. I could hear him moving around but couldn't see what he was doing. He suddenly bent over and reached into my pocket and pulled out my car keys.

"On your knees," he said. For a second I thought he was going to put a bullet in the back of my head, the same way maybe he or one of his buddies did to Leon Qualls. It's not easy to get from your belly to your knees with your hands behind your back, but somehow I managed.

"Over there," he said, pointing with the gun at a partly disassembled engine in one corner of the room. I shuffled over to it on my balky knees. He removed one cuff, then snapped it onto the block.

"Mr. Gracey," I said, "I don't know why you think I'm here, but you're only making it worse for yourself. The best thing for you to do is—"

He yelled furiously and incoherently and jammed the gun into my temple. I felt his hand tremble. "Don't talk," he said, leaving enough space between each word to drive a Beethoven symphony through.

I stopped talking.

He began pacing back and forth and waving the gun around. He ranted, his voice starting low, then getting louder and angrier with every word. "Jesus Christ," he said, "I stay away, and I stay away, and I stay away … then I come back here for ten minutes and goddammit, you show up!"

Each time he turned his back, I looked for something to bean him with. There were heavy car parts all over the place but nothing within reach. After a minute, he seemed to come to a decision. He pulled the cot away from the wall. Underneath was a toolbox. Evidently, it was heavy because it required some effort to pick up. We walked over to the workbench and grabbed a padlock that had been sitting there. "I should shoot you," he said.

"Why don't you?"

He muttered something that I couldn't understand. Before I could ask him to repeat it, he was out the door, carrying the padlock and lugging the metal box. He slammed the door behind him. I heard him secure the padlock, then the sound of a car trunk opening and closing. Footsteps led back to the building, then came the sound of liquid splashing against the outer walls. The smell of gasoline got stronger. There was a sudden "whoosh," like the sound a pilot light makes when you light it with a match.

He'd set the place on fire.

I looked around for anything that might help affect my escape.

If the engine block had been made of iron, I never would've been able to move it, but it was made of aluminum, so with every ounce of my normal strength, plus the extra strength I possessed from not wanting to die, I managed to drag it across the room to the workbench. My lock-picking tools were in my gun belt, which Gracey had taken, but I thought I might find something else I could use. With my free hand, I rummaged through the mess until I found a small length of copper wire. I made a couple of little bends in it then slipped it into the handcuff's lock. It took a few seconds to disengage myself; I didn't have much more to spare.

I twisted the knob, but the door wouldn't open. I was right; he'd padlocked it shut. I threw my full weight against it, to no effect. I looked around for something heavy I could use to bash against the door. The smoke got thicker by the second. Underneath the workbench was a pile of disassembled parts. I tossed them aside, one after another, until I found something I could use: a sledgehammer.

It took one swing to splinter the latch, and two to bust the door completely open. I covered my face with my arms and launched myself out the door. I dropped to the ground and rolled to make sure I wasn't on fire.

I got to my feet and took stock of myself. Parts of my uniform shirt were charred. My forearms felt a little like they were sunburned, but that was it. The rest of me was fine.

Gracey's shack sure wasn't. It was lit up like a torch. He'd taken my keys and my .45, but my pickup was still there. I checked the glove compartment and saw my little .38 was there, too. My police band was powered by a secondary battery I'd installed so I could use it when the engine was turned off, so as not to run down the primary battery. I was too far from home to raise Karen or Joel, but I switched to a highway patrol frequency and got hold of someone right away. A unit was in the vicinity. He told me he'd be there in five minutes, which is more time than it took for the Waynoka Fire Department, the Waynoka police chief, and a Woods County sheriff's deputy to get there.

It only took a few minutes for the pumper truck to extinguish the fire. The sheriff's deputy and police chief weren't happy I'd intruded on their turf without permission, but once I'd told my story, they were generally sympathetic. I gave them all a description of Gracey's car and its plate number. The county fella and the highway patrolman put out an APB. I asked the deputy to have his dispatcher call Red and tell her what was going on. "Make sure she knows I'm alright," I added. He said he would.

An ambulance showed up a little later than the rest. The medics fussed over me until I put my foot down and said I was fine, and they needed to leave me alone. After answering a few questions to the deputy's satisfaction, the highway patrolman offered to drive me home. I was happy to accept.

After I got back to the station, it took a while to convince Red my hide was as intact as it would ever be. I changed into a spare uniform I had on hand, then started to recount what happened. I'd only just begun when a call came over the radio saying the Woods County sheriff had picked up Jimmie Gracey. I called the sheriff on the telephone. He said they were holding him for false imprisonment, and I was welcome to come and talk to him if I wanted.

I definitely wanted.

***

Kevin Bruce, the Woods County Sheriff, greeted me when I arrived. We knew each other a little from working together on a cattle rustling case a few years ago. He commiserated with me over being held captive and asked me what brought it on. I wasn't comfortable going into detail; I liked Kevin, but I didn't know him very well and couldn't be sure who he was friends with. All I said was that I suspected Gracey had defrauded a couple of old men and I wanted to question him about it. Kevin said he'd hold Gracey as long as he could, but he you never know what kind of bail a judge is going to set. I said I was pretty sure a charge of attempted murder would be enough to hold him for a while. He laughed and said it was probably so, then led me to an interview room.

He tapped on the door. "Gracey's in there."

"Have you read him his rights?"

"I did. He said he had a lawyer but wanted a different one. I called over to the courthouse for the public defender, but he was in court. I left a message that he had a new client. You'll have him to yourself until he gets here."

He opened the door and let me in. "Knock when you're done," he said.

Gracey sat in a metal chair at a wooden table in the middle of the room. His hands were handcuffed behind his back, so he had to sit on the front edge of the chair.

"Mr. Gracey, I'm here to—"

"I'm not talking until I get a lawyer."

"You don't even know why I'm here," I said. "Before you tried to barbeque me, you could at least have let me explain."

"Listen, Barney Fife," he snapped, "I know why you're here and I'm telling you, I'm not talking until I get a lawyer."

I told him they'd called the public defender, but he or she was in court. He said, "Then I guess we're all going to have to wait, aren't we?"

So we spent some time sitting and staring—sometimes at each other, although he got tired of it before I did and dropped his gaze. After a few minutes, I got sick of it, too.

"Why would you rather use a public defender than Chester Hooks?"

"Why would I want Chester Hooks?"

"Because he's your lawyer."

"How do you know?"

"He told me," I said. "In fact, he told me quite a few things." He didn't tell me hardly anything, if I'm to be truthful, but Gracey didn't know that.

Gracey scoffed. "You're lying. Chester knows better than to tell you a damn thing."

"What do you mean, 'he knows better?' Are you saying Chester's scared of you?"

"He's scared about what I know," he said, which I thought was interesting. I kept after him a little bit, asking about SWOOP and Pete Kuhlman and Earl Calvert. I even threw in Walter Fessler and Betsy Hill, trying to insinuate I knew more than I actually did. He wouldn't bite, except to blurt out "lawyer" once in a while. I thought he flinched a little when I mentioned Leon Qualls, but it could've been my imagination.

I reckoned I was wasting my time, so I knocked on the door for them to let me out.

The sheriff saw me. "No go, huh?" he said.

"He won't talk until his new lawyer gets here."

"I just got a call. He's on his way over."

"Ok, we'll see what happens when he gets here." I asked what guns they'd taken off Gracey. He said a Colt .45—which was mine—a Ruger .357, and a .25 caliber Beretta.

"It's kind of strange," he said. "The .25 was wrapped in a plastic bag, like he was trying to preserve evidence or something."

The slug Dr. Childers took out of Leon was a small caliber: either a .22 or a .25. It looked like we might have our murder weapon.

I asked if there was somewhere I could sit while I waited. He led me to an empty desk in the squad room, then asked if he could get me anything. I said I'd love a cold Tab. A young deputy brought one right over.

I'd only taken a couple of gulps when a harried-looking fella in a light blue summer suit brushed past me. The deputy guarding the door outside the interrogation room let him in. A little while later, he stuck his head out and said a few words to the deputy. The deputy came to me and said Gracey was ready to talk.

Someone had brought in a third chair. The lawyer used it to sit beside Gracey. I sat across the table from them. The lawyer told me his name, which I forgot almost immediately and still can't remember. He started in before I could say another word.

"Chief Hardy, my client has evidence of a criminal conspiracy that involves people living in your community."

"I'm all ears."

"It involves some well-connected people who are in a position to do my client harm. It is his contention that they intend him to frame him for crimes they themselves committed."

At this juncture, I reckon the fella was unaware that his client was a willing participant in those crimes. But part of a defense lawyer's job is to believe the lies their clients tell them, isn't it?

I said something to the effect that I could help protect his client, which made Gracey laugh. I couldn't blame him. The lawyer said they intended to contact the Attorney General. I said I thought that was a good idea. The AG was no great shakes, but he was bound to be more trustworthy and competent than Harry Hawpe.

The lawyer said, "So if that's all—"

"Not quite," I said. "I respect your position, but we still got your boy for what he's done to me. I'll make you a deal. I'll talk to the Woods County DA and ask him to take it easy on him if Mr. Gracey tells me the name of this fella." I pulled out a photograph of the men surrounding Kath at Burt's funeral and pointed to the figure of the red-headed fella—the one with his back turned.

The lawyer looked at Gracey, who shrugged. "Would you give us a moment?" the lawyer asked. I knocked on the door for someone to let me out. They called me back in after a couple of minutes.

Gracey said, "The guy's name is Jess Skeehan."

"The *vet*?" I said. "It's not Walter Fessler?"

Gracey looked at me like I was crazy or stupid or both.

In one corner of my mind, it dawned on me that Skeehan was the redheaded fella I'd recently seen but could not remember, but at that moment the rest of my mind was stuck on a single track.

"Then who's Fessler?" I asked.

Gracey opened his mouth. The lawyer reached his arm across his client's chest like he was trying to physically restrain him.

"That's all we're prepared to give you at this time," he said.

Gracey half-grinned and shrugged.

"I guess it'll have to do, then." I got up to leave. "By the way," I said. "Where'd you get that little Beretta? I've been looking for one of those." Before the lawyer could stop him, Gracey said, "Don't ask me. That was Murray's gun."

The lawyer's face turned red. "Alright, chief, if that's all—" I tapped on the door. Someone let me out.

Sheriff Bruce asked me how it went.

"So-so," I said. "I told the lawyer I'd ask your DA to take it easy on him for what he did to me, if Gracey would give me a name."

He asked if Gracey gave me the name. I said he did. He said he'd pass along my request. I held my index finger and thumb a half-inch apart. "I was this close to getting him to spill."

"Close don't count, though, does it?"

Sometimes it does, but then again, I never could play horseshoes worth a damn.

CHAPTER TWENTY SEVEN

Karen had a Swanson's fried chicken TV dinner in the oven for me when I got home. She asked if I felt like eating. I didn't say so, but I felt like I needed a drink.

The thought startled me. I'd been thinking less and less about booze. Now all of a sudden it reared its head.

"I could eat," I said. We sat down at the kitchen table.

"So what did Jimmie Gracey have to say for himself?"

"He gave me the name of the fourth man in those pictures I took at the funeral."

"Who was it?"

"Jess Skeehan."

"The *vet*?"

"Yup. Jess Skeehan, the vet."

She frowned. "We won't be taking Mr. Paws to *him* again." Mr. Paws heard his name and meowed. Red got up and fed him a can of beef mush.

I said, "Of course, there's no reason to think Skeehan is related to any of this."

She said, "Didn't you say he was a weirdo?"

I thought of the mechanic who had just recently replaced the starter on my truck, who's a genius with a wrench, but is unwilling or unable to talk in-depth about anything except University of Oklahoma football. "Wes Harmon's pretty weird and I don't suspect him of conspiring to kill anyone. Unless it was by talking them to death."

"I guess," she said and sat back down. "I was sure you were going to say it was Walter Fessler."

"I was sure that's what Gracey was going to say. But he didn't."

The oven timer dinged. She got up again, got me a fork, unwrapped the foil off my dinner and sat it down in front of me. Call me crazy, but I really like the smell of the fried chicken in Swanson's Hungry Man TV dinners. It was almost enough to make me forget the smell of bourbon.

"Gracey tell you anything else?" asked Red.

"Not a lot, although I think he was about to give me Fessler before his lawyer butted in. The lawyer says they're going to the state Attorney General to try to make a deal. He says this is a big conspiracy, and it involves a lot of prominent citizens in Tilghman County."

"We kind of figured as much," she said. "Why didn't he go to Hopalong?"

"I expect because Hawpe is involved."

"In which case, working with the Attorney General is Gracey's only option."

"My impression is Gracey is afraid he's being set up to take the fall for this whole thing all by himself. Whoever else is tied up in this, it's not their names on the documents. It's his."

"And Walter Fessler's."

"And Betsy Hill's," I said. "But she's not going to talk."

Red made an I've-got-an-idea face. "You know what?"

"What?"

"I might know someone she'll talk to."

"Who?"

"Cindy."

"Why would she talk to Cindy?"

"Well, for one thing, she doesn't know her."

"How do you know?"

"I don't, for sure. We'll have to ask Cindy."

"Alright then, but why would Betsy share intimate personal details with someone she doesn't know?"

Red chuckled. "Obviously you've never been to a beauty parlor."

The next morning both Red and I got up bright and early and went in to work together. First thing we did was call Cindy back to my office.

"What's up?" she said.

Red asked her if she knew Betsy Hill.

"Betsy who?"

Red beamed triumphantly. "Don't you go to bed every night thanking your stars you're married to me?"

***

The plan was to send Cindy to Jesus is Lord Salon and have her trick Betsy into talking about the case. We gave her a crash course in what we needed to know and sent her over there, figuring she ought to be able to get right in, since these days Betsy's only customers these days are blue-haired old ladies, and they've become almost as scarce as certain white-haired old men who made their fortune in oil. Betsy's young enough to be my daughter, but as a beautician, she's still living in 1955. The downturn in her salon business is why Betsy got her notary license in the first place.

"Just ask for a trim," advised Karen. "Sometimes women come out of there looking like they're wearing a French poodle on their head."

Cindy said: "Thanks for the warning."

Cindy left for the salon at about 10:00. She came back a couple of hours later having gotten a lot more than a trim. As long as I've known her, her hair has always been long, brown, and straight—the kind you don't have to do much with except brush. In fact, before today she'd never been to a beauty parlor. Her mom always cut it, she said. Now, it was short, cut barely to her collar, and kind of messy-looking, with bangs feathered across her forehead. She looked a little like Henry Fonda's daughter, which isn't a bad thing.

"It's called a shag," she said. "She wanted to give me the poodle treatment, but I wouldn't let her. You like it?"

I deferred to Karen.

"I love it!" she said.

I said, "I guess I like it too, then."

"All in the line of duty," said Cindy. "At least I got what you wanted, information-wise. Some of it, anyway."

"How'd you get her to open up?" I asked.

"By talking about what idiots our boyfriends are."

I'm not sure I knew Cindy had a boyfriend. "Did she mention her boyfriend's name by any chance?" I remembered how upset she'd been at Burt's funeral, so I had a pretty good idea.

"She didn't. She said he'd broken up with her, but the way she talked, I'm pretty sure she meant Burt Murray."

"I reckon dying is a way of breaking up," I said.

Betsy and Cindy got to talking about things in the way men sitting around a barber shop do. They talked about everything from Rock Hudson to the names of the nurses on the General Hospital soap opera. Real subtle-like, Cindy worked Jimmie Gracey's name into the conversation; I think she remarked how good-looking he was, which was taking a chance, since she'd only seen the pictures I took of him at Burt's funeral, and they were kind of blurry. Fortunately, Betsy agreed he was quite handsome and seemed ready to talk about him in some depth. Cindy asked her how she got to know him. Before you know it, Betsy was telling a story about Gracey calling her up and asking if she'd notarize some documents for him. She met Gracey, Earl and his lawyer at Earl's place.

"Did she tell mention the lawyer's name?" I asked, sure that if she did, it would be Walter Fessler.

"She said Earl's lawyer was Chester Hooks."

That confused me so much, I thought my head might explode. "But the name on the documents is Walter Fessler."

"I know."

"So why'd she say it was Hooks?"

She shrugged. "Because it was Hooks, I guess."

"Apparently Walter Fessler is Chester Hooks," said Karen.

"Hooks was Fessler all along," I said. "How about that?"

"So Chester's involved in this, too," said Karen. "Oh, what a tangled web we weave."

I asked Cindy if Betsy mentioned what kind of documents they were.

"She said Earl was selling Gracey some kind of property."

Gracey, meaning: Southwest Oklahoma Oil Partnership. "I'm sure if we could track down the names of the partners in this SWOOP thing," said Karen, "Chester's name would be on it."

"There's more," said Cindy. "Betsy said that not long after that, she notarized Earl's will."

"Prepared by Chester Hooks—"

"—signing as Walter Fessler."

Things were starting to clear up. "Why would Betsy do such a thing?" I asked.

"Betsy made it sound like they paid her more than her regular notary fee."

"I'll bet they did," said Karen. "A lot more."

I said I hope it was worth the jail time she's going to get. "Did you ask her about Pete Kuhlman?"

Cindy shook her head. "I didn't want to push my luck."

I agreed that was probably for the best.

My phone buzzed. It was Joel, who'd been holding down the fort while Cindy was out. He said he was swamped, so I thanked Cindy and sent her back to her usual post.

Karen asked me if I thought we should talk to Chester about misrepresenting himself. "Not yet. I don't want to tip him off we're onto him. He'll be disbarred over this. He's already richer than God. I mean, how much money does one man need?"

"Maybe he has problems we don't know about," she said.

I thought for a moment. "You know, this makes me wonder what Jess Skeehan has to do with Chester, Hawpe, and Zimmerman." I paused. "Maybe I'll take a run out to his place. See if he knows anything about all this."

"All you have is a picture of him in their company. It could just be a coincidence."

"It probably is, but you never know."

"I think you might be reading too much into it."

"Maybe," I allowed. "What do we really know about Skeehan, anyway?"

"Not much. He moved here about a year ago, as best I remember. That's about it, I guess. I don't even know where he comes from. Until we got Mr. Paws, I barely knew who he was."

I was struck by an idea. "You know who we haven't talked to in a while? Isabel Cruickshank."

"Yeh. So?"

"I wonder if she might be able to give us information on him."

"I doubt the FBI keeps files on veterinarians."

"Not normally, maybe, but what if he's got a record?"

She shook her head dismissively. "There's no reason to think he's a criminal, Emmett."

"Maybe he's not, maybe he is. Anyway, the FBI keeps records on folks you wouldn't expect they would."

"So you think Mr. Paws' doctor is some kind of arch-villain?"

"I don't know. He is strange." I paused. "I guess I'm kind of grasping at straws here."

"Go ahead, then. Call Isabel. Leave no stone unturned."

The last thing Isabel did before saying goodbye to Red, was to tell her how to get in touch with her in Virginia. Before I could ask, Red was dialing the number. She got through without too much trouble. They chatted for a minute, and then Red handed the phone over to me.

"Hey Isabel, how is everything?"

"Good, Chief. How 'bout you? Did anything ever happen with the Burt Murray shooting?"

"Actually, that's what I'm calling you about. You got a minute?"

"Sure."

I told her the story right up to the second. When I finished, she chuckled and said, "That's quite a situation, for sure. What can I do to help?"

"Like I just told Karen, this is probably going to seem like I'm grasping at straws, but there's this fella named Jess Skeehan. He's new to town—a small animal veterinarian—but other than that, we don't know anything about him. I saw him in the company of Hawpe, Hooks, and Zimmerman, and I'm wondering if he might be involved, as well. I was hoping you might be able to use your connections to get some information on him."

"Well, Emmett, to tell you the truth, I'm not sure what I can do. The bureau hasn't exactly given me the keys to the car yet, but let me look into it and I'll get back to you."

"I'd appreciate it," I said and gave her the little information we had on him. She called back around quitting time. As it turned out, she was not yet authorized to access that kind of information, much less share it with local law enforcement. She said she'd keep digging, though, and let us know if she found anything.

"So much for that," said Karen. "You going to go out to talk to him?"

"Yeh, think I will."

"Want me to come?"

"Nah, that's alright. You go home and start supper. I shouldn't be long."

She looked at me skeptically. "You should take Joel."

"He's only five minutes away if I need him. Anyway, I'll be fully armed."

She shook her head. "Take your .38, too."

My encounter with Jimmie Gracey was still so fresh it was raw. "I won't be making that mistake again."

Of course, I did not hesitate to repeat the mistake of visiting a possible suspect all by my lonesome.

CHAPTER TWENTY EIGHT

The sun was dipping low on the horizon on my drive out to Skeehan's, but there were still a couple of hours of daylight left. I wasn't wearing a watch, but I'd guess the time was something like 6:00 or 6:30.

It had only been a matter of days since I'd taken Mr. Paws to get vaccinated, so I had no trouble finding the place. The same Pontiac was parked in the carport like it had been the last time. Well-mannered gentleman that I am, I parked on the road so as not to block it in. I touched my .45 for luck, then lifted my left pants leg to make sure my little .38 snub-nose was where it was supposed to be. On the way to the door, my eye fell on that strange-looking dumpster with what I supposed was a chimney attached. *He must burn his garbage*, I thought.

I rang the doorbell.

He opened the door a crack and stuck his face through, smiling just the same as when he tried to pretend he didn't want to kill Mr. Paws.

"Yes?" he said.

"Dr. Skeehan, you remember me? I'm Emmett Hardy. I brought in my cat a couple of days ago?"

"Oh, of course. Chief Hardy." He looked out at my truck. "Did you leave him in your pickup? Go get him and bring him in."

"This isn't about my cat, Doctor Skeehan. I wanted to ask you a few questions about a case I'm working on. Mind if I come in?"

He took a furtive look behind him. "This isn't the greatest time, Chief Hardy. I've got a chestnut-fronted macaw on the loose. I'm afraid if I open the door, he'll fly right out."

"That's fine. I can wait until you get it squared away."

"That would be great," he said and shut the door.

I assumed a chestnut-fronted macaw was a bird, although for all I knew, it could've been some kind of flying squirrel. There were noises from the inside of the house, like the sound of furniture being moved. Dr. Skeehan yelled and cursed a bit, then everything went quiet.

He opened the door. "Come right in," he said.

He was considerably more disheveled than when I'd seen him a few days before. The Dippity-Do or whatever he used to hold his thinning red hair in place had given up the ghost. The strands he'd combed over the top hung limply on one side of his head. Sweat stains showed through the underarms of his lab coat. His shirttail was only tucked on one side, like he'd gotten dressed in a hurry. The building's smell was the same: Lysol-mingling-with-cat-pee-and-cigarettes.

"Sorry about that, Chief Hardy," he said, gesturing toward a cage in the back of the waiting room. Inside was a bright green bird. "Roscoe's been a bad boy."

I'd halfway thought his story about the bird was just a way of trying to get rid of me. Evidently it was not. "Is Roscoe a recent addition?" I asked. "I didn't see him the other day."

"He belongs to a client," he said. "He's very sick and about to die. His mommy wants me to stuff him."

Roscoe squawked a couple of times, then broke into song. To the melody of the University of Texas Longhorns fight song, he sang, "Texas bi-ites, Tex-as bi-i-ites. Oh, Tex-as can bite my ass!"

Skeehan tut-tutted: "Roscoe's mommy is a big OU fan."

"Old Roscoe seems pretty frisky for being about to die."

"Oh, trust me, Roscoe doesn't have long. I'd be surprised if he lasts through the night."

Roscoe burst out again. Skeehan said, "Let's go someplace where we can hear ourselves think."

My guard was up. Obviously, Skeehan was a few sandwiches short of a picnic. I thought of Dracula again—Bela Lugosi this time, not Christopher Lee. Skeehan had the same jittery manner as Lugosi's insect-eating assistant, Renfield. I wouldn't have blinked an eye if he'd pulled out a jar of dead flies and helped himself to a mouthful.

I followed him into the same examination room where he'd given Mr. Paws his shots. "I'll be right back, I need to go make sure I locked Roscoe's cage," he said and walked out.

The room was small. The only seat was a red plastic chair like those in the waiting room. I tried sitting on it. I felt like a two-year-old trying to balance myself on the grown-ups' toilet. I decided to stand. There wasn't much in the room to look at: an examination table equipped with a small scale; a jar of cotton balls, a cabinet stocked with bottles of pills. There were two doors—the one we'd come in through, and the one Skeehan had left by. On the counter was a paperback. *Enjoy Your Hamster*. I began thumbing through it. I'd barely gotten past the first page when the door opened behind me. Before I could turn around, I felt a sharp poke in my rear end. My legs went out from under me, and I felt myself slipping into unconsciousness. I glimpsed Dr. Skeehan standing there with a syringe in his hand and his Cheshire Cat grin.

My last thought was: *Yup, that boy's crazy*.

***

I woke up on my back in the dark, paralyzed from head to toe. I felt almost the same was when the dentist gave me laughing gas that time—as if I was lying in my grave, waiting for someone to shovel dirt in my face. My heart hammered so hard I thought it might tear loose from its moorings. It felt like I had a stack of cinder blocks on my chest. Every breath was a life-or-death struggle.

I couldn't see well enough to get a fix on where I was. The only light was a thin line shining underneath what seemed to be the bottom of a door several feet above me. I realized I was in some kind of basement or cellar. The silhouette of a small animal passed in front of the light and for a second, I thought I felt something nibbling at my feet. *No telling what he keeps down here,* I thought. Whatever it was, I wanted to kick it away, but my muscles wouldn't cooperate.

Calm down, Emmett. Nothing's chewing on you. It's your imagination.

I forced myself to focus on my breathing. It seemed apparent that the sharp poke in my butt I felt before passing out was Skeehan shooting me full of something I wasn't supposed to wake up from. But I did, so I was ahead of the game.

Obviously, Skeehan would have taken my .45, but maybe he'd missed the .38 in my boot. If he did—and if I got enough feeling back in my arms and hands—maybe I could get out of this. I tried to raise my head to see if the gun was still there, but found that I couldn't.

Footsteps clomped above. Roscoe sang "Texas Bites." Skeehan joined in.

There was a second set of footsteps. A familiar voice said: "Where is he?"

It was Harry Hawpe.

"In the cellar," said Skeehan. "On the ping pong table."

So that's what I was lying on.

"You got him down there all by yourself?" asked Hawpe.

Skeehan giggled. "I'm stronger than I look."

"Is he dead?"

"If he's not, he soon will be."

"You gave him the same stuff as the others?"

"Yeh."

"You sure you used enough?"

"It was enough for them," Skeehan said. "It'll be enough for him."

"Them" meaning Calvert and Kuhlman, I assumed.

Hopalong asked, "What're we going to do with him?"

Skeehan said, "Cremate him."

It suddenly hit me. That strange-looking dumpster wasn't where Skeehan burned his trash. It's where he cremated the animals he put down—those he didn't stuff and mount on his wall. I probably should've realized that from the beginning, but most people who burn trash do it in 55-gallon drums. I guess if burning things is a major aspect of your business, you need something bigger and fancier.

"If we'd done that with the other guy," said Hawpe, "we wouldn't be in this mess."

"I told you. I couldn't," said Skeehan. "I was due for a state inspection. I couldn't risk traces of human remains being found in it."

"Why is it ok now?"

"The inspector came last week. I got a whole year to clean it."

I was gradually having less trouble breathing. I tried to wiggle my fingers and toes. I thought I could detect some movement in the middle finger of my right hand.

A door slammed. The bird squawked. A third pair of feet stomped across the ceiling.

"Is he dead?" asked Chester Hooks.

"Yeh, he's dead," said Skeehan. I felt like saying, "Not yet, you bastards," but even if I could, that wouldn't have been a good idea.

"Ok, this is what we're going to do," said Chester. "Harry, you need to drive Hardy's vehicle to this address."

There was a pause, then Hopalong moaned, "Chester, dang it, that's in Boise City. How am I supposed to get back? I've got to be in court in the morning."

"So do I," he said. "I'll talk to the judge. He needs to know what's going on here, anyway. He'll give us a continuance."

Hopalong whined, "Ok, but how am I supposed to get back?"

"For God's sake, Harry," Chester shouted over Roscoe's caterwauling. "You're a grown man. Figure it out!"

Texas bi-ites, Tex-as bi-i-ites. Oh, Tex-as can bite my ass!

"I'll need some help moving the body," said Skeehan, straining to be heard over Roscoe.

"I thought you said you were stronger than you looked," sneered Hopalong.

"Harry," said Skeehan, "you might not realize this since you've never done a lick of work in your life, but getting a heavy weight *down* a flight of stairs is a lot easier than lifting it *up*."

The two men hollered at each other. Roscoe sang. Chester yelled, "Can't you make that bird shut up!" to which Skeehan replied, "He sings when he's nervous." Chester said, "Did you take his gun?" Skeehan said, "Hardy's? Yeh, of course." Chester said, "Give it to me." There was a pause, then heavy footsteps, a gunshot, then quiet. Roscoe warbled no more.

"Anyone else want to sing?" thundered Chester. Apparently, no one did. "Harry," he said, slightly calmer now: "Take Hardy's pickup to that address."

"What'll you be doing?" asked Hopalong.

"Cleaning up your mess," said Chester.

"Can't one of y'all help me get him upstairs?" begged Skeehan.

"Harry needs to get rid of that truck and I have no intention of dirtying my suit. There's no hurry. Bill will be here shortly to help you dispose of the body."

Bill? I thought. *Who's Bill?*

There were sounds of feet scuffling, engines starting, and vehicles driving away. Eventually, only a single pair of footsteps walked across the floor above me. Skeehan's, I assumed.

I lay there in the dark on that ping pong table and tried to estimate how long I'd been there. It depended on how long I'd been unconscious, and I had no idea how long that was. I half-hoped it had been long enough for Red to start to worry and come out to check on me. On the other hand, I didn't want her walking in on this fiasco all by herself.

I tried again to move my extremities. I'd made some progress. Little by little, the feeling in my hands and feet was coming back. I could feel the ping pong net under my back, which was uncomfortable, but welcome under the circumstances. Breaths were coming easier. *How long before I could move well enough to defend myself?* I wondered. Skeehan could check on me at any time. If he did, I was sunk; he'd discover he hadn't given me enough dope and shoot me up with more. If I wanted to live, I'd either need to be rescued, or I'd have to overpower Skeehan and whoever was sent to help him. In my present condition, I wouldn't have been able to overpower Mr. Paws.

The phone rang. Skeehan seemed to argue with whoever it was. He slammed it down and got back to humming "Texas Bites."

My fingers and toes started to feel tingly, like they'd fallen asleep. I wiggled them, trying to get the circulation flowing. I thought about Red and remembered Chester said he was on his way to clean up Hawpe's mess. Was he talking about her? She knew everything I knew. Hooks knew that. What's to stop them from doing to her what they were doing to me?

The numbness continued to slowly abate. I could raise my head a couple of inches. My legs and arms were getting better, too.

The doorbell rang. Another pair of feet crossed the ceiling. A woman's voice said, "Alright, what do you want me to do?

It was Betsy Hill.

Chester didn't say *Bill*. He said *Hill*.

"I need you to help me get the body up the stairs," answered Skeehan.

"How'd you get him down the stairs in the first place?"

"How does that matter?" he snapped. "The fact is, I need someone's help, and you're it."

"I don't know why y'all keep bringing me in on this," she groused. "Why didn't you call Gracey?"

"Because Gracey's in the Woods County jail," he said, then explained in brief how that came to pass.

"When am I going to get paid?" Betsy asked.

"Ask Hooks," said Skeehan. "He's the money man. I'm just the scientific genius." He laughed one of his braying-donkey laughs.

The doorknob turned and the door above me opened. The lights came on. I lay as still as I could.

Through mostly closed eyes, I watched Betsy descend the stairs, using her hands as bumpers to protect her gigantic hair, and ducking so it could clear the top of the door frame. Skeehan followed, humming "Texas Bites."

I closed my eyes completely, but I could sense them standing across from each other on either side of the table. "Are you sure he's dead?" said Betsy. "He kind of looks alive."

Skeehan grabbed my wrist and held it for a moment. "Hmmm," he said.

"What's the matter?" said Betsy.

"He's still got a pulse," he said. "Help me get him up. We'll dump him in, anyway."

"What?" said Betsy in an alarmed voice. "There is no way in the world I'm going to help you burn a man alive! I don't care what he did."

What did I do?

"Listen, Miss Hill," said Skeehan, "he's as good as dead. His nervous system has shut down. He can't feel a thing."

"Can't you give him another shot?"

"I used the last of the drugs."

"Then do the Christian thing and shoot him!"

"Don't be ridiculous," he scoffed. "He's basically dead already."

I tried to gauge whether I had enough feeling in my limbs to make a break for it if I got the chance. My arms and hands seemed almost normal. My legs and feet were another story.

"I'm going to go check the cremator," he said. I waited for him to climb the stairs and go outside. I'd gotten most of the feeling back in my head and neck, so I felt I might be able to speak. While Skeehan was gone, I thought I'd try to appeal to Betsy's better nature and convince her to let me go. I've seen it work in movies.

I opened my eyes to find myself staring directly into Betsy's. Before I could get a word out, she erupted in screams and bolted from the room. "Jess! Jess! Jess!" she shrieked. "He's alive! He's alive! He's alive! Shoot him! Shoot him! Shoot him!"

Apparently, Betsy didn't have a better nature.

I tried to raise myself. My arms cooperated, but nothing else would. I was laying toward the middle of the table. I tried to inch over to where I could swing my legs off the side and onto the floor, but I still didn't have enough strength. Within a few seconds, Betsy and Skeehan were stumbling down the stairs. She came first, protecting her hair with one hand and pulling along Skeehan with the other. Skeehan was in the middle of telling Betsy there was no need to shoot me when he stopped in his tracks at the bottom of the stairs and witnessed my attempts to move.

There was no use playing possum anymore. "Listen, Skeehan," I said, surprised that I could make myself heard. "You don't want to do this."

I was wrong about that. He leaned in close and gave me a big ol' Alfred E. Neuman grin. "Chief, you know that saying: 'Nothing is certain but death and taxes?'" A thread of drool dripped in slow motion from his mouth to my nose. "I've got some good news for you. After today, you'll never ever have to worry about paying taxes again. Isn't that great?"

"What are you going to do?" Betsy said uneasily.

"What I said I was going to do. Dump him in the cremator."

"Oh my God, no!" she said. "Just shoot him! Why can't you—"

Frustration with his balky co-conspirator boiled over. He slapped her and said, "Because I don't have a gun."

Chester must've taken mine with him after he shot the bird. I was more scared for Red than ever. On the other hand, that might mean they hadn't found the .38 in my boot.

"Can't you just put a pillow over his head and smother him or something like that?"

"Yeh, but what's the point? We'll have to carry him out to the cremator anyway."

He pulled a scalpel from his smock. "Look," he said and poked me in the thigh. It hurt but I managed to keep a straight face. "Feel that, Chief?" he asked. I didn't so much as twitch. "See?" he yelled in Betsy's face, then, in a calmer voice, added, "He won't even feel it. He's still paralyzed. Now help me get him up the stairs."

Whatever drugs he'd used on me were wearing off, if not as fast as I would've liked. Exhaustion was starting to replace paralysis, but maybe if I expended what energy I had for one concentrated burst, I could make some kind of final stand. If that gun was still in my boot, I had a chance.

Slim, but a chance.

Skeehan lifted my trunk into a sitting position and looped my left arm around his shoulder. He motioned for her to do the same on the other side. At the count of three, they tried to lift me off the table. Skeehan's knees buckled. He fell, banging his head on the edge of the table.

"God*dammit!*" he yelled, checking his head for signs of bleeding.

Betsy let go of me and folded her arms like a petulant child. I flopped backward across the table and lay there on my back. "Why're y'all always shoutin' at me?" she sobbed. "I never wanted to be rich. I just wanted to bring back the bouffant!"

I believe "bouffant" is the technical term for the way she wears her hair.

"Alright, alright, I'm sorry," said Skeehan, shaking his head sadly. "It's been a long day. Getting arrested for murder was the last thing I expected when I got up this morning."

"Why would that be the last thing you expected?" she asked. "You did kill a bunch of people."

"That's a lie," he said. "Three people ain't a bunch. Ten's a bunch. Three's a couple."

She shook her head. "Nuh-uh. *Two* is a couple. Three's a *bunch*."

"Three's a *few*, alright?" Under his breath he repeated: "Three's a few."

"Ok," she sniffed. "You've killed a *few*, then."

"Exactly," he said, sounding pleased. "And one of 'em I didn't even do myself. I just kind of planned it out."

"Oh, well, I guess that's different," she said sarcastically.

He put his hand on Betsy's shoulder. She shrugged it off. He put it back. She shrugged it off again. He started to put it back. She gave him a threatening look. He gave up.

"Listen," he said, his voice a lame attempt at being soothing. "I'm sorry. I know I can be a real dickens sometimes."

A dickens? I thought. *Really?*

"Listen," he cajoled, "we need to get this done. The longer we wait, the more likely that his strength comes back."

Betsy produced a compact and began wiping away the long black streaks of mascara spider-webbing down her face. "You like me, right?" she said. "I mean, you find me attractive."

Skeehan looked around, then at me, clearly thinking she had to be talking to someone else. When he realized she was talking to him, he said with a psychotic grin, "Why, of course I find you attractive. You're the bee's knees. The cat's pajamas."

"Thank you," she said primly and turned her back. Skeehan looked at me and made a twirling motion with his index finger at the side of his head. "She's crazy," he mouthed. He tapped Betsy on the shoulder. "Now, can we—ok, we really need to get this done, ok?"

"Ok," she said with a sniffle.

They pulled me to the edge of the table and propped me up, letting my legs dangle over the side. Skeehan sat on one side of me, Betsy on the other. Each took one of my arms and wrapped it around their neck. Skeehan counted to three and they lifted. This time they got me off the table without falling down.

I wanted them to think I was even more incapacitated than I was, so I let my legs dangle, forcing them to do every ounce of the lifting. I dropped my head and looked to see if the gun was still there. I couldn't tell.

My arms were feeling close to normal. My legs were another matter. I didn't think they could support me. Somehow I needed to get a hold of that gun, assuming it was there.

It took them a while, but somehow, with me flopping between them like a dead octopus, they managed to lug me up the stairs and out into the backyard. It had gotten dark while I'd been in that basement, but it was still hot and humid. The air was thick with smoke, and I coughed, which startled my escorts. They labored forward, my feet digging a path in the dirt. The smoke thickened and everything around us turned orange and felt very, very hot. Within seconds, the open cremator door was inches from my face.

The name of a Charlie Parker tune came to mind.

Now's the Time.

CHAPTER TWENTY NINE

My seventh-grade math teacher, Mr. Anderson, had a terrible temper. He had this strange way of wearing his hair—in stiff bangs cut at a weird diagonal across his forehead—and we used to tease him about it. He'd go along with it and smile and joke with us for a while, but if we kept it up too long, he'd blow a gasket. "If you boys don't shut up," he'd sputter, "I'm going to knock your heads together!" He never did, of course. Even back then, there were things teachers weren't allowed to do.

In fact, the only people I've actually seen knock heads together are professional wrestlers on TV. I'm pretty sure that's fake, but I always thought it would hurt like hell if you did it for real.

Ask Jess Skeehan and Betsy Hill. They would know.

***

They stopped in front of the cremator. I felt them relax for a second—long enough for me to squeeze my arms tight around their necks and bang their heads together. Betsy must've felt it coming. She ducked; Skeehan's face smashed into the top of her head. Blood gushed from his nose. He released me and I dropped to the ground. He staggered backward, then fell next to me. Betsy stumbled backwards and called for Jesus to save her. I raised the cuff of my pants and reached for the .38.

It wasn't there.

I looked up. Betsy was turning it over in her hands like it was a priceless jewel.

I tried to stand but couldn't. "Give it to me, Betsy." She shook her head, still looking at the gun in awe. "C'mon, Betsy. You're in enough trouble as it is." She turned to me in a daze, like one of Count Dracula's hypnotized maidens. I heard a car engine approach. *The cavalry?* I thought. "Give me the gun, Betsy." She pointed and pulled the trigger—three, then four times. The air buzzed around me, but the bullets only clanged off the cremator. She stopped, gave the gun an *Et tu, Brute?* look, then raised it again. This time, instead of shooting wildly, she cocked the hammer and aimed. Somewhere behind her, a voice hollered "Drop it!" She turned slightly. A body flew from out of the darkness and tackled her to the ground.

Joel.

He wrested the gun out of Betsy's hands and looked over at me. "You alright, chief?"

"I'm fine, as far as I can tell." I tried and was able to get to my feet, albeit on shaky legs.

He turned Betsy over, pulled together her hands, and cuffed her. She lay gasping on her stomach.

Lying in the dirt next to her, like a headless and legless French poodle, was her hair.

She'd been wearing a wig all along.

***

Skeehan's nose looked like a piece of smashed ravioli. As he lay on his back, he put a hand in front of his face and spit out a few bloody teeth.

I guess I didn't know my own strength.

Betsy saw her hair sitting there in the dirt and went nuts. "My hair, my poor hair!" she cried, sounding so bereaved, I was tempted to test her soiled wig for a heartbeat. Instead, Joel picked it up and handed it to her on their way to his cruiser.

I felt dizzy so I sat back down, taking care to put some space between myself and the cremator and Skeehan, who was still humming "Texas Bites" but using the lyrics to "Boomer Sooner." I felt a fair amount of pain, which under the circumstances I considered a positive sign.

As for Skeehan—lying there on his back, coughing up blood and broken teeth and singing that silly song—he looked like he wouldn't hurt a fly.

Joel pulled the cruiser around to the back of the house, got out, and walked over to where I was sitting on my butt. He offered me a hand. "Thanks, but I think I'll stay where I am for the time being. Where'd you come from, anyway?"

"Mrs. Hardy got a call from Isabel Cruickshank. She said Skeehan had been convicted in Tulsa County back in '69 for possession of drugs with intent to distribute and served five years in McAlester."

I turned around and said to Skeehan, "Why didn't you tell me that?" but he was too busy singing at the stars and jabbering like an idiot.

"Anyway," said Joel, "she told me to get out here. So here I am."

I asked him to take Betsy back to the station and while he was at it, call Red and tell her how things turned out. Joel asked if I'd be alright left alone with Skeehan. I told him I'd about recovered all my faculties and that I'd be fine.

"I'll leave this, just in case." He loaded my .38 from his ammo belt, handed it over and sped away.

Skeehan's never-too-pretty face was much the worse for wear; his formerly white smock was caked in blood and dirt and ash. He alternated jags of whimpering with quiet giggles and singing; at some point he segued to "You're So Vain." I got to my feet and shut the cremator's door. The roar of the fire decreased enough that we could hear crickets chirp, which I considered a much more pleasant sound, all things considered.

Neither Skeehan nor I spoke for a while, until out of the blue, he said, "I never wanted to be a veterinarian."

I went along with it. "That right?"

He rose to a sitting position, grimacing at the effort. "I wanted to be a marine biologist."

I started to tell him I'd been in the Marines, but I held off. I got the impression he was talking about something else.

"Why didn't you do that instead?"

He put a hand to his forehead and pretended to peer into the distance. "Hmmm, genius, I don't see any oceans around, do you?"

I gathered that being a marine biologist had something to do with the ocean.

"We got lakes."

"Not the same."

"Nah, I guess not."

A siren blared in the distance. One of Keith's boys, sounded like.

"Listen, Dr. Skeehan, I'm not going to pretend you're not in trouble, but I expect if you help us with our inquiries, the judge will cut you some slack. Tell us what you know about the deaths of Earl Calvert and Pete Kuhlman and that young man whose body we found at Indian Valley, and I'll do my best to help you."

He put his hand to his mouth, spat out some more blood then wiped it on his smock.

"Why'd you have to bang our heads together like that? It really hurt."

"I'm sure it did."

He leaned back on his elbows and looked at the sky. "Oh well. I suppose I'd have done the same thing if I were you."

"What I'd like to know is why I'm not dead."

"Yeh, what the hell? I'd like to know that, too. I've put down hundreds of dogs and cats using that mixture. Never failed once." He sighed. "I gave you more than the other guys, but I guess it still wasn't enough."

Presumably, he meant Earl and Pete. "Maybe it's because I'm younger and stronger."

"Probably. You're lucky, though."

"How's that?"

"I gave you the last of my stock. If I had any more, I'd have shot you full of it." He smiled. "Bye-bye, Chief Hardy."

"I guess I am lucky, then."

The siren got nearer.

"So what about it?" I asked.

"What about what?"

"You going to help us out?"

"You mean cooperating in exchange for a lighter sentence?" He shrugged. "Sure, why not? It's not like they're going to kill me or nothin'."

Emergency lights lit up the night. I cuffed Skeehan and escorted him to a sheriff's department vehicle. "How about giving me a preview of what this was all about?" I asked as I put him in the back seat.

"Money, power, sex. You know. The usual." He seemed to think about it for a moment. "Well, maybe not sex." He thought some more. "And maybe not power. But definitely money."

***

Instead of driving all the way to the sheriff's office in Temple City, Keith and I decided to transport Skeehan to Burr for questioning. Keith drove. I rode in the backseat with the prisoner. None of us said much. When we got there, I called Karen and told her what we were up to. She asked if I wanted her to join us. I said Keith and I had it covered. She told me she was coming anyway.

One of our new facility's few drawbacks is a conspicuous lack of closet space, so we'd mostly used the interrogation room as a place to store office supplies. We gave Skeehan some aspirin to alleviate the pain in his mouth, then locked him in the holding cell while Keith and I moved out boxes of pens, manila envelopes, and bottles of Liquid

Paper, so we'd have room to question him. I retrieved the little cassette recorder we keep around for such occasions and loaded a fresh tape. We escorted Skeehan into the room. I asked if he'd like anything to drink. He wanted a coffee with two milks and five sugars. It made my teeth hurt just hearing him say that, and I don't even drink coffee, but I obliged his request.

I asked Skeehan if he was ready. He nodded. I hit the record button. Keith read him his rights. Skeehan waved it off. "I don't need a lawyer. I'll tell you what you want to know."

"Don't say that unless you mean it," I said. "We're getting this on tape."

"Who the hell cares? Paint it on the water tower if you want." He took a sip of his coffee and smacked his lips. "Let's do it," he said.

We let him talk.

***

"Jimmie Gracey met Burt Murray in prison," he began. "They weren't cell mates, but Gracey knew who Murray was, and I guess he figured they had a few things in common. Politicians are nothing but con men, anyway, and that's what Gracey was. He sucked up to Murray. I don't think he pitched a particular scheme at first, but he must've known that if and when Murray got out of jail he'd be in a position to do him some good.

"As for Murray, he was working the angles, trying to get out of jail and not having much luck. His first lawyer was worthless; he called him 'All hat and no cattle.' But Murray was loyal and kept using him for years and years. It's kind of funny, because when he finally ran out of money, the guy dropped him as a client. That was actually lucky for Murray, because he ended up with Hooks, who ended up getting him out."

Red slipped in and stood behind us with her arms crossed.

"Unfortunately, he didn't have the money to pay him. All he had left was his house, and he didn't want to sell that out from under his wife. He needed another way to get money. One day he was bitching and moaning to Gracey about it, and Gracey said he knew a way for him to make enough money to pay his lawyer and a lot more, besides. Murray called it, 'Stealing from the rich and giving to the poor.'"

"Burt being the 'poor' in this scenario," said Keith.

"I remember one time he called it 'a redistribution of wealth,'" replied Gracey. "I told him he sounded like a commie. Murray said, 'It's communism when they do it. When we do it, it's free enterprise.' He got a big kick out of that."

Karen said, "I'll bet he did."

"Alright then," said Keith. "What was the plan?"

Skeehan seemed surprised at the question. "Well, you know it, don't you? I mean, that's why Chief Hardy came after me, right?"

"Let's pretend we don't," I said.

"Gracey's idea was to steal those old men's mineral rights. Not Calvert and Kuhlman specifically, at least not at that point. His idea was to form a business partnership with him as the managing partner—"

"Which turned out to be SWOOP," I said.

Skeehan looked at me blankly for a moment, then smiled. "Oh, SWOOP. Yeh, I get it. The initials." He tapped his head and grinned. "Dang, you're smarter than you look, chief. Good for you!" He took a sip of coffee and smacked his lips. "Anyway," he said, "this business would offer to buy some old oilman's mineral rights for a guaranteed amount, payable every month for the rest of the guy's life. We're talking crazy money here—more than twice what they were making. The only catch was: The payments would cease upon the guy's death. To make that work, they'd need a mark who didn't have a family to leave his money to."

"Because an ordinary rich person would want to take care of his family after he died," said Karen.

Skeehan smirked. "I've never met a rich guy I'd call ordinary, but yeh, that's the idea."

"I trust there was never an intent to pay them anything," said Keith.

"Not a red cent. The plan was to kill them before they could collect and make it look like natural causes or an accident or something." He took another sip of coffee. This time he winced. "Gol' dang, Chief, you really did a number on my mouth."

Red pressed on, ignoring Skeehan's complaint. "But why would Pete Kuhlman go for something like that?" she asked. "He didn't spend the money he already had."

"Greed. Guys like that are never satisfied. They always want more."

I nodded like I understood, but I'm not sure I'll ever truly understand what makes people that way.

"How'd you settle on Earl and Pete?" asked Red.

"First, they needed someone without a family, like I said. Second, they needed someone who trusted them. To make this work, they'd have to tell some real tall tales. Murray could do that. No one I ever knew lied better than him."

"What kind of tall tales?" asked Red.

"Did you ever in your life meet a rich man who liked to pay taxes?" he asked instead of answering directly. "Because I sure haven't. Men like that'd rather burn their money than give it to the feds."

"They'd still have to pay taxes," said Keith. "Probably more than they would if they were getting regular royalties."

"Yeh, but you're living in the real world. Hooks and Murray sold them on a fantasy that they'd actually pay less. They bought it, hook, line, and sinker. Anyway, they'd be dead before they could collect. All Hooks, Hawpe and Gracey needed was for Calvert and Kuhlman to trust them enough to sign on the dotted line."

"I guess you were counting on Burt's powers of persuasion," I said.

"That, and Chester Hooks' powers of legal mumbo-jumbo. If you ask me, any halfway intelligent six-year-old would've seen through it, but between the two of them, ol' Burt and Chester could sell ice to a polar bear."

"Pete Kuhlman was mean, but he wasn't stupid," I said. "You'd think he'd know better than that."

Skeehan waved me off. "Listen, Chief, Kuhlman was already losing his marbles by the time they got to him. Anyway, he was no accountant, and he sure as hell wasn't no lawyer."

"And Chester was."

"That's right," said Skeehan, "and you know who else was?"

"Harry Hawpe," said Keith.

He guffawed and cackled, "You guys really are pretty smart."

"Tell us exactly how Hooks and Hawpe came to be involved," I said.

"Like I said: Murray wanted Hooks to represent him but didn't have any money. He said to Hooks, 'I can't pay you now, but how about this?' and told him Gracey's plan. Hooks liked it but said they couldn't pull it off without Hawpe and the judge overseeing the case."

"Zimmerman," I said.

"Right," he said.

"That's another thing I don't get," I said. "Chester's already richer than God. Why would he sign on to something like this, and risk going to jail?"

He gave me a surprised look. "You mean you don't know?"

"Know what?"

"You ever heard of the Dixie Mafia?"

I did. "They're the outfit behind the murder of that sheriff's wife in Tennessee about ten years ago. What about them?"

"Hooks owes them money, that's what. A lot of money. Gambling debts, mostly." He leaned back and yawned. "Damn, I'm tired."

"You can sleep when we're done," said Keith in a tone of voice I would not describe as kind and gentle. "What about these gambling debts? How much did Hooks owe?"

"25 grand," said Skeehan, "and their patience was wearing thin."

I asked how long it took for Hooks to pay them off. Skeehan gave me a pitying look.

"See, Chief," he said like he was explaining rocket science to a three-year-old, "these oil leases bring in a lot of money, understand?

Calvert had two rigs on his land. Each rig earned over $1,000 profit per day. That's $60,000 a month. Chester insisted on a 50-percent cut. 50-percent of $60,000 is $30,000, which means Hooks made 30 thousand dollars that first month. With that, he could pay his debts and have enough left over to buy himself a solid-gold toilet or two."

Being treated like a moron by this blithering idiot irritated the hell out of me, but I have to admit, I didn't realize how much money an oil rig brought in. And there I was, thinking the two thousand a month I was pulling in from my daddy's natural gas leases was a lot of money.

"Of course, Murray and Gracey didn't like giving Hooks half of everything," he continued, "but they didn't have much choice. Murray needed Chester to get him out of jail, and Gracey needed him to make his plan work."

"They also needed Zimmerman, right?" said Keith.

"Right," said Skeehan. "Zimmerman had just taken over the case after the original judge retired. The first guy was a straight arrow, but Zimmerman could be bought, and Hooks knew it. The main issue was how much to give him. Hooks insisted Zimmerman's cut come out of Murray's and Gracey's end. Murray didn't like it—he planned on using his share to run for Congress—but there wasn't anything he could do but give in."

Keith said, "So now, one half is going to Chester and the other half is split three ways."

Skeehan shook his head. "*Four* ways," he said. "They needed someone to kill those old bastards without getting caught."

"Which is where you come in," I said.

"Yup," he said. "They needed someone with the necessary expertise. Gracey knew me from McAlester and brought me aboard."

"How'd Betsy Hill fit in?" asked Red.

"We needed her to fake-notarize some documents. She'd been sleeping with Murray, so it was easy to get her in on the deal. Hooks made us pay her out of our half, too, but there was no way we were giving her a full share. We paid her a flat fee. I'm not sure how much. You'd have to ask Hooks."

I did some quick math in my head and said, "I can hardly believe Zimmerman was ok with one-eighth of a share."

Skeehan looked aghast. "Why wouldn't he be? It was free money. All he had to do was order Murray's sentence vacated. After that, Hawpe would announce Murray had suffered enough or some other bullshit, and that he wasn't going to retry him. That was it. Gracey was already out and cooling his heels until Murray was released. Once that happened, the plan could go forward."

Red asked, "Who did what, in carrying this out?"

"Murray did most of the recruiting. Earl Calvert had been a big supporter of his over the years, so Murray reckoned he could talk him into anything. Calvert was old and senile, had lots of money, and those lovely mineral rights raking in all that money year after year with nobody to leave it all to. They offered him a deal: 130 grand a month for as long as he lived. When Calvert needed a lawyer to handle his end, Burt recommended Hooks. Calvert hired him. Betsy came around to notarize the Calvert's and Gracey's signatures when the deal was made. Hooks signed later."

"As Walter Fessler," said Karen.

"Right. Afterwards, when Calvert needed to redo his will, Hooks took care of that, too, again signing as Walter Fessler. No reason for Calvert to be suspicious. Once he signed it, he probably never looked at it again."

"Then you killed him before he could collect," said Keith.

He sighed. "Those guys were every bit as guilty as I was, but yeh, technically I did the actual killing."

I asked. "How'd you do it without setting off alarms?"

"You mean, how did I make it look like he died of natural causes? I gave him a potent elixir of my own invention." He winked. "I'd tell you what's in it, but then I'd have to kill you."

I did not point out that he'd already tried and failed.

Karen asked him to walk us through the process.

"What do you mean?" he said, like it was a stupid question. "Gracey and Murray held him down. I gave him the shot. Calvert died. That's it."

"You must've assumed there'd be no autopsy," said Keith.

"I didn't especially care one way or the other. The stuff I gave him is undetectable. Even if it wasn't, Hawpe had the medical examiner in his pocket." That would be the permanently vacationing Dr. Morston.

"I assume you did the same thing with Pete Kuhlman," said Keith.

He grimaced. "Kuhlman wasn't as easy."

"Put up a fight, did he?"

"Not exactly. He tried, but he was too sick to put up much resistance. Nah, killing him was the easy part. The problem was what came after."

"What came after?"

"His grandson showed up."

CHAPTER THIRTY

I'll tell the rest of the story myself. I reckon I could just transcribe the tape we made, but the way Skeehan told it—with so many side-stories and regressions and non sequiturs—I'd wear out my typewriter getting it all down and bore you to death in the process.

A few months had passed since they killed Earl Calvert. Royalty money was pouring into SWOOP's coffers, but not enough to satisfy the four men getting partial shares. Especially Burt Murray. He still owed Chester for getting him out of jail. He didn't have the cash, so it was being deducted from his monthly cut of the oil revenue. After that, there wasn't much left for campaigning.

Desperate for more, Burt nominated Pete Kuhlman to be the next victim. Pete didn't have any living relatives—or so they thought—and he was sick in body and mind.

He also owed Burt. All his life, Pete was known to take potshots at trespassers. Back in the early '50s, he shot a teenager cutting across his property on his way to a fishing hole. Burt got him out of that mess, refusing to arrest him, using the old "a man's home is his castle" saying as an excuse. Thankfully, the boy didn't die. Pete paid off the family and Burt talked the DA out of pressing charges. Based in part on that, Burt figured if anyone could get close enough to Pete to get him to sign-off on a deal like this, it would be him.

At first, everything went as planned. Pete swallowed the bait and signed over his royalties, delighted at having all that extra money to stuff under his mattress. After Chester drew up a new will to reflect the change in Pete's circumstances, they planned to kill him the same way they did Earl: Gracey and Murray would hold him down and Skeehan would shoot him up with his super-secret drug cocktail. Nobody squawked or thought anything was suspicious when Earl died. The SWOOP-sters reckoned it would be the same with Pete. If an evil plan ain't broke, don't fix it.

Except Pete Kuhlman wasn't Earl Calvert. Pete was mean enough to disinherit his grandson because the kid was mentally ill, so you'd better believe he was ornery enough to fight back when someone tried to kill him. Knowing his history, you'd think they would've been more careful when they showed up to finish him off.

Things started going to hell as soon as they pulled into Pete's driveway. Before they could even get out of the car, they found themselves pinned down by gunfire from Pete's bedroom. While they ducked for safety, Burt shouted out to Pete, identifying the group, and telling him they only needed him to sign some papers. Pete ceased fire before anybody got hurt, although a slug did pierce one of the car doors, and another put a nice clean hole in the crown of Burt's businessman's Stetson. Skeehan said that Burt turned as green as Kermit the Frog. Pete asked what in hell they thought they were doing, sneaking up on him like that, then tossed his house key out the window.

They let themselves in. The place was a mess. They found Pete in his bedroom, lying in a hospital bed, and gripping a Winchester .30-30. He moaned in pain; Skeehan thought the recoil from the rifle might've dislocated his shoulder. His bedsheets were stained yellow and brown. The room smelled like raw sewage. Breakfast cereal was scattered all over the floor; all Pete would eat in his final days were the little marshmallow pieces in Lucky Charms—yellow moons, green clovers, etc.

Burt knew Myrtle Dennis had been taking care of Pete; he asked Pete why she'd let the house fall into such a mess. "I fired her," said Pete. "Bitch was trying to poison me." Burt tried to defend Myrtle, saying she was a good Christian woman who only wanted to help him in his time of need. Pete was having none of it. He said she knew he'd left her his house in his will and wanted to kill him so she could move in.

According to Skeehan, Pete was so far gone and in so much pain, they were doing him a favor by killing him. "Hell, we were putting him out of his misery," he said. "You should be giving me a humanitarian reward, not throwing me in jail." I said he was welcome to explain that to the judge, if he thought it would help his case.

Skeehan was carrying a little bag containing the syringe and drugs and whatnot. Pete asked about it. Skeehan said he was a diabetic and had to give himself a shot. Pete figured something was fishy and demanded they leave. Burt tried to calm him down, but that just riled Pete more. He raised the rifle like he intended to shoot Skeehan. Gracey jerked it out of his hands, so Pete pulled a handgun from under the covers. Burt took that away and pointed it at Pete, intending to shoot him then and there. Gracey took it from him. Pete, knowing his goose was cooked, tried to get out of bed, but his legs were too weak for him to stand, never mind run. He fell to the ground and screamed. Burt and Gracey pinned Pete to the floor and Skeehan injected him. Pete stopped breathing within a minute or two. That was it.

For Pete, that is.

Burr's answer to Moe, Larry, and Curly, had more adventures in store.

***

They needed to get out of there quick, in case the mailman or Myrtle Dennis or Santa Claus or whoever else suddenly showed up. They picked Pete up off the floor, stripped him of his filthy pajamas, carried him into the living room, and laid him down on the coffee table.

Gracey found a box of giant-sized Hefty bags in the kitchen under the sink; Skeehan found a broom and a dustpan in a hall closet. They went into Pete's room and swept up the cereal, gathered up the empty boxes, pulled the dirty sheets off the bed and stuffed it all into one of the garbage bags. It was Burt who insisted they change the sheets, thinking it would look bad if Pete was found lying in his own filth; he didn't want to give anyone ammunition to question Pete's state of mind at the time of the SWOOP deal. They couldn't find any fresh sheets, so they used a slightly less-soiled set they found stuffed between the cushions of Pete's couch.

Skeehan and Gracey were about to go out to the living room to get Pete and put him back in bed, when all of a sudden Burt shouted, "Holy shit!" and ran outside. Gracey and Skeehan followed hot on his heels. They watched Burt run down and tackle an unhealthy-looking young man, sit on him, and pin his wrists to the ground. Skeehan asked where the fella had come from. Burt said he'd seen him peeking in the window. He shook the man and demanded he tell them what he saw. The man wouldn't answer, just shut his eyes, and struggled without success to get out from under the 250-lb. crazy ex-sheriff. Suddenly, Burt stood up, still holding the man by the wrists. "Son of a bitch!" he shouted. "Did you piss on me, you little bastard?" He craned his neck, trying to get a look at his backside. He asked his partners if the kid had pissed on him. "A little," said Gracey.

Burt growled, "Help me get this sumbitch inside." They dragged the man into the living room and threw him down on the couch next to where Pete's body was laid out naked on the coffee table.

"Who the hell are you, and what are you doing here?" asked Burt.

The man was a disaster: thin to the point of being undernourished, with long greasy hair and dirt covering every inch of skin that wasn't covered by his urine-soaked blue jeans and yellowed Keep On Truckin' t-shirt. The man stunk. "That house already smelled like shit and piss," said Skeehan. "He smelled even worse."

The three unwise men stood around the man. Burt screamed and badgered him, but he wouldn't answer. He couldn't take his eyes off

Pete. At one point, when Burt finally stopped to take a breath, the man asked in a small, high voice: "Is that my grandfather?"

"No, he ain't your grandfather," said Burt. "Pete Kuhlman ain't nobody's grandfather."

"He's mine."

Burt looked like he'd been struck by lightning. "What's your name?" he asked the man.

Still staring at Pete, the man said, "Leon Qualls."

Burt appeared relieved. "If Pete did have a grandson, he'd be named Riley."

The young man looked away from Pete and up at Burt for the first time. "I was born George Riley, Jr."

A look of sick realization crossed Burt's face. "This ain't good. This ain't good at all."

Gracey asked what he meant. Burt said, "He ain't lying. Pete's daughter and her husband died in a car crash years ago. The husband's last name was Riley. George Riley. They had a kid, who was a baby at the time. Pete was his only kin, but he didn't want to take him, so the state put him up for adoption. Holy shit!" He stomped his foot hard enough to shake the house. "What a son-of-a-bitching day this has turned out to be."

It was about to get worse.

For everyone, but especially for Leon Qualls.

***

While Gracey searched for something they could use to tie Leon up, Burt continued to hector him, demanding to know why he'd come and what he'd seen and if anyone else knew he was there. Leon shut down, too scared to answer. Gracey came back with some clothesline he'd cut down in the backyard. They dragged a chair from the dining room into the living room, sat Leon in it, and tied him up. Before they could tie his writs, they had to take off Leon's gloves. Skeehan remembered them. "They were different-looking, with a strange blue pattern, and the fingertips were cut out off."

"He cut off the fingertips so he could count out his change," I muttered.

"Count out his change?" said Skeehan.

"Never mind," I said.

He shook his head and went on with his story.

Burt, Gracey, and Skeehan went into the kitchen to talk things over, leaving Leon in the living room with the body of his dead grandfather. Gracey asked Skeehan if he had enough drugs with him to kill Leon. Skeehan didn't, so Gracey volunteered to shoot him. Skeehan says he thought that was a bad idea. They got to arguing. Gracey suggested they vote on it, which essentially meant Burt would get to decide. While they sat around the kitchen table waiting for him to make up his mind, they heard the sound of running feet.

Their knot-tying had been sub-par. Clearly none of them had been Boy Scouts. They rushed outside to find Leon running across the backyard toward the barn, 30 or 40 yards away. Leon had a considerable head start, but he was no athlete, and Burt moved pretty well for someone of his build. The gap closed. Leon looked back, saw Burt gaining on him, then dropped to flat on his stomach. He lay there with his hands covering his head. Murray sat on him. He had a gun, a little .25-caliber Beretta. "Grab his hands," he said. Gracey pulled Leon's hands away. Burt shot him in the head. Skeehan said he screamed and cussed at Murray, telling him he'd messed up and that they were going down for murder. (For the record, I believe this last was an embellishment by Skeehan designed to make him look better.) Burt kept calm and said, "Don't worry, I done this before, I know what I'm doing," or words to that effect. I asked Skeehan what they did with the gun. He said Murray gave it to Gracey to get rid of. Evidently, Gracey held on to it and wrapped it in plastic to preserve Burt's fingerprints. I guess there's no honor among murderers.

They decided to leave Pete's body inside the house. Of course, they needed to dispose of Leon's body elsewhere. Gracey and Murray wanted to use Skeehan's cremator. Skeehan refused, telling them he was expecting a state inspection any day and didn't want them finding human remains. They all agreed it would be a mistake to act too hastily, so they stowed Leon in the trunk of Gracey's car and went back in the house to finish cleaning.

Burt thought it was important that they make the house neat but not too neat. It was common knowledge that Myrtle had stopped taking care of Pete. If they made things too spic-and-span, folks might get suspicious. Skeehan claimed to have been the one who cleaned the bathroom, but he didn't mention the Klan hood; I reckon at the time he didn't know what it was. Somewhere along the line, one of them—Skeehan insisted it wasn't him, which probably means it was—tossed Leon's gloves in the drawer where Joel and I later found it.

Burt had a deep freeze in his garage large enough to stow a body; Karen was right about the body being frozen, only it was Burt who did it, not Pete. They decided to store it there for the time being. Skeehan said he asked Burt if having it there would make him nervous. Burt grinned and said, "Not really, I've never once had anyone come by and ask to see the contents of my deep freeze."

A couple of days later, Burt called up Skeehan and Gracey and said he had an idea: They'd burn the body, but instead of using Skeehan's cremator, they'd cart it to a deserted building and set it on fire. It would be burned beyond recognition, making it impossible to identify. Burt had a place all picked out. The old Indian Valley School was far enough from the nearest house so they could operate without being discovered. They'd head off a murder investigation by staging it to look like Leon accidentally did it himself.

They bought a jug of denatured alcohol, a can of Sterno, and a bottle of Boone's Farm Strawberry Hill. They liberated Leon's corpse from Burt's freezer and thawed it out. At Indian Valley, they arranged things like they would a movie set—posing Leon's body a certain way, leaving the wine bottle next to him so it would look like he'd been drinking. They weren't sure if a bottle of Boone's Farm would get a fella drunk enough to pass out. If I'd been there, I would've said:

Maybe, but most likely not. Skeehan offered himself up as a guinea pig. He was obviously a lightweight when it came to drinking; he chugged the bottle and got totally plastered. Thus reassured, they spilled the denatured alcohol around the premises, lit the can of Sterno, and let the flames spread until they consumed the entire building. With luck, whoever found the body would read the scene as they intended: Some bum got drunk and fell asleep while he was making his dinner.

That's exactly what Bernard and Dr. Childers and I believed at the time. In retrospect, I could hardly believe we bought into it so easily. I'm disappointed mainly in myself. The other two probably couldn't judge whether someone like Leon would pass out after drinking a bottle of Strawberry Hill.

An old drunk like me should've known better.

***

That was basically the end of Skeehan's account. I turned off the tape recorder, feeling relieved we'd gotten the story out of him, but a little sick to my stomach, all the same.

Keith asked him, "I reckon you figured you'd gotten away with it, huh?"

Skeehan smirked. "Which part?"

"All of it."

Skeehan shrugged and turned to me. "I did. It wasn't until you brought your cat in that I thought we were in trouble."

"Why is that?" asked Karen.

"Obviously, Chief Hardy was using it as an excuse to check me out. Nobody vaccinates their cat. Dogs, sure, but cats? Hardly ever."

"You're not going to like hearing this," I said, "but before that day, I'd never given you a second thought."

"No kidding? I was sure you were onto us."

"Nah. Heck, with Burt being shot later that day, I forgot about you completely. I eventually came to be suspicious of Chester and Hawpe, but it didn't occur to me that you might be involved until today."

He shrugged and asked how we identified Leon Qualls. I told him about the class ring, and how it led to everything else. Skeehan said: "I guess y'all were just smarter than us all down the line."

I was still disturbed by how lightly he was taking this. "Aren't you worried about going to the electric chair?"

"Where've you been, Chief Hardy?" he said with a cocky smile. "There's no death penalty in this country. The Supreme Court suspended it in 1972."

Keith and I exchanged looks. He said, "Do you want to tell him or should I?"

Skeehan looked back and forth at us. "Tell me what?"

"I hate to break the news to you," I said, "but the Supreme Court un-suspended it a few days ago. It's legal again."

His smile froze. "You're kidding, right?"

We shook our heads.

"Well, hell," he said after a moment, his voice quivering. "I guess I should've kept my damn mouth shut."

CHAPTER THIRTY ONE

Skeehan was right. He probably should've kept his mouth shut, although it might not have made any difference. He would've been put away for a long time for what he tried to do to me, anyway. He did at least manage to avoid the death penalty by agreeing to testify against Hooks, Hawpe, and Gracey. Betsy Hill did the same.

As for Max Morston, Hopalong had some dirt on him having to do with the half-assed way he performed his official duties. Morston falsified Annie Childers' autopsy report then embarked on what he fully intended to be a permanent vacation. He was picked up at a Jack In the Box in San Diego a couple of weeks ago and extradited to Oklahoma. I like to imagine he was talking to the clown in the drive-through at the time of his arrest. His trial is pending; he was arrested too late to be tried with his co-conspirators.

By being assassinated, Burt Murray cheated the hangman in a different way. It is some consolation to me that his reputation is finally destroyed beyond redemption. As if revelations of his further crimes were not enough, his big 4th of July event was a colossal bust. Officially it was canceled, but word didn't get out, and hundreds of people showed up anyway, expecting to eat their fill of barbecue and line dance and watch the fireworks. They got none of the above. Such a fiasco would've caused Burt to lose a lot of votes, had his campaign not been terminated with extreme prejudice some days prior.

As for the other folks involved, John Joe Heckscher is more on track to be head of the OSBI than ever. Somehow, he managed to take most of the credit for unraveling the conspiracy, even though he hardly did anything except falsely arrest Joel and me. I complained to his boss about what he and his boys had done to Joel's house. I think he might've gotten his wrist slapped. He never would tell us how he knew Gabe Younger was Joel's father.

Speaking of Joel, he'll be running this place before you know it. I'm sure there are some folks around here who'll never forgive him for saving my life, but other than that, I do believe he's turned some heads and changed some minds. I guess people do have a capacity for growth.

Keith lost his race for reelection. His opponent made a big deal about the increase in car thefts in the county and somehow convinced enough folks that Keith was responsible. I probably shouldn't have been surprised when Keith lost, but I was. Tilghman County no longer has any elected Democrats to blame for all their problems.

Finally, Jim and Freda Qualls are going to court, trying to recover their son's rightful inheritance, with the intention of starting a foundation to provide educational opportunities for young people with problems similar to Leon's. I wish them the best of luck.

I write this on the morning of January 18, 1977. I'm reading the morning paper while Red makes my breakfast. The lead story concerns the execution of a fella named Gary Gilmore by the state of Utah. Gilmore's is the first execution in the United States since it was made legal again last summer.

The trial of Chester Hooks, Harry Hawpe, and Jimmie Gracey begins in a few hours.

I can't imagine they'll find much comfort in today's headlines.

Unless the entire jury pool gets raptured up to heaven before the trial, justice will soon be done in the murders of Earl Calvert, Pete

Kuhlman, and Leon Qualls. That's a good thing, but there's a name missing from that list of victims: Leon's girlfriend, Carrie.

I don't mourn Burt's death, but I do regret that when the bill finally came due on his lifetime of lying, cheating, and killing, someone else had to pay it along with him. Burt killed Carrie's friend, so Carrie killed Burt. I expect, in her mind, that was the only way she could get justice.

How she knew Burt killed Leon is an open question, but I have a theory.

Carrie accompanied Leon to Pete Kuhlman's place. She hid while Leon went up to the house. She saw Burt chase down Leon and drag him inside, then saw Leon temporarily escape, and watched as Burt put a gun to the young man's head and pulled the trigger.

Carrie was in the barn. She had to be. When Leon was running toward the barn, he was running to Carrie. With those men running after him, rather than lead them to Carrie, he dropped to the ground.

Leon saved Carrie's life.

Carrie avenged Leon's death.

I've come to believe that the reason Leon didn't go to graduate school—the one place in the world where he felt safe and could fully function—was because he knew it would take him away from Carrie. Theirs was a love story. Not exactly Romeo and Juliet, but it does bring tears to my eyes if I think about them too much.

There are other unknowns. For example: Where did Carrie get the antique Colt Buntline revolver she used? You're more likely to see that gun in a museum than in the hands of a street urchin. As of yet, no one has discovered how she got it.

Another thing I haven't been able to figure out is why in hell did Pete Kuhlman agree to sell his mineral rights? That old miser didn't spend a tiny fraction of the money he was already raking in. Why did he want more? The same could almost be said of Earl Calvert, although he wasn't cheap like Pete was. Still, in the course of his investigation, the new district attorney learned that Earl didn't spend anywhere near the money he was already making every month off those oil wells.

I don't know. I guess greed's a powerful motivator. Maybe as powerful as revenge.

And while we're at it, what was in that box Jimmie Gracey took with him when he set his house (or whatever that place was) on fire? The Ark of the Covenant? The Lost Dutchman's gold? Gracey didn't have it on him when he was arrested, so he must have stashed it somewhere. Strange.

I guess if your favorite thing is tying up loose ends, you'd be better off buying yourself a closetful of shoes than investigating a case like this.

Karen sat a plate of bacon and toast in front of me. "Are you testifying today?" she asked.

"Probably not," I said. "Today is mostly for opening arguments and the like. I don't expect they'll call me until tomorrow. How about you?"

"That new fella isn't sure," I said, referring to Hopalong's replacement. "He said it might not be until next week."

We sat and listened to the coffee percolate. Mr. Paws crawled up onto my lap and sniffed at my plate. I offered him a tiny piece of bacon. He looked insulted and jumped down.

"How's your tooth?" asked Karen.

I never did get that filling replaced. The tooth got worse, and last week I had to have a root canal. Dr. Rader offered me some kind of pill to help with the pain, but I turned it down. After my experience with Jess Skeehan, I thought I'd rather grin and bear it.

"It's fine, thanks."

She broke the silence. "You know who I've been thinking about lately? The little girl. Carrie."

"Me too."

"I mean, where was she during that week before she shot Burt?" she said. "Where'd she get the gun? Especially a gun like that."

I could only shake my head and sigh.

Who was Carrie, anyway? A young woman with problems, probably more than I'll ever have to face. A girl with blond hair and blue eyes who liked dogs and loved her boyfriend. Hell, with some help, she might've been a good mother if she'd gotten the chance. The odds were against it, but you never know.

Karen got up from the table. It was her turn to go in early. "When you get the time, you should try to find out who she was," she said. "Everybody has somebody."

I know better than to disregard that tone of voice.

"I'll get after it," I said. "As soon as the weather gets warm. You know how I hate running around in the cold."

She wrapped her arms around me and laid her cheek against mine.

"I know," she said.

"Don't worry. I'll find her." I offered her a kiss.

She accepted, and said again: "I know."

ABOUT THE AUTHOR

Chris Kelsey is a native Oklahoman now living in Dutchess County, NY. *Blond Hair, Blue Eyes* is his fifth novel. In addition to being an author, Chris is also an accomplished jazz saxophonist. He currently teaches instrumental music at Trinity-Pawling School in Pawling, NY.

OTHER TITLES BY CHRIS KELSEY

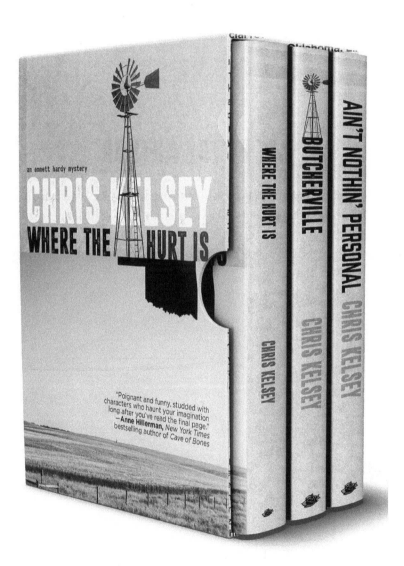

NOTE FROM CHRIS KELSEY

Word-of-mouth is crucial for any author to succeed. If you enjoyed *Blond Hair, Blue Eyes*, please leave a review online—anywhere you are able. Even if it's just a sentence or two. It would make all the difference and would be very much appreciated.

Thanks!
Chris Kelsey

We hope you enjoyed reading this title from:

Subscribe to our mailing list – *The Rosevine* – and receive **FREE** books, daily deals, and stay current with news about upcoming releases and our hottest authors.
Scan the QR code below to sign up.

Already a subscriber? Please accept a sincere thank you for being a fan of Black Rose Writing authors.

Printed in the USA
CPSIA information can be obtained
at www.ICGtesting.com
CBHW031116020524
7931CB00009B/107